FRANK GOT
ABDUCTED

For Stefan
I am definitely
not an alien.

ANDREW
HEATON

FRANK GOT ABDUCTED

ABDUCTED

Andrew Heaton

2nd edition published in the United States by Last House Standing in 2017.

ISBN-13: 978-0-9896131-7-0

For my parents,

Who never abandoned me to wolves.

And for the wolves, who treated me as their own.

CHAPTER 1

Hillary jammed a cracker into her mouth and teetered onto the Greyhound bus. She slumped into the nearest available seat, then contorted herself around the bony protrusion of knees digging into her back through the seat cushion behind her. She finished off a bag of crackers, wiped the snack debris on her pants, and then emptied a bottle of Diet Coke she had filled with tap water. She leaned her forehead against the window and whimpered. She prayed that the hangover would not stalk her any further than the border of Minnesota.

Her purse rattled across the seat beside her as the cell phone within vibrated. It was a text message from that bastard Tod. *Hey,* it read, *I just want you to know that I still think of you as a friend.*

She gripped the phone, willing male pattern baldness to course through it and the network, further receding Tod's hairline. Her thumbs furiously hammered out a response. *I just want you to know that I think of you as a non-toxic polymer who pays taxes and wasted a year of my life.* She jammed down the "send" button and hurled the phone into the dark recesses of her polka-dotted purse.

After a couple of minutes she fished it back out and began another text message. *Remember, I'm arriving at the bus station at 1:30 a.m. Don't be late! Love you!* This she sent to Frank, her fraternal afterthought of a brother. She adored and missed him, but with a peculiar combination of unconditional love and day-to-day disinterest.

She glanced out the window to watch a burly porter lug her suitcase to the bus. A cigarette dangled from his lips, then dropped, spilling sparks and ash across her suitcase. He half-heartedly slung the carryall into the luggage bay underneath the bus, flattening several hat boxes.

The suitcase contained everything salvageable from her failed attempt at life in St. Paul—mostly shoes and a handful of clothes that still fit. Everything else had been pilfered, spoiled, or abandoned during the succession of events which ultimately jettisoned her from the Land of 10,000 Lakes.

The tragedies began when her miniature roses had agreed to an apparent suicide pact, all completely and inexplicably withering within two days. Without their ferocious pink and red petals shielding her apartment from poor aesthetics, burglars finally felt at ease to climb up the fire escape, smash a window, steal everything of value, break some of her furniture apart on the off chance money was hidden in a chair leg or stool, leave the door to the refrigerator open, and shatter an entirely different window on their way out.

Two days later, Hillary's company downsized her on the grounds that they had already waited far too long to replace customer service with automated voice systems and six technicians in the Punjab. Her manager tore into her when she protested, ranting about how robots were "the wave of the future," and if she wanted to stop them she was probably some kind of communist. Fortunately, the corporation had a surprisingly large guilt complex for its size. It agreed to a severance package of two weeks paid

2

vacation, in addition to her existing hoarded sick days, then handed her picture to security.

With her lease nearly up anyway, she had called her then-boyfriend Tod to see if she could live with him until she got back on her feet. He was a slim excuse for a man who supported himself by erratically delivering mail to the denizens of St. Paul. He celebrated no major holidays, but compensated by observing dozens of minor ones, often from religions that no longer existed. He adopted a "play it safe" policy during Minnesota's ferocious winters, looking out his window every morning to determine whether or not he should get up and risk delivering mail.

When Hillary dropped the idea of an apartment merger, fears of commitment and intimacy skittered out from beneath his bed and couches to howl. Not only did he summarily dismiss the idea of residential fusion, he tried to petition down to an "open relationship," wherein both he and Hillary could freely mess around with whichever girls consented. This, after a year of monogamous dating.

Hillary refused the compromise. She broke up with Tod, purchased a bus ticket to her hometown, and crammed the remainder of her worldly goods into an engorged suitcase. She spent her last night in the city by herself, draining an industrial-sized bottle of Bailey's and flipping through *The Farside Gallery*. The following morning she roused herself, grabbed her suitcase, and fled to the Greyhound station four blocks away. She didn't even shut the door to her apartment.

Hillary would turn twenty-eight within the year, and had not anticipated entering her upper twenties with so little to brag about. Her childhood and schooling had imbued her with a deep, profound sense of impending greatness. She tempered this lofty expectation with what she considered to be a laudable sense of global responsibility. Her personal bar of achievement far surpassed mere finance; she wanted to make a *difference*. This had in fact been the cornerstone of her salutatorian address at her high school graduation, wherein she had encouraged her classmates to "make a difference, not a living," plus half a dozen other platitudes.

Yet, several years into ostensible adulthood, she had not become a social entrepreneur building orphanages in South America. She hadn't even been elected to Congress or starred in a film. She had made incremental advancement in a series of administrative or service jobs, the most recent of which had just collapsed beneath her.

Additionally, she had always assumed she would be married by now. All of her sorority sisters were. Some were pregnant. Soon they would be starting on their second round of husbands, potentially reviving Hillary's bridesmaid duties. She could feel her ring finger growing ever more naked.

As the bus lurched forward, a familiar-looking man shuffled down the aisle to take a seat in front of her. She stared at the back of his head, trying to recall the face's owner.

"James!" she cried, squeezing his shoulder and laughing.

He turned around and sized her up. He appeared to be James, but he did not appear pleased to see her.

"James?" she asked, forcing a chuckle. "What

4

are you doing here?"

"I'm not James," he explained. He turned back and rummaged through his black man-purse.

Hillary continued squinting at the back of his neck. The man *looked* like James, save a few variables. Whereas James shaved dutifully, sometimes twice a day, the passenger before her had the three-day designer stubble of a man who meticulously groomed his facial hair to appear derelict and uncaring about it. He sported chic glasses so thin that their functionality was questionable, whereas James did not require corrective *or* affected eyewear.

"Are you related to James?" she asked. It was a safe bet. The man was a dead ringer, and en route to James's home state.

"No," he said, with the same tone one might employ to turn down a prostitute or death sentence appeal.

"Really?" she prodded. Apprehension crept into her voice. She experienced a brief, mild wave of panic that she had lapsed into insanity. "Because you look just like my friend James Kelway. You could be his stunt double."

He turned around to glare at her. "Miss, I'm trying to read here. Would you mind switching seats with a screaming baby or something?" He faced forward and successfully avoided eye contact. She frowned. Her fellow bus rider was being needlessly rude. The combination of his condescension and her hangover steeled her resolve to proactively irritate him and *earn* his curtness.

"What are you reading?" Hillary asked, to spite him.

"A *book*," he offered, in a tone which conveyed

suspicions she had never seen one.

Hillary sat back in her seat to allow the man time to delve into a paragraph. She leaned forward after allotting enough seconds to interrupt him in mid-sentence. "What book?"

"Please go away," he said curtly, to clear up any confusion about whether or not they had just experienced an awkward pause or an awkward ending.

"Sure thing." She leaned back and pointed her cell phone at him. She tried to will him bald.

CHAPTER 2

Sephus strained to discern the voice of Charles Gander over the din of the Mariachi band bleeding into his favorite talk radio show.

"Hello," the host said, engaged and cool, "you're on *Midnight Chat* with Charles Gander." Stephen Hornswild, who handled *Midnight Chat* on Mondays and Fridays, usually opened phone calls with "Hello?" Not Charles, though. He met every phone call with confidence. He *knew* the caller was on the line. Sephus liked that.

"Hi. I mean, hello. Hi," a nervous woman stammered, already off to a bad start.

"Who's calling?" Charles asked.

"Mil—I'd rather not give my name out."

"That's alright, Miss. What state are you calling from?"

"Alaska."

There would have been an awkward silence as Charles waited for the mystery caller to get to the damn point and blurt out why she was calling in on call-in Thursday, but the invading fuzz of Mariachi trumpets took care of that. "What can I do for you, Miss?" Charles asked.

"I . . . well, I have a story, and if you can make any sense of it, I would like that." She had a raspy voice, a smoker. Probably in her mid-forties, though possibly prematurely grizzled by nicotine and tar.

"Sure thing," Charles said. The two syllables were self-assured and soft, as if Charles could sense her fear and embarrassment over the air, stick his hand through the microphone, reach through her cordless receiver, and rub her shoulders in a reassuring manner.

"Last week I was about to go to sleep, and I'd just put my pajama pants on, and I got this weird sensation, like someone was at the door, and I walked towards it and a light filled up my living room."

"Go on," Charles said, his hand firmly holding hers over the radio.

"Like I said, this light filled the room, and I didn't know what to do, and the next thing I know I'm somewhere else—somewhere not in my room."

Sephus noted that callers had a tendency to throw out redundant descriptions like this. What could "somewhere else" mean *other* than a different location from the room? When Sephus finally called in, he would be cool and confident like Charles. He would sound like a reporter, not a tornado victim.

"Do you know where you were?" Charles asked.

"I don't know, someplace else."

"Right."

"Anyway, some . . . " the woman's voice cracked. She held back a sob. "Something started walking toward me." She sucked in a labored breath. "The next thing I remember I was lying in my bed. My skin felt . . . tight."

Somehow, in the charismatic majesty that was Charles Gander, the radio host *nodded* over the airwaves, compelling her to continue.

"What . . . what happened?" she asked, now very close to crying, perhaps tearing up in her trailer.

Slouching in the passenger's seat, belt unbuckled, Frank groaned. "Turn the channel, man."

8

"Shut up," Sephus hissed. He self-consciously ran a hand through his new haircut. The barber had layered it in a peculiar fashion reminiscent of roof shingling.

"This is such crap."

"This isn't 'crap.'" The exchange made Sephus miss whatever platinum words Charles Gander broadcasted, very likely healing the woman from her traumatic event.

Midnight Chat gave way to a commercial break featuring Stephen Hornswild babbling about some kind of hair cream he wanted to share with the listening audience.

"She was for real," Sephus said, keeping his eyes on the road. He swerved to avoid a dead opossum, or at least an opossum convincingly playing dead.

"Just another nutcase," Frank mumbled into his Flaming Lips t-shirt. "Trying to get attention through some cock-eyed story about getting sucked up in a flying saucer."

Sephus signaled to no one in particular on the desolate county road and hung a right onto an even smaller, dustier county road. "She was for real," he repeated.

"Sure she was."

"She *was*," Sephus said, hazarding a glance at Frank. The passenger harrumphed. "For one thing, she never claimed she was abducted, and she didn't mention anything about a flying saucer. *You* inferred that. Maybe she got abducted; maybe something else happened. Whatever it is, it's real to her. She's not making it up."

"You can tell?"

"Yes, I can," he said, with the same pride other

9

men in Grant County might display if their understanding of car mechanics or lawn mower operation was questioned. "Something scared the hell out of her. She couldn't explain it, and she was too embarrassed about anything that screwy happening to her to mention her name over the radio. People like that aren't looking for attention, they're looking for answers."

"Whatever," Frank retorted, derailing Sephus's argument, at least so far as Frank was concerned. "We're here," he stated, adding further credit to his observations.

Sephus put the car into park and unbuckled his seat belt. "Are you okay to drive?"

"What?" Frank asked, then, guessing the question, "Yes, of course I am."

"Okay," said Sephus. He shook Frank's hand and unlocked the door. "Say hello to Hillary for me. Is she still dating Tod?"

"Who?"

"Tod? Isn't that his name? The mailman from St. Paul?"

"Oh, yeah. Swell guy, Rod. G'night."

Sephus nodded, climbed from the car and retreated to his farmhouse.

Frank, still slightly drunk, let himself out of the passenger's seat and walked around the car to position himself behind the wheel. He shut the radio off in irritation as Charles Gander rambled out a sermon about alternative energy, which he had somehow been reminded of by a caller with a question regarding chupacabras. He put the car into reverse and exited Sephus's driveway, knowing if he stalled for long his friend would come out and start hassling him to sleep on the couch.

Normally Frank might do this, but he had a sister to pick up, and he was no slouch, or at least he believed he was no slouch. If Frank Norbitz told his sister he was going to pick her up in Oklahoma City at 1:30 a.m., then dammit, he would *be there* by 1:45 a.m. at the absolute latest, tipsy or not.

Actually, he would be sober by the time he arrived, because Oklahoma City was a good two hours from Sephus's home in Hoople and he wasn't even that sloshed. He would be fine within the hour, and in any case could pick up breath mints when he filled up his tank.

He drove through the town of Nash and turned south onto Route 132. He accelerated the car until it reached eighty, but then thought better of it and eased off to fifty. He did not want to miss his exit, and recalled some sharp turns ahead. Also he had been drinking, and that was always a good reason to drive only slightly over the speed limit.

The road was deserted. It would be half an hour before he crossed anything other than utterly flat farmland. It would be twenty minutes before he saw any lights, unless another car happened to come from the opposite direction this late, which was unlikely.

Inky blackness rolled by. He was unsure if the miles of fields flanking him were harvested wheat or merely grazing turf for cattle. Whatever the case, they were too flat and well-trimmed to provide any reflection from his headlights at all. He could see the road stretching ahead of him, but little else.

After a few minutes of complete silence Frank grew edgy. He had grown up in Moore, a suburban ligament connecting two larger and more interesting cities, and was not entirely acclimated to the smaller population of rural Oklahoma. It was too peaceful and quiet.

He reached down to the tape deck and switched the radio back on. "—will understand that we have a limited supply of oil? China is industrializing, and that's going to put a bigger strain on the wells. What happens when China is as dependent on petroleum as we are, and we suddenly tap the Middle East dry? I'll tell you what happens. Armed—" Frank switched the station to static, then to more static, then switched over to FM to see if he could find any music on those frequencies. No luck.

He jerked the steering wheel suddenly as a flash of white hurled in front of his car. The Ford Taurus slid on its two left tires and fishtailed, finally skidding to a halt across both lanes. A deer bolted away in his rearview mirror.

"Damn deer!" he yelled. Why the hell did they do that? There was a solid half hour between him and any other vehicle. Thirty minutes for deer to cross the road, cross back, maybe even take a nap on the warm asphalt if they felt like it. Yet they waited for headlights. Were they as indecisive as they were stupid? Frank promised himself that if he ever lost his mind and sprinted blindly across a road, he would at least slow down to look for traffic.

He shook a lone menthol out of a grungy cigarette box and jammed it between his thin lips. He could feel his heart thumping from the adrenaline. He decided to take a break for a few minutes, nudging his car into a more suitable parking position along the shoulder of the highway. He was beginning to suspect that the alcohol had affected him more than he had previously thought. If he parked the car for an hour he could probably still get to OKC by the time Hillary's bus got there, and that was assuming it got there on time itself. Maybe her bus driver was taking a smoke break because of a deer *he* nearly hit. Probably not, though. Buses didn't have to worry about hitting many things besides other buses.

He turned the engine off and leaned over to search for a Zippo in the glove compartment. Several maps, none of which actually depicted Oklahoma, fell to the floorboard. The lighter peeked out from behind an empty Listerine bottle. He pocketed it and stepped out of the car, but not before checking his pocket for the keys—he was very careful about that. Frank had no desire to wait until the following morning for some farmer to take a chance and drive him to the nearest phone booth, or to pick up his sister in a car with a broken window.

He lit the menthol cigarette and sat down on the trunk of the sedan, feeling the thin metal give slightly under his ass. After a couple of drags he surveyed his surroundings to see if there was anything worth staring at for the next couple of minutes. Nothing at eye level looked even remotely interesting, but the night sky above him shimmered. The headlights and lampposts of Moore and Oklahoma City drowned out lesser gas giants and dulled the rest, but between Nash and Enid, the pulsing stars could make an astronomer salivate.

His eyelids stealthily slid shut, independent of any orders. They tried to remain inert, but he forced them to flutter open again, lest he fall asleep. He still had a job to do. He took another drag on the cigarette and rubbed his eyes.

He finished his smoke and looked around. Something was off. Something felt wobbly, as if somewhere in his general vicinity he had left the oven on. He frowned, flicking the butt away from his fingers and onto the asphalt. He was beginning to suspect that he was not a "fun drunk," as he had always hoped, but was instead a paranoid one. Paranoid drunks weren't nearly as amusing, and it bothered him to eyeball the grim possibility.

He couldn't shake the odd feeling. A hunch gradually formed in his mind, telling him that he was being watched. Paranoid or not, he didn't feel like sitting on his trunk next to Route 132 anymore.

Sephus's neighbor, Leland McCorvick, was a Korean War veteran. He once mentioned to Frank over a beer that good soldiers do not look directly at whoever they sneak up on. People could sense it. So could rabbits, incidentally. Mammals have some kind of screwy sense informing them if they are being stared at.

Frank now felt very much like someone was watching him. Not sneaking up on him, although the notion of someone or *something* crawling toward him through the field sent a chill up his spine. He hopped off the trunk and opened the door to his car. He felt an urge to turn on the cabin light and make sure no one was there, but refused to acknowledge this silly impulse.

He stepped into the car and grabbed the door handle. Then, for whatever reason, he glanced up. Had he not already flicked his cigarette away, it would have dropped from his mouth.

In the sky above his car, in a huge pie slice, big as a football field, was nothing.

No stars. Just blackness. As if a perfect equilateral triangle had been cleared away above him. He stared at it for a few moments and arrived at the logical conclusion that something huge, something *gigantic*, hung directly above his car, maybe two hundred feet up, completely eclipsing the cosmos beyond. He could not see any edges or surfaces, just the gaping silhouette looming directly over his car.

Whatever dusty instinct informed Frank that he was being scrutinized flipped an alarm switch inside his head. He slammed the door shut and locked it. The engine chortled as he jammed his keys into the ignition. He put the Taurus into drive, accelerated, and double-checked to make sure the door was locked, all in one fluid motion.

Frank pushed his foot against the pedal as his car involuntarily slowed. It rolled to a stop, then went quiet as the engine neatly shut itself off. The headlights and dashboard lighting flickered, then died. Frank struggled to rouse the engine, to hit the gas, to make an escape.

The doors unlocked.

CHAPTER 3

"Hey Frank, it's me," said Hillary, with the calm, metered speech of an axe murderer on vacation. "It's three o'clock in the morning and I'm sitting at a bus station in Oklahoma City and if you don't get here in the next *forty seconds* I'm going to wander through alleys until I get mugged just to spite you." This was the twelfth message on Frank's voicemail, although the previous four were only variations of "Where ARE you?!"

Not only angry, but desperate, she dialed up her father. It cut directly to his automated message. "Hello, you've reached Arthur Norbitz. I'm not here right now, but if you'll leave your name and number, I'll get back to you in a jiffy."

It was the same half-true greeting which aired whenever summoned since the man had disappeared in March of the previous year. The phone company reluctantly agreed to keep the account active until the police removed him from the Missing Persons list. The irony was that Arthur had never paid the bills regularly enough while bodily present to keep his mobile phone coverage consistent for three months, let alone for the year and a half of his absence. She decided not to leave a message. If her father ever did reappear, he already had several hundred recordings waiting for him.

The bus station was not the happiest of places to wait for a ride after midnight. The lights were harsh, fluorescent, and prone to flickering. Fast food wrappers and other travel flotsam lay strewn across seats and the grungy tiled floor. A shifty man in a beanie hacked a cough into the crook of his arm, then glanced at Hillary suggestively.

At the opposite side of the station, the impolite James doppelganger sat cross-legged, reading his book. He was also waiting for someone, but with more patience and ease than her. He glanced her way, prompting Hillary's eyelids to narrow to slits in a gaze of unmitigated hatred.

The entrance to the bus station opened and a man with a bright houndstooth blazer stepped in, grinning. "James!" she blurted out, then slapped a hand over her mouth in response to his quizzical look.

No, she thought, *it* is *James!* This man looked even more like James than the last one! It had to be him. You could not look any more like James than the man on the bus without *actually being* James. It just wasn't possible.

"James?" she ventured meekly. Maybe he didn't recognize her; it had been six years since they graduated, or spoke. Apparently he had grown a mustache.

"Nope," he said, smiling, and gestured toward the stubble-faced jerk from the bus. The jerk in turn glanced at Hillary, looked at the newcomer, then leaped up from his chair. He grabbed his black satchel and hurried in a sprint toward the exit, following the houndstooth mustachio outside.

This was too weird for Hillary. They were clearly avoiding her, and they both looked like James. She jumped up from her own chair, hoping no one would touch her bag, and hurried after them. Outside, the constellations of skyscraper windows glowed in the otherwise black night. Somewhere in the distance a car honked, but for the most part the city slept.

The men saw her exit the building, and dashed. They pounded the cracked pavement beyond the sidewalk, galloping away from the station. Hillary pursued them, noticing their peculiar syncopated dash. They strobed in and out of the early morning darkness as they passed beneath successive streetlamps. "Stop him!" she yelled. She had not planned on doing this, but considered it a good idea now that she had. Maybe some altruistic hobo would leap out from behind a garbage can and tackle them at the knees.

The two men jogged passed the city's luminous Botanical Gardens and hazarded brief looks back at her over their shoulders. Crossing the street again, the man in houndstooth ferociously waved his arms. A silver Volvo screamed around a corner and squealed to a stop in front of them. The door to the backseat flung open and the two hurled themselves inside. The car lurched forward as the grinning mustachio swung the door shut behind him.

Hillary stopped running and stood on the sidewalk as the car careened down the street towards her. As it passed her by, she caught a brief glance of the driver.

He looked an awful lot like James.

CHAPTER 4

"Those mathematician sonsabitches," Leland McCorvick growled. "Damn bastard sonsabitches number crunchers." The haggard farmer spat a glob of masticated Copenhagen chewing tobacco next to his boots. He squinted in the bright, shadeless lake of wheat.

"Who?" Sephus asked.

"Sombitch mathematicians," grumbled Leland, altering the grammatical formula he had been using to fashion expletives.

"You think . . . mathematicians did this?" asked Sephus, dumbstruck. He stood at the center of a perfect flattened circle amidst the wheat crop. *Absolutely* perfect. Beautifully so. Around it, increasingly smaller circles formed a spiral, and north of them another circle with a key-like outcropping gestured to an additional ring with a smaller, inversed projection.

"Who the hell else'd do it?" Leland demanded, hands on hips. "Cows?"

"Well," Sephus said, still surveying the crop circle around him, "extraterrestrials, maybe."

The farmer snorted. "Nah, I watched a special on these here crop circles. 'S mathematicians. College students with boards 'n ropes through 'em come out and walk around all funny-like and beat down the wheat to make these stupid designs."

Leland, like many from the region, possessed questionable grammar, but watched the History and Discovery channels every night after the news, and was consequently a fairly educated man with broad knowledge in a variety of fields. He expertly wielded his homemade contractions as brain camouflage to the detriment of northern businessmen who underestimated him in wheat negotiations.

"Why would mathematicians want to stamp circles in your field?" Sephus asked.

"Dunno," Leland replied. "Drunk, probly." This was Leland's explanation for a lot of deviant behavior, and was, more often than not, spot on.

Sephus suppressed a grin. *Crop circles!* He couldn't believe he was standing in one, on a neighboring farm, no less. It was like he was in a story from *Midnight Chat* with Charles Gander! "There aren't any colleges near here."

"No, but they can drive, can't they?"

Leland walked back toward his equipment shed. Sephus followed, then stopped to answer his cell phone, turning away from the wind. "Hello? Frank?" he asked. A Frankish static fuzzed back over the phone. "How's Hillary?"

"I'm in Utah!" Frank shouted, finally bursting through the interference.

"What?" Sephus asked. "No you're not." Sephus had no problem arguing with people about basic information they ought to know. He worked one summer in his youth as a host and waiter, and had sometimes corrected people on how to pronounce their own names.

"I'm in *Utah!*" Frank repeated. "Park City, Utah."

Sephus furrowed his eyebrows and cupped the receiver on his Stars & Bars cell phone. "Listen, Frank, it's seven o'clock in the morning right now, and you dropped me off around ten last night. That's nine hours. Utah is at least fifteen hours away. You could not have driven that far in one evening."

"Well I must have, Sephus," Frank said. Annoyance poured in through the static.

"Must have?"

"Yes, I . . . I don't actually recall driving to Utah."

Sephus looked around the inside of the crop circle for help. "Are you guessing that you're in Utah? Hand the phone to someone around you. You're probably just in Guymon." Frank couldn't find his way out of a refrigerator box.

"I know where I am, Sephus! I just don't know how I got here. I woke up a few minutes ago parked on a runaway truck ramp. All of the license plates here say 'Utah.'"

Sephus frowned. It was not odd for his friend to wake up at strange locations, surprised to find himself there. Usually next to some beer cans, maybe an ex-girlfriend. But at no point had Frank ever woken up in a different state, with logistical amnesia. "What do you remember?" Sephus asked, almost as confounded as Frank.

Frank silently skimmed his memories of the previous evening. The long stretch of road, the deer, the cigarette. The lack of stars, the sudden panic, the rapid acceleration and deceleration. His door unlocking, and a soft light growing brighter inside of his car, like a spotlight dribbling in through the windows. Then Park City, Utah.

"Nothing," Frank said. "One minute I was in—" he corrected himself, "I was near Nash, the next moment, Utah." Sephus said nothing on the other end of the phone. "Sephus . . . I think I'm an alcoholic."

"Maybe," Sephus agreed. "What are you saying, that you blacked out and then drove all the way to Utah, too drunk to remember?"

"Seems like the best explanation to me."

"But . . . That's fifteen hours away."

"Right," Frank said with a touch of pride in his voice. He was still confused and a little frightened, but there was a growing chance that he had made the best time on a road trip in the history of mankind.

"What did Hillary say?" Sephus asked.

"Hillary?" Sephus could picture Frank suddenly remembering his sister. Hillary, standing at a bus station for nine hours, tapping her foot, slowly transforming into a five-foot-nine dynamite keg. "Oh no."

"Call Hillary," Sephus advised. "Your family probably thinks you're dead."

"Right," Frank said. "Okay, I'll see you in a couple of days."

CHAPTER 5

James yawned and slipped into his bathrobe before descending the stairs of his home. He drifted towards the clinking of silverware and humming, drawn to the odors of breakfast wafting out from his kitchen. An exact duplicate of himself, with the addition of a mustache, stood flipping pancakes next to his stove. "Good morning, sir!"

"Good morning, Monty," James said, awarding him two pats on the shoulder. "I'm surprised you're up."

Montgomery scraped the pancakes off of the frying pan with a spatula and dropped them onto a plate next to a pile of steaming scrambled eggs. "James, this is a lovely house. I'm glad you volunteered to host us this year."

The homeowner shrugged and poured himself a cup of coffee from the bubbling pot. "Just happy to help. It works well logistically, what with being in the middle of the country and everything."

"Right," said Monty, sliding sausage links onto the pan. "Oh, that reminds me—thanks for picking me up from the airport last night."

"Not a problem. If I hadn't been so sacked I would've rode with you and Karl to the bus station."

"About that," said Monty, tapping the spatula as he spoke. "Something happened last night which—"

"Morning all," announced Vincent. This dead ringer for James sat down at the kitchen table and inhaled the surrounding aromas. "Glorious. I've been looking forward to your pancakes, Monty."

Montgomery grinned and held his spatula up in salute. "Are those new silk pajamas, Vincent?"

The man nodded, scratching his stubble. "I was at Macy's the other day and thought, 'You know, I sleep nearly every night. I might as well invest in decent pajamas.'"

James sat down next to him and squeezed his elbow. "Vincent, it's good to see you. How have you been?"

His double shrugged. "I'm doing very well. Nearly out of ideas, but I don't think anyone who reads my column will notice. Yourself?"

"Fantastic. Couldn't be better."

"Good morning," another double said, freshly emerged from the couch. He too looked identical to James, sans laugh lines. "Monty, that smells delicious. James, Vincent," he said, seating himself at the table.

Montgomery tipped his head toward the table. "Good morning, Karl. Dig in, fellas. I've been sampling breakfast the whole time. The sausage will be out momentarily."

Karl set three pancakes onto the plate in front of him and divided them into squares with expert precision. "James, has anyone spoken to you about last night's incident?"

James raised his eyebrows. "Incident? No, Karl, I just woke up."

The identical man nodded, depositing a small layered cube of flapjack into his mouth. He munched on it appreciatively and swallowed. "Delicious, Monty. You've outdone yourself."

"Thanks," Montgomery said, setting down the sausages and joining the three at the table.

"Last night a young woman recognized Vincent. She mentioned you by name. And, when Montgomery entered the bus station to signal Vincent, she chased them both until I came around with your car." He pointed toward the front door. "Your keys are on the rack, incidentally. Thanks."

James set his fork down. "Did anyone catch this woman's name?"

"It was Hillary Norbitz," said Vincent. "I recognized her from the dreams."

"Oh, *that* one," grinned Monty. Everyone except James chuckled.

James blushed. "Are you sure it was her?"

"Tall, lithe young woman." Vincent smiled and looked into the distance. "Flaxen hair dusted with copper, teeth whiter than albino piano keys. Hillary Norbitz, Jimmy."

Karl appeared less than nostalgic. "Is this woman a security threat?"

"Who, Hillary?" returned James. He shoveled some scrambled eggs onto his plate. "No, why would she be? We were very close in college, but we haven't spoken much since."

Karl sliced his sausage into tiny coins of fried pork. "Is there any chance she'll drop by your home while we're here? I don't want her asking a lot of questions."

James shook his head. "No, she doesn't know where I live. She's probably just visiting her family for Labor Day weekend. Don't worry about it."

"Good," said Monty. "Let's move on to something else, then. Why not kick off the weekend with a toast?" He raised a glass of apple juice. The others raised their coffees. "Gentlemen," he said,

looking each in the eyes, "to ourself."
  "To ourself!" they answered.

CHAPTER 6

Frank clinked his seventy-eight cents onto the counter and thanked the clerk, an apologetic-looking teenager, for the coffee. Java had definitely improved in quality since Utah. It was still bad, per se, but at least the natives did not intentionally make it worse. When you get into small Mormon communities no one visits except perhaps other Mormons (and even then reluctantly) the people resent selling coffee at all. They still offer it, for whatever reason, but it tastes like they're adding salt to it, just to teach the heathens a lesson.

Park City had decent coffee, but only because it was a tourist town. Even so, Frank had been relieved when the pleasant ski resort village faded into the mountains behind him. Park City was so kempt and organized it was creepy, like the inhabitants were planning something. To Frank, it was Disney World through the eyes of Tim Burton.

He put the gas station cup to his mouth and blew on it, letting the air bounce off of the brown wetness and carry the smell of stale coffee beans up through a forest of nose hair. He had no idea how people drank coffee right out of the machine. Maybe folks who downed boiling hot coffee hated the flavor, so they didn't mind having their taste buds scalded off. Frank somewhat enjoyed the taste of coffee, but he did not like searing pain in his mouth from blistering hot liquids.

He walked over to the condiment dispenser beside the slushie machine and stirred two packets of sugar and a little cream into his drink. Satisfied that it was of acceptable temperature and modification, he sipped a little, then took a gulp. He nodded to the clerk, who was scanning an inventory binder with a covert *Playboy* magazine tucked inside, and walked out to his car.

The theorized fifteen-hour drive was probably going to turn into a twenty-hour drive, because Frank had made a wrong turn and very nearly ended up in Las Vegas, where he wished he had randomly awoken that morning instead of Utah. It was already dark and he was in Colorado, and unsure of how many more hours it would be before he got back to his trailer in Hoople. Probably at least six.

It did not bode well for work the following day. Tired as he would be after the long drive back, he would still need to go to work bright and early. He had not expected to take an unpaid vacation, let alone do so in Utah. His boss at the grain elevator had been reasonably forgiving about Frank's absence when they spoke over the phone, but that was probably in part because Frank had feigned food poisoning. Actually, Frank had surprised himself with the quality and pathos of his performance in regard to fake vomiting and moaning about expired tuna. If his job working at a grain elevator didn't pan out, perhaps he'd head to California and become a movie star.

Six hours, he thought. *At least.* He took a deep breath and quit beating himself up about the wrong turn. Yes, he had made a mistake, and yes, the extra time incurred was a blow to his manhood, but there was nothing he could do now but press on and avoid falling asleep at the wheel.

Also, there was the shortcut.

That would save some time. At his previous coffee stop at the Utah-Colorado border, he had picked up a map and charted an ingenious method of abridging his trip through a series of strategic back roads. Most people wouldn't do this sort of thing, because it's easy to speed on highways, whereas back roads tend to be made out of dirt or gravel and therefore not conducive to speeding. Fortunately, Frank's Ford Taurus was dinged up enough that he felt comfortable subjecting its underside to a little sandblasting from the road. Hell, it might even peel off the remains of the unfortunate skunk he hit near the state line.

The last few drops of coffee oozed into his mouth, sluggish with partially stirred cane sugar. He chucked the cup into the car's wastebasket, which was the driver's side window. He tried to hum a Garth Brooks medley but could not remember what came in between the bits about wild horses, and resorted to the radio instead. He twisted the dial back and forth aimlessly, combing the barren airwaves. Outside, the familiar sight of wheat whistled by, as the mountains of Colorado yielded to more gentle fields that would eventually roll into Kansas.

At last a voice punctured through the void, prompting Frank to groan. It was that crackpot Charles Gander, whom Sephus listened to religiously. Frank had a brief internal debate between silence, static, and *Midnight Chat*, reluctantly choosing the paranormal talk show.

"—has struck again," said Gander. "Both state and federal officials are baffled by the recent murders, and remind citizens to report any information they might have about the Rectum Thief to authorities. Investigators now believe the serial killer is responsible for the deaths of eighteen people, although more are possible." *Midnight Chat,* which extended well beyond midnight and occasionally skipped it entirely, began each show with an hour of news tenuously connected to the world everyone who did not listen to *Midnight Chat* lived in, then some calls from listeners.

The Rectum Thief was a mysterious serial killer who thwarted law enforcement officials and kept mothers all over the Southwest in the grip of terror. Police claimed the victims were killed relatively quick, with minimal pain. This was weird in and of itself, as homicidal maniacs usually incorporate a morbid artistic flourish into their sadistic habits. Yet, forensic investigators reported that his victims died before hitting the ground, let alone before their dismantling.

Once the murderer killed the victims, he surgically removed various parts of their bodies. No calling card, no cryptic messages pieced together with letters from magazines, no pattern. Just a series of stolen eyeballs, spleens, appendixes, and on two occasions, rectums. The final stolen pieces led to the serial killer's nickname, unflattering even by serial killer standards.

"What I don't understand, ladies and gentlemen," continued Gander, "is why the police don't call in psychic investigators. There are multiple, proven, *documented* cases of psychics locating missing persons and discerning the identities of murderers, and it's high time—" Frank

30

slapped the tuner. Charles Gander's voice drowned in a flood of static. He did not like Charles Gander. So far as Frank was concerned, Charles Gander was the Rush Limbaugh of Bigfoot experts, occultists, and a string of "scientists" educated exclusively within the Caribbean.

Out of the static came a new sound, almost like speech. It was distant and eerie, like baritones trying to gargle and speak Portuguese at the same time in the back of a cave. The sound made Frank shiver, and he turned the radio off altogether. Gravel plinked the undercarriage of his car.

As he rounded a curve onto one of his strategic Colorado backroads, he felt the hairs on his neck stand on end, then, even more impressively, his arm carpeting do the same. It felt similar to the sensation which heralds being struck by lightning, which Frank had experienced twice through a combination of interesting meteorological phenomenon, golf, and amazingly poor planning.

He turned the air conditioning up as he felt a bead of sweat form on his forehead. His heart rate increased. *Damn that Charles Gander,* he thought. The news report about that creepy serial killer must have given Frank the willies. He found himself checking his rearview mirror to make sure no knife-wielding psychopath sat in the back, waiting to filch his sphincter.

As the car bumped off a pothole the radio turned itself back on, this time with even louder Portuguese cave gurgling. Frank pounded the dashboard with his fist until it fell back into silent submission. He found himself quite spooked. He did not know why, and this made him even more frightened. He focused on controlling the coffee sloshing around his bladder, looking for an opportunity to leave, and this miniscule amount of control over the universe made him feel a little better.

The momentary relief abated as a new wave of paranoia washed over him. He did not sense, like the previous night, that he was being watched. He was being *chased*. He was a deer in a crosshair, running. He jammed his foot against the gas pedal and throttled down the road, barely keeping the Taurus's traction on the gravel beneath.

His dashboard lights died. The engine began to sputter. "No, dammit!" he yelled, hitting the steering wheel with his hand. He pumped the gas pedal up and down and shifted into a different gear. The engine flared into life once more, lurching forward. He kept speeding, hitting seventy miles per hour, eighty. Again the engine nearly died, and he repeated the gearshift maneuver, swerving back and forth on the road as if trying to keep his car awake.

Frank leaned to his right as the road curved. His car strained to keep all four tires on the ground. It straightened, then nearly hit a gray blur as something ran in front of the headlights. It startled Frank enough that he did not have time to react to the next curve. He jerked the steering wheel to the left and squealed the breaks, but the Taurus careened off of the gravel and sailed through a rotting wooden fence.

The car shook and rattled like a doomed roller coaster as it launched through a field, hit a bale of hay, skidded on two wheels, and slammed into another bale of hay. This one brought the Taurus to a stop, although Frank, not wearing a seatbelt, bounced inside of the automobile for a couple of additional, painful seconds.

The impact threw him to the passenger side of the car with his legs draped over the driver's seat, jammed beneath the wheel. He painfully dislodged them and made sure nothing was broken. He seemed to be in one piece, but with several bruises, and many proto-bruises waiting their turn to announce themselves.

In particular, his head hurt. He touched it and drew back blood—the steering wheel he had pounded for years had finally struck him back. His left eyebrow needed stitches, and blood was starting to drip into his eye. As he wiped a few errant drops away he saw movement beyond the left side of the car. He unlocked the door and fell out, discovering a tender ankle. He picked himself up and half ran, half limped, into the field.

His car was parked in a grazing area, but he ran past this, over a fence, into a wheat field. Stalks scraped past him, making him grunt. He kept running until his ankle and a throbbing side-stitch compelled him to stop.

He crouched down in the wheat and forced himself to breathe slow, hushed breaths. A rustle a few yards away made his head jerk. It jerked again, painfully, as he heard quick, light footsteps behind. He looked at the ground around him for something he could use as a weapon. A rock, or, God willing, a revolver some careless gun enthusiast had dropped whilst threshing wheat. A stick, a little thicker than a pool cue, was all he could find.

He stood up and gripped the wood like a baseball bat, taking a step toward the sound of footsteps. Something rushed ahead past his line of sight, then ducked down in the wheat. He took another step forward and cocked the stick back. Aiming where he thought the sound came from, he flung the wood. It didn't release.

Something was holding it.

Something behind him.

CHAPTER 7

Hillary opened the little drink fridge by the checkout line, scooped out a Mocha Frappuccino, popped the top off, and emptied it down her gullet in one frat-inspiring gulp. She set it down in the basket of the shopping cart so that she would not forget to pay when leaving the store and be prosecuted for shoplifting.

Exhaustion bubbled in her plasma. She had slunk back to the bus station the previous evening only to find her luggage missing. After half an hour of frantic searching, she located it in the women's restroom, unzipped but with everything accounted for. This was almost as disturbing as never seeing it again. What the *hell* had the thief done with it? Why, she marveled, would someone steal a suitcase, take it to the middle of the ladies' room, unzip it, and then leave? When she arrived at her mother's home via taxi at 4:00 a.m. she scoured the bag for a bomb or cocaine or small animals a lunatic might have stuffed into it. Nothing. Just a mysterious whiff of hazelnut.

Frank, the idiot, called her not only in the middle of desperately needed sleep, but also at the exact moment in her dream when Hugh Grant was about to embrace her. Hillary had been too groggy to have a good conversation about why exactly her brother was in Utah instead of at the front door with a consolation six-pack of beer or chocolate or a new DVD, so she had contented herself with yelling at him for a few minutes before slamming the phone down and concentrating on the English movie star with her head buried beneath the pillow.

Sleep did not return. At nine o'clock her mother knocked on her door while simultaneously swinging it open, then placed a tray of orange juice, French toast, and a comprehensive list of errands and chores on top of the nightstand. By ten o'clock she was at a grocery store in Oklahoma City.

Helen, Hillary's mother, refused to buy groceries. Her husband Arthur had disappeared on a grocery run. Helen filed a missing persons report, but most of the family and police department were confident that he walked out on her. The grocery run had come after one of the many ceasefires that marked the highlights of Arthur and Helen's marriage. The previous night had been a marital Ragnarok, involving broken plates, woken neighbors, the reputations of several dead relatives, and a wounded tabby cat.

Helen, in a perverse coping mechanism, found the prospects of a dead husband far more appealing than an AWOL one. She referred to him in the past tense, set a spot for him at any family function worthy of the good china, and wore black on the single anniversary of his disappearance. Once, when drunk on Uncle Vernon's bourbon-nog, she had made a vague reference to her suspicions of "death by Rectum Thief."

Hillary assumed he had gone to a bar, peered into his gin like a crystal ball, and reflected on his life. After a few minutes of deliberation, he declared it a sinking ship filled with people he would not share a rowboat with, and took off. Maybe he had gotten the groceries, maybe he hadn't. They would never know.

Hillary glanced at the list in her hand and mentally organized her route through the store. As she tried to remember if tea and "that one type of bean dip I like, not the kind with the blue label," were on the same side of the building, James pushed by in a creaky cart. Hillary eyeballed him and considered whether or not to blurt his name out, ultimately thinking better of it. She had already accused two other people of being James, had spied a third in their getaway car, and was not about to make that same mistake again.

He stopped in front of a wall of Cheetos and smiled at her. "Hillary?"

She cocked her head and double-checked to make sure he was actually James. Same well-worn tweed sports coat, same immaculate khaki pants, same unimposing loafers. "Yes?" she responded, playing it safe.

"It's me. James?" He extended his palms and did a little jazz hands maneuver to somehow jog her memory, in case any memories of him featured half-assed dance moves. Hillary returned his smile.

She pushed her shopping cart out of the way to give him a hug, wrapping her hands around his waist and leaning back. "James, what are you doing here?"

He glanced quickly to his left and then back at her. "Labor Day weekend."

"Me too!" she exclaimed, disengaging from the embrace. "I'm here visiting Mom and Frank, except that Frank is driving back from Utah because last night he drove there instead of Oklahoma City to pick me up, the moron."

"Really?" James asked. "You'd think he'd realize

he was going in the opposite direction once he left the state."

"Frank is an idiot," Hillary said, settling the matter. "Why are you here for Labor Day?" James glanced to his left again, prompting Hillary to look in that direction. "Do you have family here?"

James had no idea how to handle this. If he said yes, she would probably bring up the fact that identical versions of himself, save fashion and hair styles, were bumping around the metro area bus station. This might encourage questions about twins, even though she knew he was an only child.

"I..." he glanced around the aisle in search of a good reason to be in Moore. "Left my cow here." *Where had* that *come from?* Did not "I live in Oklahoma City" make more sense? Or even "I'm buying groceries?"

"Your cow?" Hillary asked.

"I mean," he said, as inspiration struck, "I mean my girlfriend lives here. Or her family does, anyway. Girlfriend, not cow. Girlfriend."

Hillary's smile tightened as the natural impetus behind it died away. "Is your girlfriend fat?" she asked.

James took a deep breath. "She's voluptuous."

"Oh. Maybe I know her, I'm from here. What's her name?"

James thought about this for a second, which did not make him look like a very good boyfriend. "Susan Miller?" he asked. It was the first name that popped into his head. Sounded more specific than "Smith."

"Yes, actually, I do know her." She closed her eyes to summon the image of a girl from her adolescence. "When we were in high school she went by Susie Miller, but it's probably the same girl. A head shorter than me and blonde?"

Crap, James thought. How difficult was it to come up with the name of a girl who *didn't* exist, or at least didn't know the person he was talking to?

"She dyed it last year," he admitted. "You know that sort of hair that's, like, blonde, but it's got darker colors in it, so it sort of looks textured? Like girls on magazine covers? It looks like that."

"Oh," Hillary said, now rifling through her shopping cart. She started reading the ingredients on the back of a milk carton, which were "milk." "Please tell Susan I said hello."

"She says 'hi,' too," James said.

"What?" Hillary asked, setting the milk down.

"I mean I'll bet she'll say hi, so you can just assume she said 'hi' back. That's how nice Susan is, always saying hello and such. Nice girl. Voluptuous," he added.

"Okay, well, it's good to see you. We're having a barbeque tomorrow night, so if you're not doing anything, you and Susan should come by. Mom asks about you occasionally, and I wouldn't mind catching up."

"I'd love to, but Susan's Jewish."

"We're not serving pork."

"Ah, I'm on a 'pork only' diet right now. Polish nutritionist thing."

"Then . . . but then you and Susan . . ."

"Okay, well I gotta go." James backed out of the aisle and waved to Hillary. He raced down another aisle, shoved the cart aimlessly, and ran out of the store.

CHAPTER 8

A solitary car exited the highway and rolled into the town with quiet purpose. It continued past small houses to slightly larger houses with bigger yards. It pulled up to one in particular and stalled as the driver grabbed a newspaper from the seat beside him and flipped a few pages back.

The article featured a picture of a crop circle found on a farm near an obscure town in Iowa two days earlier. It was a massive spiral of disparately sized rings. Tiny straight lines and forks extended from some in various directions. A few of the circles connected with bars and double bars.

The driver checked the picture a third time and folded up the newspaper with resolution. He turned the car off, pocketed the keys, and put on black leather gloves. He picked up an unlabeled kit and a ridiculously sophisticated, self-heating, battery-powered thermos and exited the car. Slow, deliberate steps clinked against the cracked sidewalk in the humid summer air.

He stepped onto the porch, a sort of squat trailer park imitation of a Victorian landing, and glanced behind him. Satisfied that he could see no neighbors or other houses, he knocked on the door, once, twice, thrice. His figure loomed motionlessly in the doorway, listening to the sound of creaking floorboards as its owner approached from within.

Somewhere in the house a light turned on. Footsteps padded to the entry. A large wooden door opened behind its screen forerunner. A man who had obviously just woken up at three in the morning stared at the visitor on his front porch. Boxer shorts hung beneath an undershirt that had probably never been under anything, yet still desperately needed retirement. Graying stubble was smeared across his face. His thinning comb-over leaned completely to his left, as if it had tried to escape while he was sleeping. Short, dark-gray hair covered much of his ears, giving the appearance of mold.

"What?!" he demanded, angry and bewildered, but mostly angry.

"Darryl Sworsen?" The man asked in a quiet, metered voice.

"What the hell do you want?"

"Darryl Sworsen?" he repeated.

"Do you have any idea what time it is?"

"Darryl Sworsen?"

The man closed his eyes. He was tired, he was getting older, he didn't want to play games. "Yes, now what—"

The visitor's hand shot through the screen door and into Darryl Sworsen's extensive beer belly. Sworsen staggered back and looked at the fist and syringe poking through the torn screen. He slammed the wooden door shut and locked it behind him.

The intruder bent down to open his kit and placed the used syringe in a small hard case where it couldn't poke anything. He zipped the kit up and opened the screen door. His gloved hand grasped the doorknob firmly as he put his shoulder against the wood to test the door's strength. He withdrew his wallet, took out a credit card, and slid it through the doorframe. It wiggled back and forth in his hands until the latch clicked, and he returned the card to his wallet.

He picked up his kit and let himself into the house, then shut the door behind him. He glanced around the hall as a crash echoed through the house, then walked toward the noise. The hallway opened into a dining room with an attached kitchen. Sworsen lay on the floor, facedown. Blood slowly collected beneath him. A little could be seen on the edge of the counter, where he had hit his head as he passed out. A cordless phone sat on its side a few inches from his outstretched left hand.

The man paced over to Sworsen's body and bent down to examine the phone. "Hello?" a voice asked from the receiver. "Hello?" the same woman repeated, this time concerned. "Sir, is everything ? Do you need us to send help?"

The man picked the phone up and held it a few centimeters from his face. "Yes?" he asked calmly.

"Sir?" the voice came back. "Is everything alright?"

"Yes," he responded in an even calmer voice. "Everything is fine. Thank you. Dad was choking, but I just got in and gave him the Heimlich. He's fine now."

"May I speak to him?" the voice asked, relieved.

"No thank you," he said, as if turning down fries at a drive-through. "We appreciate your help. Have a pleasant evening." He disconnected the phone and set it back in the charger. With no noise or passion, he flipped Sworsen over and inspected his face. He had hit his nose on the way down, which now bled profusely. The body's eyes were half open and dim, unblinking.

The intruder left the kitchen in search of a

bathroom and returned shortly. He hoisted Sworsen up and looped his arms under the body's shoulders before dragging him down the hall. He placed the body inside of the tub, then returned to the kitchen to retrieve his kit.

CHAPTER 9

Frank awoke to the meaty hand of Leland McCorvick gripping his shoulder and rocking him back and forth. "Get yer ass up, you drunken sonvabitch!"

Frank pulled his head up from the steering wheel and looked at the wheat stalks engulfing his car. McCorvick leaned in through the open door, jerking him into consciousness. "Am I in Colorado?" Frank asked. His body was sore all over, as if he had run the length of a marathon and decided that stretching was for losers.

"What?!" Leland spat. "Yer on my farm, you whiskey-guzzling sombitch!"

Frank rubbed his eyes. "In . . . in Hoople?"

"Yes, dammit!" Leland yelled, as infuriated at Frank's geographic idiocy as his overtly incompetent parking job. The farmer motioned for Frank to unbuckle his seatbelt, because he wasn't going to put his hand that close to another man's groin during peacetime. As soon as the belt was unlatched he hoisted Frank out of the car by his neck and let him scramble to his feet on the fallen wheat stalks.

"Son," the man said, red faced, "I would beat you within an inch of yer life." His eye twitched. "Within a *centimeter* of yer life you *damned drunken sonvabitch hippy!*" (Frank did not know the metric system any better than Leland McCorvick did, worse, in fact, but he did not want to argue with the man.) "But you managed to pass out in the one part of my crop already destroyed by those," here his face

45

turned purple as another interloping group popped into his head, *"damned sonsabitches mathematicians!"* He spewed out chewing tobacco in contempt.

"Mr. McCorvick," Frank said apologetically and with a hint of mirth, hoping he might somehow funnel this otherwise sour meeting into a humorous "Wow, what a night I had!" story.

"Shut the hell up!" barked McCorvick. "Son, you speak when spoken to, you got that?"

Frank was not sure if it was appropriate to answer this orally, so he nodded.

"Good, you lush sonvabitch. Now listen, I don't know how the living hell you got your car all the way into this here crop circle without leaving a trail, but you do the exact same thing to get out, ya hear?" Frank gulped, nodded. "Take her slow, don't hurt the wheat. When you get onto the road you drive the speed limit as fast as you can away from my property or by living hell I will *end* you, son. Y'understand?"

Frank nodded furiously and reached for his keys. He noticed that his pants were on backwards, so he switched hands and fished them out of his de facto left buttocks pocket. He climbed into his car and started it, then rolled at a speed he guessed would neither plow through the wheat nor stay long enough to compress it. Once he hit the road, he drove the specified forty-five miles per hour until the McCorvick farm disappeared from the horizon, then he sped toward Sephus's home.

He looked at himself in the mirror. The gash on his forehead had disappeared. A hairline pink sliver marked where the otherwise gaping wound should have been. Checking the rest of his face in the mirror, then glancing at his arms, he could find no wounds or scabs from the previous evening's unforeseen collision with a bale of wheat.

He pulled up to Sephus's farmhouse and parked next to his friend's pickup. He pounded on the front door, waited impatiently, then let himself in. Roswell, Sephus's cat, stared him down a few feet from the door. Cats creeped the hell out of Frank, so much so that the wide-eyed tabby was more effective at keeping him at the door than a Doberman.

"Sephus!" he yelled.

"What?" a voice called from the opposite end. "Frank, that you?"

"Yes!"

"How was the drive?" he called back.

"Really weird."

"That's nice." Sephus wandered down the hall in a green towel. Little specs of red dotted his face where a dulling razor had nicked him. "Is Hillary going to kill you?" Sephus had met Frank's sister only once, two years ago at Christmas. A month prior to the holiday Frank had mentioned that the picture of the willowy strawberry blonde hanging in his trailer's kitchen was not, as Sephus previously assumed, cut out from an issue of *Cosmo*, but was in fact his sibling. The farmer could not believe Frank was related to anyone so striking or intelligent-looking. He joined the Norbitzes that Christmas specifically to see if her photo had been airbrushed.

"She'll get over it," Frank said, dismissing the question. He pointed the conversation back to himself. "Something's happened to me." He looked at his friend imploringly.

"Your pants are on backwards, Frank." Sephus

turned around and walked down the hall. "Which reminds me: pants." He stepped into his bedroom and closed the door. Frank unbuckled his belt, which was surprisingly difficult from behind. He was about to drop his pants and put them on the right way, but the cat kept watching him. He forced himself to disengage from the feline's stare, gazing instead at a family picture of the Fitzbaur family taken in Sephus's late adolescence. The happy family posed in front of a blue backdrop, all grinning, all wearing matching sweaters, and all holding pistols.

Sephus returned in a work shirt and overalls. He synched an orange Oklahoma State University cap over his damp, thinning hair. "You want some orange juice, Frank?"

Frank nodded and followed him into the kitchen. He sat down and slumped against the table.

Sephus handed him a glass of juice. "Okay, so what's the problem?"

Frank took a deep breath. Sephus was his best friend, or at least his best friend within reasonable geographic distance. He needed to talk to someone about the strange things happening to him, if only to sort them out in his own head. But he did not want to tell Sephus. Not because Sephus would laugh at him—that was okay. He could handle that. Rather, Sephus would nod and get excited and come up with a screwball theory to explain it.

"Last night on my way back from Utah, I was driving through Colorado and I got this weird . . ." he searched for the right word, "feeling." He swallowed, continued. "I got all panicked and started speeding, then I went off the road and crashed into a hay bale."

Sephus took a long sip of orange juice and licked the pulp off his smooth upper lip. "Are you all right? You must be, if you drove here."

"But I didn't!" Frank blurted out. "I didn't drive here!" He drew a long gulp of his own orange juice and a deep breath. "I ran out of my car—I felt like a deer being chased—and I ran into a wheat field." Goose bumps popped up on his arm like itchless mosquito bites as an echo of the terror dripped out of his memory and down his spine.

He could not recall much of what had happened afterwards. He remembered the jumpy things in the field, swishing around in the wheat, and he remembered trying to hit one with a stick. After that, he could only recall screaming. In fact, in his mind he could see *himself* screaming, but that didn't make any sense. He decided the stick and the field monsters were too much to tell another human being. Especially Sephus.

"After that?" Sephus asked.

"I woke up on Leland McCorvick's farm, and he nearly killed me." He touched his left eyebrow. "When I crashed the car, it split my eyebrow open. A really big gash, too. I needed stitches. But when I woke up this morning there weren't any scabs on me. Not even bruises, just sore muscles. And my car was parked . . ." he calculated the time in his head, "a good six or seven hours from where I crashed it."

Sephus digested all of this. "And your pants were on backwards?"

"Right," Frank added uncomfortably. "And my underwear too, I think."

"Can I see your watch?" Dumbstruck, Frank unfastened his Casio and dropped it on the table.

Sephus picked it up and compared it to his own. "Twenty-three minutes behind." He handed the watch back and clasped his hands. "Yup, you've been abducted by aliens, Frank."

"Dammit!" the man cursed. "No I haven't, Sephus. Only fruitcakes and aging hippies think they get abducted."

"Actually," Sephus said, swirling his cup with his hand and watching the orange juice spin, "there are a lot of very respectable people across a wide range of professions who claim to have been abducted. Probably a lot more than we know, since a lot of folks are afraid of losing their job or standing in the community by going public."

Frank put his head in his hands. "Look, Sephus, that's a load of crap. Leland McCorvick would burn down your house if he heard you talking like that."

Sephus's back stiffened defensively. "Well, why don't you go talk to Leland, then?"

"Because if I go back there within seventy-two hours he'll probably chase me down with his tractor."

"Then you're stuck with me, and I'd appreciate it if you didn't make fun."

"Okay, sorry." Frank thought about his situation and tried to come up with other logical alternatives. "Couldn't I have just been drunk and imagined everything? Then passed out and driven myself to Leland's farm?"

Sephus bit his lower lip. "Had you been drinking?"

"No, not since two nights ago when we went to the bar."

"Then, no, I don't think so. Alcohol doesn't go

dormant and then pop up on you a day or two later."

"Maybe I'm an alcoholic."

"Right, you probably are, but that doesn't explain any of this."

"Maybe I got so drunk I don't even *remember* drinking," he said, with a touch of awe.

"I don't think it works that way."

"Maybe . . . maybe I . . . saw a hitchhiker . . . and he . . . drove me home?"

"Frank," Sephus said soothingly, "the more you deny you've been abducted by aliens, the more suppressed your memories are going to be and the worse it's going to get." He got up and walked toward his bookshelf. "I have a couple of memoirs by abductees that I think you might find helpful—"

"I read *three* books a year and I've already reached my quota."

"Have you? Or did you read the same erotica novel again three times?"

Frank looked at his shoes. "That's three book . . . readings."

"Aliens," affirmed Sephus.

CHAPTER 10

Helen Norbitz had the chronically frazzled look of a woman who raised two children and married a third. Years of vigilance for dangerous activity had strained her eyes until one day, at the age of fifty-two, they lost all tension. Large bags hung under them, which, coupled with the frizzy mats of hair framing her face, made her look a little like an Irish setter.

She took a sip of the watery coffee she preferred and gazed at the daughter sitting across from her. As she had many times, she wondered how exactly something so pretty and elegant ever clawed its way out of her. "How's St. Paul?" she asked, sensing that her motherly gaze was becoming awkward.

"Prolific," Hillary said absently.

"No, I meant St. Paul, Minnesota. How do you like it up there?"

"Oh," said Hillary, staring at the tiny rack of thimbles and trinkets on the wall that is obligatory throughout the Midwest. A doily with the family name, also compulsory, hung above it. "It's nice." She continued staring at the trinket rack with the same glazed-over precision evening people use at breakfast, morning people use when hung over, and zombies use whenever depicted. "About that. Is it okay if I stay here for a few days, maybe a week or two?"

Helen sucked down the last of her coffee, making a whiskey face as the brown grit at the bottom slid down her throat. "Of course, dear, always. Don't you need to get back for work, though?"

"Not for a while," Hillary said. "I'm going to use some of my vacation time."

"Oh, that's wonderful!" exclaimed Helen. She could think of nothing more enjoyable than having a child return to the nest for awhile.

"Actually probably two or three weeks," Hillary added.

"Wonderful!" Helen repeated, all smiles. "Did you invite Tod to our Labor Day barbeque? I'd love to see him again."

"Tod and I broke up," Hillary relayed in an overtly professional tone.

"Oh, sweetie, I'm sorry. Are you doing okay?"

Hillary nodded. "Pretty good. It was for the best, and we parted on good terms."

"That's nice. It's better if you can be friends afterwards."

Hillary felt her own cup of coffee cool in her hands. The disasters of St. Paul and the ensuing retreat to Moore had all happened in such rapid succession that their impact on her only now began to take shape. Mostly in the form of shock. She found herself staring through the wall toward the north, gazing out over the smoking, flattened Maginot Line that was her life.

"Sweetie, what are you thinking about?" her mother asked after a few minutes of silence.

Hillary glanced at her mother and decided to lie. "Just thinking about Dad, Mom."

Helen nodded sympathetically. "I think about your father a lot, too. I was talking to Reverend Thunderpop the other day, and he made an excellent point, that God lets everything happen for a reason. We don't know why the good Lord permitted the Rectum Thief to murder your father, but somehow his savage killing will be for the greater good."

"What?" Hillary asked. Previously the family had employed an unspoken agreement that Arthur simply walked out. It was interesting how, in Helen's world, the past was in as much of a state of flux as the present. "Mom, let's not talk about that."

"Okay, dear." Helen put her mug in the sink. A clever phrase once adorned its green exterior, but time had stripped some of the lettering, leaving only "Mllfg FF!" if you took the gaps out.

"Have you seen James Kelway recently?" Helen asked from the counter.

"Several times, actually, but it was only really him once."

"Oh?"

"Yeah. He's a travel writer now. I gather that he's very successful, but he usually dismisses his books as thick brochures, so I'm not sure."

"Oh, that's right," Helen said, looking toward the bookshelf in the den. "He sent me a copy of *I Kicked the Gator* last Christmas. He left a very sweet note inside if you want to read it. I didn't know he grew up in the city."

"He actually lives there, I think. He travels a lot, but keeps a house in Nichols Hills as sort of a home base."

Helen lit up a cigarette and let it hang from her fingers after a few puffs. She believed she looked sexy while holding a cigarette, and only inhaled enough to keep them lit. She was not fat, but looked as though she might become so at a moment's notice.

Her body was poised to swell, as if smoking alone forestalled the outcome of pulling the pin from a grenade.

"Did you know he's dating Susan Miller?"

Her mother's jaw dropped. "Susan Miller from high school?"

"Yes."

"That *bitch!*"

"I know!"

She leaned over, jamming a hand on her hip. "Now what's James doing with a catty girl like that?"

Hillary sighed. "You know James. Nice guy, smart. He's the guy we all planned on marrying back when we were dating guys we had no intention of marrying. Looks like Susan was smart enough to snag him."

"You know," Helen said conspiratorially, "I always thought you and James would've made a good couple." This, despite her best intentions, made Hillary feel no better.

"She's Jewish now," Hillary said, referencing James's barbeque rejection. "Not that that matters," she immediately added, feeling nervously close to racism or anti-Zionism or whatever it is if you think about a convert to Judaism in a negative context. "Susan Miller," she said in exasperation to no one in particular, but by default, her mother.

It was unthinkable. Doubly so, since some part of Hillary had always been aware of James's interest in her. She had not returned this attraction, but that didn't matter. It was comforting to know that, if she ever ran out of options, he was there, waiting. Her knight in shining backup. But Susan? The prototypical varsity cheerleader you're-not-cool-enough-to-hang-out-with-us girl?

She snatched a Wily College yearbook from the bookshelf in the den and returned to the kitchen. She flipped it open and rummaged through the pages until she saw a picture of herself and James. They were apparently the President and Member-At-Large of the Luge Enthusiast League, which she had no memory of. She suspected they had cooked it up to get into the yearbook.

They met while attending Wily College, a proud institution of higher learning that once awarded an honorary doctorate to a horse. They first encountered each other next to the fire escape of his fraternity, Pi Kappa Upsilon, the Kosovo of the Greek system, on the way to her own sorority, Gamma Gamma Delta, the blonde Brahmins of the college. Their friendship was instantaneous.

At that time James had not yet discovered his own sense of style, nor any. He dressed similar to a professor they knew on campus who once relied on a wife to dress him, but was now divorced. To his credit, James forced himself to make direct eye contact at all times, regardless of what top Hillary wore. She saw in James not only a bizarre exception to the rule of frats, but someone so unimposing and harmless that she need never fear him.

James, conversely, saw his first approachable sorority girl. Hillary was good-looking, but had not yet realized it. Lack of confidence clung to her fuzzy sweaters like dew. At some level all girls in Hillary's sorority questioned whether or not they were pretty, but James did not know this, nor even suspected it was the case. With Hillary, at least, self-doubt simmered more towards the top.

She stood at five foot nine, an inch shorter than James. Her body made her uncomfortable for the same reason it did her sisters, but from a different angle. To them she possessed a balletic figure, tall and unforgivably slender. To her it was boyish and morbidly flat-chested, with an unnervingly cruel height that scattered half the men she met. She stooped slightly in conversation to downplay what she considered a gargantuan stature, and James found the gesture endearing.

At that time Hillary's father, Arthur, worked as a dispatcher at a trucking depot and did not make a terrible amount of money. Hillary attended her college and sorority through a series of scholarships and part-time jobs. She shopped exclusively at thrift stores throughout high school and college before doing so was trendy.

She had felt out of place amidst the more glamorous girls of Westmoore High, like Susie Miller. Sorority girls, which were, if anything, more glamorous, fashionable, and glittery than anyone encountered at Westmoore, still made her feel out of place. She feared that someday her sisters, many of whom already resented her sylphlike build, would realize she was not "one of them," and push her to the periphery of the social universe. As a result, she felt more comfortable around nerds, dweebs, and oddly proportioned people. James had been all three.

On top of that, James adored her. He showered compliments on her fashion and prettiness, which her sisters were unwilling to do, and appreciated her brains and wit, which they were unable to. He was a bookish homebody, almost always in his room, available to her whenever she wanted company or compliments. He became Hillary's friend, confidant, and surrogate house cat. James found in her enthralling female companionship, and a glimpse into a world of lip gloss and eyeliner the lower castes of Wily College only speculated about.

The friendship hit a snag their senior year when Hillary dated Francisco, an Italian Adonis who swept her off her second-hand stilettos. Francisco, like most habitual cheaters, turned out to be the jealous type. Hillary's contact with James lessened and completely ceased by the end of the spring semester. A year later, when Hillary found Francisco in bed with Trish, one of her pledge sisters, she threw a vase at him, knocked everything off his bookshelves on her way out, and dropped his engagement ring in his pet goldfish's tank, which died of unrelated matters the following week.

She had not seen Francisco since, and hoped she never would. She had not physically seen James either, but they sent each other Christmas cards that usually included sweet, hopeless promises of an impending reunion.

And now he was dating Susie Miller.

"Mom, where's the phone book?"

Helen let out a cloud of smoke. "On top of the gun case. Why?"

"I might want to order a pizza or something." She walked into the den and hunted for Susan Miller's listing through the Yellow Pages like an antidote for snake venom. Despite her simple and common names, the phone book had only one entry for Susan Miller of Moore. She poked Susan's digits into the handset and bit her lip.

The phone rang twice and made a *click* before a

woman's voice piped in. "Hello, you've reached Susan," it said, happily, confidently. This was a sexually satisfied woman, Hillary could tell, and it made her hate Susan even more. "I'm not in right now, so—"

"Hello?" Susan asked, breaking in over the message. "Hold on, I'll turn it off." She fumbled with something on the other end but her pre-recorded voice droned on. "Hello?" she repeated upon the message's conclusion.

"Susan Miller?" Hillary asked, sweetly and innocently, the cancer lurking in every packet of artificial sweetener.

"Yes? Who's this?"

"This is Hillary Norbitz. From Westmoore."

"Hillary!" the woman squealed in delight. "It's been so long! How are you? Oh, it's wonderful to hear from you! Yay!" *That bitch*, Hillary thought. She was so excited and nice that Hillary felt bad loathing her. "Did you keep your last name, or are you still single?" *Better.*

"Still single, actually, although I hear *you're* not."

"Why, no, no I'm not," Susan said bashfully. "I'm surprised you know that, we just became partners recently."

"I ran into James at the grocery store and he mentioned you were together."

"Who?" Susan asked.

"James? James Kelway?"

"Sweetie, I believe you're thinking of a different Susan. I'm, uh, a lesbian."

"Oh. That's interesting."

The conversation became increasingly fascinating from there. Susan brought up how snide she had been to Hillary, and how she had hoped to run into her someday so she could apologize. Then she asked what Hillary was wearing, which was weird, but Susan sensed it and backed off. They ended on a good note and agreed to have lunch at an unspecified date.

Hillary hung up the phone and set the yearbook down. She sat on the couch for a few minutes, letting the new information about James and psychological healing from high school sink in. After a trip to the bathroom and downing some yogurt from the fridge, she picked up her mother's copy of James's latest travel book and opened it to his handwritten note.

Mrs. N, it said in cluttered script, *I'm terribly sorry to hear about Arthur's disappearance. I only met him once, when I spent Thanksgiving with your family, but I really liked him. We watched a football game together and didn't talk at all, and that was nice because sometimes I like just sitting with people and not talking. My thoughts are with you and your family. Please let me know if I can do anything to help.* A number hung beneath his signature, which Hillary punched into the phone.

It rang twice before he picked up. "You've got James."

"You're a liar," Hillary said, all breath and smile.

CHAPTER 11

Leland McCorvick sprang upright in bed mechanically and with resolve, like the hinge of a panzer. His eyes narrowed to slits as he scanned his room for anything disturbing.

Something was amiss, and whatever it was, wherever it was, it had snapped one of the hair-trigger wires in his brain, rousing him from sleep.

He got out of bed and slipped into an old jumpsuit. He jammed his feet into sturdy boots, grunting. As he walked out of the room he stamped his feet to position them correctly in the footwear.

He strode through his house suspiciously, finally arriving at the front door. His home was secure; he would have detected any intruders by now. He opened the closet beside the entry and picked up his shotgun. Sephus, who came over once a week to drink beer and watch the History Channel with him, had once suggested he name the shotgun "Harold" because, according to Sephus, "it looks like a Harold." Leland had replied that only queers named guns, and had resumed his practice of referring to it in a purely functional manner.

He loaded the chamber, made sure the safety was on, and walked out of his house. The farmer stood on his front porch, head slowly swiveling like an oscillating fan of doom.

Leland McCorvick did not trust government officials, the liberal media, or "feelings." He *did* trust his instincts, which he saw as a biological phenomenon wholly independent of things like moods. They now told him something weird was happening on his farm, and damn it all if he wouldn't find whatever it was and kill it.

From the porch he could see his truck in plain sight, which was fine. A quick and silent walk to his freestanding garage yielded nothing out of the ordinary. He had yet to inspect his wheat fields, or his grazing land and sleeping cattle across the road. Although he knew the government could and would attempt to steal his land, it used lawyers and congressmen and worked only during daylight hours. This left the wheat and cows on it, but Leland did not sense cattle rustlers. He determined that whatever interlopers had roused him were idiot high school students, now either awkwardly groping each other in the back of a car in his field, or drinking whiskey and trying to tip over cows.

Although he would not allow any damnable youths to defile his crop, protecting his livestock took precedence. He gripped his shotgun and marched across his front yard and onto the road, then to the cattle guard a few yards away. Cattle guards consist of several pipes laid across the ground with gaps in between. Cows, which are otherwise stupid beyond all reason, are smart enough to realize that if they start screwing around with the pipes they will break a leg or two. The result is that trucks can drive over them but cows cannot, both in the sense that cows cannot drive trucks and they cannot walk over the guard.

Leland, who did not have hooves to worry about, stepped past the cattle guard and into his pasture with relative ease. He should not have been able to do this, however. Leland had built himself a dependable cattle guard, but he knew enough about life and cows to include fail-safes like gates. The entrance had a metal gate that normally latched into a fencepost, but was presently open. He had never bothered purchasing a lock for it because he assumed that in northwestern Oklahoma if you shut a gate, people knew it was supposed to stay shut, and if they were the sort of dishonest miscreants who would let themselves onto your property without your permission, they probably wouldn't care about breaking a lock anyway.

He strode across the short grass, organically mowed by cows, until he saw the reflection of moonlight bouncing off of an old blue Lincoln sedan. It looked entirely out of place in the middle of a grazing pasture at night. *Teenagers,* Leland thought. He clicked the tiny button releasing the shotgun's safety mechanism and walked a little closer to the car. He fashioned no plans to kill them, just to fire into the air and yell something. The little hoodwinks would jump back into the front seat, start the car, and get the hell off of his property. Then, if all went according to plan, they would tell all of their horny friends that Leland McCorvick tried to kill them, and he wouldn't have to scare his cows with gunfire again until a whole new batch of reprobates entered high school.

His finger prepared to pull the trigger and pepper the night sky with lead pellets when he noticed something out of the corner of his eye. He lowered the shotgun and turned his head toward movement. About thirty feet from the car, crouched over and working with his hands, squatted the figure of a man beside a cow. Those little degenerates *were* cow tipping!

Quiet wrath, the most frightening of all wraths, bubbled inside the farmer. His eyes and nostrils widened in horrifying unison as he marched toward his downed heifer. He would see to it that the brats righted the livestock and that she was okay, or he would grab them each by the ear and march them to his house, where they would call the police to come pick them up, then do chores until a car arrived.

"Hey!" Leland barked, approaching the man and cow.

He was about to say something else when he noticed blood oozing through the grass. The cow was dead, with the man up to his wrists in its entrails. "What the hell are you doing?" Leland asked, horrified, shocked, and ready to thrash the marrow out of whoever had mangled his property.

The squatting man jumped in surprise. He looked at the cow, hunkered down again, and stared directly at Leland, eyes glinting in the moonlight. With gross intensity, he thrust his hand up to his elbow inside the downed animal. After fumbling for a few moments he withdrew his limb, then dropped something into a thermos. He jammed a lid onto the cylinder, leapt up, and ran towards his car.

Leland fired his shotgun at him. The cow mutilator ducked and continued running. He flew into his vehicle, gunned the ignition, and peeled out. The Lincoln made a wide loop and headed back toward Leland, who was directly between it and the cow gate.

Many people in similar instances would have run out of the way and called the cops. Most men in his position probably would have gotten out of the car's trajectory before firing a shot at it. Not Leland McCorvick. Leland McCorvick charged a hill in Korea by himself and killed fourteen armed communists. Later that night he snuck out of the hospital with three bullet wounds and limped on crutches to the saloon half a mile away, because that morning he had promised to buy his sergeant a drink. On the way home he shot an American he found trying to rape a twelve-year-old Korean girl, and would have finished him off, too, had the crutches not slowed him down.

He stood his ground as the Lincoln bounded over the field toward him. He raised the shotgun to eye level, bracing it against his shoulder. When he could finally see the driver's eyes, he fired. The blast shattered the front and back windshield. The Lincoln veered as its driver ducked down to avoid the discharge, missing the farmer by the width of a Band-Aid.

Before the car hurtled out the cow gate, Leland McCorvick was already chasing after it. He cleared the pipes in a single leap and jogged after the swerving Lincoln, memorizing its license plate number as it zoomed away. He jumped into his truck and sped in the sedan's general direction, reloading his shotgun. But it was too late—his truck was built for reliability, not acceleration, and the Lincoln had a significant lead.

The cow killer got away.

CHAPTER 12

James wore a pair of Groucho Marx glasses with attached bushy eyebrows and plastic nose. A cheap Sooners baseball cap hung low over his forehead. He scrunched his shoulders forward in a suspicious manner. The other three wore similar outfits, except that Monty and Vincent, who could never relinquish style, wore a fedora and backwards cabby hat, respectively, instead of baseball caps. Everyone had on the Groucho Marx glasses.

"These disguises are useless," James said after a moment. "If we don't want people asking questions about our mutual identical appearances, mutually identical disguises aren't going to help any. We still look the same, but with silly glasses and fake noses." He took his glasses off and deposited them into a blazer pocket.

The four were situated in "The Retaurant," so called because no one had replaced the light-up neon "s" since the Carter administration. Montgomery and Vincent sat next to one another, as usual. The former was an affable blowhard who loved himself with the ferocity of a hundred self-help books. Vincent did not so much love himself as feel awed and a little humbled to be himself. He was slightly unnerved by all of the non-Vincent people around. Naturally the two got along beautifully, based on the mutual assumption that no one could appreciate the sheer awesomeness of either as much as the other. Karl and James sat across from them, friends by default.

Monty smiled and adjusted his glasses. "James,

where's the best place to hide something from people?"

James shrugged. "Right in front of them."

Monty stirred some sugar into his iced tea and took a sip, then wiped some residue off of the mustache. "Do you know what I did in college?" he asked.

James clinked together the ice cubes in his glass of water. "Drank like it was your job and drifted between shallow relationships?"

Monty nodded. "And, when I *was* drinking, if I got really sloshed, I'd tell people I was an alien."

His three dinner companions were aghast. "You *what?*" Karl demanded. "Why didn't you ever tell us there was a security risk?"

"Because there never was," said Monty. "Everyone in college, just like today, thought I was a gasbag. I had a reputation as a very funny guy who liked attention. On the rare occasion that I claimed I was an alien, it was laughable. Nobody took me seriously; it was just something amusing I said at parties after a few martinis."

"You let secrets slip while intoxicated?!" Karl raved, albeit quietly. "You've jeopardized the entire mission!"

"No," Monty said, perfectly composed, "I protected it. As I said, it was a joke. And as a result of it, whenever some questionable part of my identity came up, they assumed it was part of the *same gag*. But I can tell you, no one ever *really* thought I was an extraterrestrial. And if they found out some other incriminating fact about me today, they would write it off as a practical joke. Some comic yarn I started years ago with lingering tendrils." He took another sip of his iced tea. It dripped onto the table from his fake mustache, which began to molt. "I made the clandestine ridiculous."

Vincent nodded. "Hence the disguises—so ridiculous anyone would dismiss us offhand. We look silly."

"Exactly," Monty responded.

"Just the same, I'm not going to wear it anymore," James said.

"Suit yourself."

Vincent cleared his throat. "To change topics, when exactly do we want to leave?"

"Assuming that there are no indications of medical problems," said Karl, "I say when we hit thirty-five."

"Thirty-five?" asked James. "Pretty young, don't you think?"

Karl shook his head. "No, pretty safe. This is a dangerous little planet, James. There are all sorts of unforeseen accidents that get people killed. Diseases, car wrecks, heart failures, terrorist attacks."

"And mountain lions," Monty added helpfully.

Karl continued. "All it takes is one faulty capillary, and we're out of luck. I don't want to pick up the phone one day and find out we're going to waste away because Montgomery played racquetball too long. All four of us have to go back alive."

"That's part of it, though," James argued. "Mortality. That's part of being human. I think we should at least stay until we're in our sixties. Otherwise we won't really know what it's like to get older. Or have a family, for that matter. *One* of us needs to get married and reproduce."

"Not it," Vincent said.

"Not it," Karl repeated.

"You have to get married to reproduce?" asked Monty.

James's idealistic perception of their mission had been a frequent source of derision from his cohorts. Each of them operated under a different sense of motivation on Earth, but James's was the most vulnerable to mockery. Karl viewed their time in strictly professional terms, as a task to be executed. Vincent understood his stopover on the planet less as a period of personal growth and more as a gift to its inhabitants themselves. Monty saw it as an extended opportunity to shack up with exotic locals and collect anecdotes for an eventual memoir. Only James saw their sojourn as an explorer. It had compelled him to devour entire encyclopedias, and to plumb the depths of human emotion through literature, music, and reality television. It had led to his career as a travel writer. It had forced him to find out what "Canada" was.

"Still," James commented, "love and marriage are an important thing to much of humanity. Most people do one or the other before they die."

Monty got serious long enough to look sincere. "Listen James, if you can find a nice girl and marry her and have kids, I'm all for that. But before you do, you need to keep in mind that your wife will be marrying more than she bargained for. And your children might not have a father for more than a decade. Maybe long enough to raise them, but not to see their own kids or spouses."

James nodded. "I'm not planning anything, I just think if we're going to do this, we need to go all the way."

The waitress, a hefty woman with more of a makeup palette than a face, slid the check onto the linoleum table top and walked away. Montgomery snatched it before anyone else could and laid some bills on the table. "Gentlemen, I think it's time we split up. I've got a flight back to California at four, and I'm sure Vincent will be leaving for New York soon." He winked at the group and gave a mock salute. "Until next year."

CHAPTER 13

Jim Thunderpop had been the senior pastor of Third Baptist for sixteen years, which was an astounding amount of time to stay at one church. Baptist churches are congregational, which means they can hire and fire their preachers for any reason they feel like, and do. Upon arrival, Reverend Thunderpop struck up an alliance with the Old Women of the church, and no one had been able to get rid of him since. It was theoretically possible that these old women might someday die, but Reverend Thunderpop knew that most of them were too stubborn to kick off before the Rapture.

Two churches called Third Baptist existed in Moore, which confused a lot of people who, coincidentally, had no interest in attending either. The reason for two was because Thunderpop's immediate predecessor, Tom Marcky, had not left the church quietly when the Old Women (or "crone-ocracy," as he had referred to them in his final sermon) pulled the plug on his regime. There had been a cataclysmic battle between the liberal Marckyites, who wanted to spend the bake sale's money on some interior decorating to make the converted gas station feel a bit more like a church, and the conservative Old Women, who wanted to use the same money to finance missionaries to convert the heathen Russian Orthodox, who smelled Catholic and reportedly worshipped pictures.

Marcky took off before they could remove him, along with three pews, a coffee machine, and a pickup truck full of hymnals. His radical liberal followers purchased a new building out of their own pockets and declared it the new location of Third Baptist before the Old Women knew what was going on. The Old Women and the husbands they spoke through caught wind of the move, threatened a lawsuit, and removed Marcky from his position.

Marcky, with his radicals in a new church across town, refused to recognize the vote of no confidence on technical grounds, and set up a sort of Third Baptist in Exile. Ever since then the two Third Baptists of Moore refused to acknowledge each other as actually existing, although both got along fine with the older congregations of the First Baptist Church of Moore and Second Baptist Church of Moore.

When Thunderpop's regime replaced the radical Marckyites in the wake of the coup, he did not particularly care about the congregation's sordid squabbles. He had no desire to lock horns with the Third Baptists in Exile over a legal battle to determine who got to keep the name, which sounded stupid in the first place.

A week after his confirmation by the parish council as senior pastor, he and his wife, Becky, visited Marcky and his wife, Tabby. Both reverends agreed that, in general, their congregations were pretty dumb. They theorized that the denomination tended to break in half every decade or so anyway, so there was a good chance the two Third Baptists might wind up in different General Conventions and keep their coveted names anyway. The two pastors hit it off rather quickly, and e-mailed each other lame jokes or comical ideas for their church billboards every couple of weeks. Once a month they drove an hour north to Guthrie in separate cars to drink a beer and a half each, posing as Lutherans under the names of R.J. Kilroy and Phillip McPilkerton. Sometimes they wore fake mustaches.

Frank made an appointment with Reverend Thunderpop on his way to Moore earlier in the day. He knew he should probably visit his family first, but his unexplained nightly terrors bothered him. Additionally, he postulated, any expectation they had for him in regards to Labor Day weekend had been dashed some time ago.

The preacher sat behind a simple oak desk, something an elementary student might use if they weighed one hundred and sixty pounds. He wore a brown suit as old as his second marriage, and had slicked-back hair which no one had ever seen grow or shorten. On the surface in front of him rested a small desk lamp, a spiral notebook and pen, a Bible, a backup Bible, and an NRSV Bible that he never taught out of but sort of liked the wording of.

"Frank," he said, "I'm glad to see you." Thunderpop was the only preacher Frank could remember from his boyhood at Third Baptist, which stretched from the age of six, when he started putting up a fight about going to church, to the age of eighteen, when he left home and lied about going to church in Hoople. Thunderpop remembered Frank fairly well, and was proud of him, because he had always secretly suspected the kid would wind up in prison. He leaned forward. "Are you doing with your dad's disappearance?"

Frank nodded, surprised at the question. "Sure, I'm fine." Arthur never really accepted his role as a paternal figure in the family, so Frank and Hillary grew up with a sort of oblivious avuncular character who slept with their mother and drifted between jobs. He had kicked off his fatherhood by, in lieu of hiring babysitters, opting to rent out the children to grad school students looking to pick up girls by playing with kids in a park. His absence was disheartening, but he had never been fully present to begin with.

"Glad to hear that," said Thunderpop. "So what's on your mind?

"Well, some weird things have been happening lately, and I want to just, you know, sort of pick your brain to make sense of them. Run a few ideas by you."

"Go ahead." Reverend Thunderpop leaned back in his chair.

"Okay, well, the first question is this: if a man is doing something bad, sometimes God will, you know, like, jerk him around and stuff?"

"How do you mean?"

"Like, do more than just send preachers to talk to him. Perform a miracle, or scare him."

"Sure, God could do that."

"Okay, good," Frank said. Premise one established. "Alright, and angels work for God, right?"

"Yes. But demons are angels too, just fallen ones, and they don't work for God."

"Okay. But angels do."

"Yes."

"So God could, hypothetically, order his angels to visit someone and shake them up or something to get His point across?"

Thunderpop answered slower this time. "Yes, God could do that."

"See, that's what I thought." Premise two, done. "Okay, so then, let's say I'm an alcoholic."

"Are you?" Thunderpop asked.

"No, not anymore. And, between you and me," he leaned forward and whispered in case God was listening, "I don't think I really had a problem before they started screwing with me."

"Before who started screwing with you?"

"The angels. I'm getting there." He took a deep breath. "Anyway, I wasn't in trouble or anything, just drinking more than I ought, like on weeknights and stuff."

"And so angels told you to stop?"

Frank thought about this. "No, not exactly. They sort of . . . Well, they picked up my car when I was about half an hour out from Enid and dropped it off in Utah. Then, when I started driving back, one of them ran across the road and I swerved into a field and I crashed my car, and then they chased me into the wheat and I tried to kill them with a stick, but they wouldn't let me, and then they dropped me off at a farm up in Hoople."

Thunderpop digested this new information, which was a good deal more bizarre and meaty than the previous "yes or no" snippets. "Come again?" he asked, probably the best question.

Frank endeavored to retell the story, this time more clearly.

The preacher leaned back in his chair and sucked his cheeks in. "Okay," he said. He leaned back further, making the chair creak. "Okay," he repeated. "So . . ."

"Well, hey, I can see that's a lot to think about. Listen, what I really want to know is if God's going to quit bothering me if I stop drinking. Or his angels, anyway."

"Uh," Thunderpop said, groping for words. "Well, Frank, God doesn't ever really 'bother' us. He always helps us and He always loves us."

"Right. But if I quit drinking, is He going to quit loving me in such a way that makes freaky gray angels chase me around in fields?"

"See," Thunderpop said, reaching for a Bible, "see now *that's* where I get confused about this. Did the angels ever actually tell you to quit drinking?"

"Yes," Frank said. "By picking my car up and leaving me in Utah."

Thunderpop shook his head. "No, that's not really them giving you advice or anything. In the scripture they usually say stuff. Half the time it doesn't make sense, but they still *say* something. Did they mention that they were angels, or say anything about God?"

Frank sighed. He picked up a Bible from the desk and flipped through Leviticus as if actually searching for some legitimate passage pertaining to the situation. "They didn't really *say* anything," he said, pretending to read. "Not that I remember."

"Well now, maybe they were demons, then. But there's no real reason to think that they're angels. I mean, even if they said they were, they could still be lying." Thunderpop removed his glasses and cleaned them on his plaid tie.

Frank sighed, deeply, tiredly. "So . . . what happened, then?"

The preacher scrunched his lips together and

raised his eyebrows. "Heck, Frank, *I* don't know. Were you drinking when you saw all this stuff?"

"Only the first time, but I wasn't even really drunk, just feelin' it."

"Well, I'll pray about it and call you if I figure anything out."

Frank fought his urge to dog-ear what he had been looking at in the Good News, but resisted the urge and set the Bible back down on the desk. "That's about it, preacher. Thanks for your time."

He departed from Third Baptist paranoid and irritated, afraid Sephus might actually be right.

CHAPTER 14

Hillary struggled to remember which light switch activated the bulbs in the living room. Her mother collected and installed them all over the house. To Helen, each room had a single switch and a myriad of charming, completely decorative ones attached to the walls like tiny paintings. To everyone else the house was filled with frustrating duds.

She located the correct switch, four switches from the door, and drove the darkness of the living room under furniture and into corners. Through a combination of strategic mood lighting and completely non-strategic burned-out bulbs, the room rested at a cozy twilight. It was funny that a house with so many light switches had so few working bulbs. Several well-placed aromatic candles added to the home's ambience, masking the ghosts of a thousand cigarettes through fruit odors. It smelled like the smoking section of a cherry farm.

A bottle of Friends in Merlot Places, vintage a month ago, breathed on the kitchen counter. James developed an affinity for the sweet wine in college. He did not like drinking wine in general because it seemed pretentious, but the brand came from a vineyard owned by one of his frat buddies, and purported to be the least affected winery on the planet. Plus he liked sweet drinks.

She hoped he still enjoyed the taste. When they shared a bottle one night in his frat room, watching reruns of *Seinfeld*, the wine had cost about eight dollars. It was entirely possible that his palette and price range had improved, and that Friends in Merlot Places would complement Helen's house all too well.

As she drifted around the home emptying ashtrays, brushing crumbs onto the carpet and adjusting details in general, she did her best to suppress a few unhelpful thoughts. She censored her motivation for wearing a killer outfit as she masterfully applied makeup. Formally, she told herself that she simply enjoyed dressing up. Informally, she knew James would salivate as soon as he saw her, and it made her giddy. This self-deception was transparent, almost playful.

What was threatening, and strictly forbidden to surface in her inner monologue, was the vast extent of her budding interest in James, and the impetus fertilizing it. What had begun as catching up with a college friend had ballooned into wine and cosmetics. Did she really even *like* James? Had she ever? She was fresh out of a relationship. She had retreated home, jobless. James, clean and stable, represented not passion, but redemption.

This shameful idea lurked next to its older, long-suppressed brother. An aged, quiet longing that she might finally fall in love, walk down the aisle, cuddle next to her husband by a fire, watch movies in soft pajamas with him, and be contented and loved. She refused to entertain this latent hope, partly because it embarrassed her, and partly because it *was* so important. She meant to conceal and protect it from the universe itself.

James, quite inadvertently, was flirting with the crosshairs of this desperate wish. She avoided probing her interest in him for fear she would discover only the dusty hope of falling in love, and that she was deluding herself into thinking she found it again. Her thoughts obliged and sunk back into her subconscious.

A timid knuckle rapped the front door. James suffered from a chronic fear of doorbells. Some part of him believed that maybe, somehow, the doorbell was connected to a huge speaker system set to wake everyone in the house. It was the same strange phobia that made him nervous whenever he passed through the detectors at movie rentals.

"Just a moment!" Hillary called, darting to the bathroom. She searched for the proper light switch, gave up, and turned a flashlight on to inspect herself in the mirror. Stunning. Hillary had held up rather well in the six years since college. She still had her figure, although she suspected the real test would come after she concluded her twenties. Tiny red frills traced the edges of her blouse, beckoning attention to the intriguing topography they obscured. Rather than attempting to showcase her minimal cleavage, the blouse pushed up and amplified her bosom, making her breasts compact but marvelously energetic.

She walked to the front door. She saw James through the spy hole, looking around the porch with mock interest as if he did not mind being locked out of the house observing spider webs. She opened the door and flashed a smile so full of shiny white teeth that rodents in the vicinity wet themselves and scattered. "Hi James!"

James smiled back, although his grin was more relaxed and less frightening to tiny woodland creatures. "Hello, Hillary. You look lovely this evening." He brushed passed her and entered the

80

house.

She escorted him to the den and gestured for him to sit on the couch. A fresh silk fabric acquired from a hobby store earlier in the day was draped over the sofa to conceal menthol burns and an interesting, mysterious stain shaped like a crowbar. James sat down but did not loosen his spine. He was dressed well, as always, but not dressed up, as Hillary.

His body language hinted at discomfort with the open flames and low luminosity. When Hillary called him a week ago she had made it sound like they would eat a pizza and maybe watch a movie if something good was playing on Helen's stolen cable. This had all the auspices of a romance.

"Is your mother around?" he asked. "I'd like to say hello to her."

"She's on her shift at 7-11. She gets off at four."

"Ah, I see. Where's Frank?"

Hillary shrugged. "Theoretically within the state. He called me this morning to tell me he was back in Hoople. My guess is that he'll roll in tomorrow at the barbeque. Excuse me." She went into the kitchen and returned with a fondue pot and some long, skinny forks. She had read somewhere that fondues were sexy, although molten cheese did not particularly arouse her.

The merlot and accompanying wine glasses followed the cheese. She filled them and handed one to James, who stared at it like it might contain poison. She considered making a toast, but could not come up with a suitable subject. They were too young to be toasting memories or departed friends or any of that, and "possibilities" seemed asinine and

81

obvious all at once.

"Do you hear much from your frat brothers?" she asked.

James nodded and laughed, cutting the tension in the air like a hatchet through tent cords. "Jerry called me from Missouri three weeks ago for bail money." Hillary laughed. "Besides him, I only keep in contact with two or three regularly. Saul is off in Switzerland or something, hot for a girl. Is this Friends in Merlot Places?" he asked hopefully.

"Yes, it is."

He took a sip and let the drink catch in the pockets of his cheeks. It made him smile. "Fresh, too. Kudos."

Hillary nodded. "A good week, I hear. Glad you like it. What's your next travel book going to be about?"

"Wales, I think." He skewered a small sausage and plunged it into the steaming cheese. "I was in the British Isles over the summer. I only visited Wales for four days; Cardiff, Swansea, and a host of little towns with excessive syllables in the North, but I fell in love with the place. They still speak Welsh up there, you know."

"Not English?" Hillary asked. She was not entirely sure where Wales was, other than it was a part of England, which is factually inaccurate and could definitely start a bar fight with a Welshman if stated loudly.

"No, it's a Celtic language, sort of like Gaelic. But unlike Gaelic, it's not on government life support. Twenty percent or so of the population speaks it, especially up north."

"Odd name."

"But a wonderful place," James replied. "It's not touristy like Scotland or Ireland. The English hang out in the region during the summer, but they only come for the scenery. So when Americans show up it's something of a novelty and they're glad to see you. Very friendly people, very real. My last night in Wales I ate Chinese food on top of an old stone circle like Stonehenge, only smaller. It was just sitting in a playground in Porthmadog."

"St. Paul is nice," she said, immediately regretting it. He was talking about stone circles in Wales, and she was regaling him with stories about Minnesota. Minnesota, where her remaining days of respectable employment rapidly slipped through her fingers like a fistful of olive oil.

"What do you like about it?" he asked. He did so calmly, with no rush to blaze over silence or force conversation. It was a measure of confidence she had not seen in James during his stint at Wily College.

"Um, nice people. And I like wearing scarves." She inwardly grimaced. *Scarves?* Clearly she was underwhelming in the evening's small talk. She resolved to do better in the next portion of the dinner. The seductive part.

"More wine?" she asked.

CHAPTER 15

Karl sat in a taxi futilely trying to assuage his irritation. Temporarily without a car, he had stood like an idiot on a corner in downtown Oklahoma City for an hour waiting to hail a cab. Eventually a friendly homeless-looking man asked if he was waiting for someone, or if he would like to buy any weed. After Karl replied that he was waiting for a cab, the homeless man laughed and suggested he call a taxi service, because that just wasn't how public or private transportation operated in Oklahoma City, and seriously, it was good weed.

Karl had sat on a park bench and called information on his cell phone, wishing he had a functional car at the moment. The operator connected him to a cab service, and after fifteen minutes, one finally arrived.

Karl now sat in the back, allowing his indignation and frustration with the universe to melt away into the streets. "Are you sure you want to take a cab to Nichols Hills?" Ryan the driver asked.

Karl nodded. "Yes."

"Okay, but that'll be a fifteen-minute ride. If you have any friends in the area you might just have them pick you up and buy their dinner. I think that'd be cheaper, and you'd get to have dinner with a friend."

"Sage advice," Karl said, staring out the window and wondering how this particular driver stayed in business. "But I only know one person in the area and he's out with a woman tonight."

"Jerk," Ryan retorted. As a cab driver he had a stern policy of unquestionably favoring whoever was in his car, with minimal effort in determining their circumstance or situation. He frequently sided with people who had convinced themselves of the ethical necessity of adultery.

"No," Karl sighed. "It's fine. He's a friend, and that sort of thing is important to him. I wouldn't be so agitated if I'd had a better understanding of how transportation works in this part of the country." The car looped onto the highway and accelerated rapidly. Ryan secretly enjoyed pretending the cab was a fighter jet.

"Well don't you worry, man, I'll get you to Nichols Hills in no time flat."

"It's quite alright," Karl said. "I'm not in a hurry."

"You said you'd been waiting for an hour, man," the driver turned back and smiled impishly. "We'll make that time up, no problem." Karl was confused. Wasn't it going to be twenty to thirty minutes, as stated?

The car swerved in between two pickups in varying shades of mud. Karl buckled his seatbelt. "It's not that I'm late, I just hate waiting."

"Ah, I see," Ryan said. He flicked the radio on. "Do you have any music preferences, man?"

Karl shook his head. "No, not really. I just like good music in general."

Wuss, Ryan thought. Everyone disliked certain kinds of music; they might as well say so. "Alright," he said, turning the dial to country. He thought better and changed it to talk radio. "Ah, *Midnight Chat,*" he said.

Karl rolled his eyes. "It's barely dark out. Why do they even call it that?"

Ryan shrugged. "It probably started out at midnight before it got a following. Have you ever listened to it?"

Karl nodded. "With that crank Chuck Gander and his patsy, Stephen Hornswild?"

Ryan nodded, but secretly began to dislike the passenger. "You don't care for them?"

"They're both morons."

"Or maybe they're onto something," Ryan suggested. "Groundbreaking thinkers look like idiots sometimes."

"The only thing Gander is onto is painkillers."

"I think you'd be in for a shock if it turned out he was right about aliens."

Karl smiled. "Yes, I suppose I would be. So would the aliens, considering what he has to say about them." The taxi lurched as it weaved behind a semitruck. "Seriously," he said, as his uppity nature made room for survival instincts, "I'd prefer a safe, leisurely ride over a fast one."

Ryan grinned into the rearview mirror. "Don't worry about it, man. I'm a professional. You have to be aggressive in traffic."

In the last few days Karl had discovered that this was not true in Oklahoma City. Traffic in any city was annoying, but it was not particularly *bad* in this state. Aside from a general lack of congestion, the homophobia which gripped the population transferred beautifully into proper distancing between cars. The only real traffic irritants were the occasional octogenarians who wandered into the passing lane because they were frightened of being flanked by faster cars on both sides.

The car suddenly slowed down as Ryan tried to pass a minivan but pulled back at the last moment. "So what do you do for a living, man?"

"I'm a human resources manager," he said. He smiled to himself, forever amused at the irony of his position.

"That sounds boring," the driver observed, in stunning honesty.

"Well—" Karl started, but before he could either correct the assumption or reveal some fascinating hobby that somehow separated him from all other boring HR personnel, the taxi cab plowed into the Nissan in front of it, mounting its bumper like some kind of horrible automobile pornography.

"Shit!" Ryan yelled. The cab dismounted and careened to its right, thoroughly pissing off another entire lane of traffic. It would not have been too bad, but half a swear word later a Baptist preacher from Moore quite inadvertently slammed into the cab, sending both cars hurtling across the median and very narrowly through three entirely brand-new lanes of traffic headed in the opposite direction, then into an embankment.

In his smoking car, Jim Thunderpop very briefly debated whether or not he wanted to die Baptist, but passed out on the steering wheel, bloodied, before reaching a conclusion.

In the back of the taxi cab, now more compact than when it had left the garage that morning, Karl spat blood out before slumping over.

In the cab, Ryan unbuckled his seatbelt and got out of the car. There was no scratch on him. He looked out over the median and the five lanes of traffic his car had just hurtled through, and was very impressed with his luck. He wanted to call someone and tell them how crazy it was that he had emerged from an otherwise deadly car accident with little more than an upset stomach, and then remembered other people were involved in the wreck.

*

"Vincent, are you alright?" Barbara the barista asked. Vincent Alderman graced only two coffee houses in New York City with his presence, and this was his favorite, which he frequently told the other. The staff knew him, and even sort of liked him now. The trick, the manager had explained to Barbara, was understanding that Vincent wasn't really the over-inflated prick he appeared to be. He was more of an endearing caricature of one. Vincent, despite a level of pretension normally reserved for French aristocrats complaining about gout, did not actually take himself very seriously, and did not expect others to. This, and a wit so sharp you could shave splinters with it, were what allowed him to exist in normal society without getting regularly curb-checked by people who did not understand the difference between pants and trousers.

The columnist stared into his coffee, wide-eyed, as if horrific visions of World War III were playing out in the hazelnut French vanilla latte steaming in his special mug that other customers weren't allowed to use. Barbara leaned over to look into his coffee to see, perchance, if there was a thumb or something. It looked fine to her. "Too hot?" she asked.

Bryce, the bistro's manager, wandered over. "Is

everything alright?" he asked. Vincent shook his head in tiny jerks. "Barbara?"

"I set his coffee down, he said 'Hello, Miss Barbara,' and then something in French, then he got this strange look in his eyes and got quiet." She shrugged.

That was not normal, not even for Vincent Alderman. People who knew him theorized that the newspaper only gave him a column in order to keep his opinions from shooting out, unfocused, into the unsuspecting populace. On the rare occasions when he did not have a seething assessment or insightful observation to ram into an unrelated conversation like a hatchet through a cheese wedge, he could always default on his favorite topic of conversation (himself).

"Mr. Alderman?" Bryce asked, resting his hand on the man's shoulder.

Vincent shook himself and looked up at the manager. "Ah, Mr. Bryce," he said, attempting to appear normal. "I . . ." he searched for a fantastic excuse that would get him out of the café quickly and with little explanation. ". . . have to go." He stood up. "Please put my coffee and a nice tip on my tab."

Before Barbara could thank him for her hypothetical tip, or Bryce could ask if Vincent's children were alright based on the faulty assumption that he had any, Vincent Alderman was out the door, cell phone in hand.

*

Montgomery Muchmore spent most of his high school career in theatre, but was merely theatrical in college. After graduating he took up improv. The combined training rendered him all but incapable of talking to anyone who did not come in groups of three or more. Outside of a handful of close intimates, he did not so much converse with others as perform, which made things like direct eye contact and one-on-one conversation both difficult and awkward. If he could not find a sizeable group to amuse at social functions he would drift from person to person in a fit of gregariousness, meeting every attendee without getting to know any.

He was at a cocktail party hosted by a fellow California radio personality. He bloomed at cocktail parties the same way certain plants open up when the lunar cycles are just right. At these soirees his own peculiar brand of eccentric bravado gave him the spotlight and attention he craved. He stood next to Cynthia, his show's producer. They both glowed; her from the rapidly assembling child in her womb, and him from the rapidly disseminating martini in his veins.

At the party, every radio talent was attempting to suck attention away from his or her colleagues like sponges thrown into a bucket of maple syrup. Each of Monty's peers made expansive hand gestures and chattered in grand, eloquent manners, conspicuously louder than necessary, so that everyone would, hypothetically, recognize their voice. No one did, because very few of the radio show hosts actually bothered listening to anyone else's program, but a couple of caterers trying to land internships recognized a few.

Monty gripped an antiquated black cigarette holder in his teeth which extended outward in a slender ebony line, oozing a strip of smoke into the air like Chinese incense. It accentuated his grin, which had been in effect since the late eighties. He had been smiling for so long it was now physically impossible for him to do anything else. He withdrew the cigarette holder from his mouth so he could illustrate his thoughts on the current president with a hand gesture in an unrelated loopy motion.

Cynthia gave an obligatory but charming laugh which awoke her unborn child, someday to be named Emilio, but currently thought to be a girl. Emilio, angry at being disturbed, ferociously head-butted his mother's uterus from the inside, which she mistook as some kind of cute infantile game.

She felt her midsection and gave a dazzling, proud smile to the crowd assembled around her and Montgomery. "She's head-butting again."

The two female interns made cooing noises and Ralph, who hosted a jazz show on Saturday afternoons, pretended to care.

"If she kicked as much, I'd say she'll grow up to be a soccer player. I don't know what to say about head-butting." She threw her arms up as if to say, "This truly is a fascinating and humorous enigma!"

"Sounds like a rugby player," Monty suggested.

"Did you ever play rugby, Mr. Muchmore?" the shorter intern asked. She had bright, blue eyes, proportional to a knockout from a Disney movie. She was petite and nubile and, Monty supposed, quite flexible. She had just moved to L.A. from Arizona and had not yet realized that people in entertainment are not only just people, but often assholes, too. Montgomery Muchmore, who was so much larger than life he used a different zip code, sucked the star-struck youth into his vortex of cardboard charisma.

"Me?" He laughed good-naturedly. "No, my dear. I was on crew team back at USC, but I never got around to rugby."

"Oh," she ventured, dazzled. "Which crew?"

"Crew team is the same as rowing team," he instructed kindly. She nodded, embarrassed. She had dated a rugby player in college, and had hoped to mention it, but the information seemed superfluous at this point.

"Ralph, how's your son?" Cynthia asked, still understandably preoccupied with the mind-blowing fact that a tiny human being was going to pop out of her in a couple of months.

"Oh, he's good," Ralph said. His son, Jason, was a normal child, except that whenever he got stressed he leaned forward until the top of his head touched the ground. Ralph, in a stunning display of parenting skills, learned when Jason was a toddler that the strange sensation of hanging upside down made him shut up and ponder the world from a different perspective. Whenever the child started crying, he held him by the ankles until the child forgot what he was crying about. Fortunately for Jason it did not damage his brain, but now the only method of coping with stress he could fathom was to try and stand on his head. It made middle school dances very, very awkward. "He's doing track, now," Ralph offered.

Monty opened his mouth to try and pack another one of his accomplishments into the conversation, but it hung like a slack hammock. He tilted his head slightly and squinted, then handed his drink and cigarette to Cynthia. "Here, can you take these?" he mumbled, walking away.

"Monty?" Cynthia asked, concerned. "Are you okay?"

He proceeded down the stairs, dazed. His face twitched as his grin fought tooth and nail to reclaim its territory. "I, uh, I just need to check on something at home." He floated out the door without shutting it behind him.

"He's so . . ." the nubile intern said, looking for a word, ". . . so *charming*," she concluded.

*

Sweet, fermented grape juice slopped out of James's glass onto one of Helen's rugs. Of these she had many. Her strategy for combating the many beer stains, cigarette burns, and dry echoes of unidentified puddles which pock-marked her den was to slap a rug over each. Small rugs, profuse in number, frequently overlapping and rarely matching, littered her den like a Turkish mosque.

James slumped back into the couch, dazed. He put a hand to his right temple, opening and closing his jaw in a cartoonish mock-speech. "James?" Hillary asked, concerned. Was he having a seizure? She shook him a little, which is exactly what you should not do with someone having a seizure. "James, are you alright?"

He stood up and surveyed the room, as if it had suddenly turned upside down, and yellow. "Hillary?" he asked.

"Yes?"

"Okay."

"You're not making sense," she said. Things had

been going so *well*, too. She had been touching his arm. He had been laughing.

James walked out of the living room slowly, out the front door, and to his car. He'd picked up his cell phone on the way out. "James?" Hillary called from the porch.

He nodded and climbed into his automobile. "I'm sorry. This was pleasant. I have to go, family emergency. Thank you. For dinner."

Then he was gone.

CHAPTER 16

Frank scrubbed the cheese off of his plate and wished he had bothered cleaning it while it was still warm, rather than letting a week's worth of rigor mortis set in. He got out a steel wool brush and put some anger into it. Satisfied that no synthetic nacho remnants clung to the plate, he set it on the rack next to his sink to air dry, wiping his brow. A new ring of salt sweat expanded the target pattern of armpit stains on his old t-shirt.

The next plate, which had some sort of red organic epoxy cemented to it, was harder still. He eventually pulled a knife out to try and slice through but quickly admitted defeat. He imagined he could wear it down with sand paper, but this might be one of those situations that warranted springing for a new plate at Wal-Mart. He did not exactly own a matching set. He had three white plates, two black plates, a white plate with a permanent scorch mark in the center from the time he tried to microwave a hamburger before taking its aluminum wrapper off, and a couple of Frisbees he feared he might give him cancer if he kept reheating pizzas on them.

He looked up from the sink and dropped the plate. It shattered into several pieces on the floor, though most of them held together via the stubborn russet sealant. A large gray face stared at him through the window. Huge, probing black eyes, a miniscule mouth, and a couple of dots where a nose ought to be dominated the frame. It looked human and at the same time utterly inhuman, and that filled

Frank with grim terror.

He and the gray creature ogled each other for several moments before he found the courage to speak. "I'm not an alcoholic anymore," he said. "Thank you for your help." The creature tilted its head slightly. "Go away!" he screamed, his voice cracking awkwardly. "Leave!"

The creature blinked and pressed its forehead against the glass to study him better. It tapped a long, bony finger against the window pane. Frank flung the plastic curtains shut. They did not close all the way, allowing the creature to shift to its right so a single black eye could gaze in at him. Frank jerked his head as he heard the doorknob to his trailer creak. He ran to the door and hurled his body weight against it as it began to open. He locked the door and bolted it, then blocked it with his couch.

Knock.

Knock.

Knock.

"Go the hell away!" Frank screamed. "Go away!" He was on the verge of tears. Some raw part of his being knew, despite all of his modernity and education, that a pale-skinned, skeleton monster stood at his front door, the same menial place he collected his newspapers every month and where his neighbors knocked. He began to shake uncontrollably, looking around his trailer in desperation. He was a small boy again, under siege by the lurking ghouls of night which take years of parental assurance to vanish from the psyche. And the monster was here, outside his door. It had watched him do dishes. Watched him with huge, soulless eyes.

He drew all of the curtains shut in the trailer and ran his knuckles through his hair. The door knocked again. *"Go the hell away!"* he screamed. He found a large butcher knife and gripped it with both hands. "I said *leave!*"

"Pizza man."

"I don't want any friggin' pizza!"

The voice fell silent temporarily. The doorknob jiggled. "It's pepperoni," it offered.

"No!" Frank screamed. What was happening? Was he living in that old *Saturday Night Live* skit about land sharks? Except with monsters, and for real? He leaned over the sink in the kitchen and vomited, shaking all over. He jumped a foot in the air as his pocket vibrated, then realized it was his cell phone and yanked it out. *SEPHUS*, the caller ID showed in pixilated letters. He flipped it open and choked back a sob over the line.

"Frank?" Sephus asked, worried.

"It's trying to get into my trailer!" he screamed. "Oh God! God! Sephus, help me!" He sunk down on the floor and found the dropped butcher knife.

"Frank?" Sephus asked again, panicking. "Who's trying to get you? Frank!?"

"It's at the door!" Frank screamed. He stood up and looked out through the slit in the curtain at the kitchen window. The black eye blinked. "GET AWAY!" he screeched, his voice popping in and out of falsetto. "Sephus! Sephus, for the love of God! Help me!"

"I'm on my way!" Sephus yelled. In the background, Frank heard his friend's truck start. "Frank, you have to talk to me—who's at the door? Are you being robbed?"

Frank sobbed into the line. He began to scream hysterically. "Sephus! Sephus, they're coming in through the windows!"

"*Frank!*" Sephus yelled. "Frank, who's after you?!"

"I'm going to lock myself in the bathroom," Frank whispered in terror. "There aren't any windows in the bathroom."

"That's good," Sephus said. "Listen, I'm ten minutes away. Do you hear me, Frank? I'm on my way!"

"No! Please!" Frank screamed. The phone made a *clink* as it fell against the false tiling on the trailer's bathroom floor. "Please," Frank cried, covering his face. "Please, please leave me alone!"

On Sephus's end of the line, everything went quiet. "Frank?" he asked, panic-stricken. "Frank?"

CHAPTER 17

Helen excelled at making eye contact with people as she spoke, but continued the practice while driving, which was bad. She also had a tendency to use expansive dual hand gestures while making eye contact, but would only do so for a moment before snapping back to attention and saving the car from veering into oncoming traffic.

Hillary sat in the passenger's seat of her mother's minivan, sighing. She had not seen Jim Thunderpop since she had converted to Lutheranism her junior year at Wily College, and did not feel obligated to visit him now. Helen had insisted they needed to make an appearance and bring a pie and a cute stuffed bear.

Hillary did like Jim Thunderpop, though. Beneath the cheap suit and stylish comb-over was a man with a firm grasp on what was important and what was frivolous bullshit. He humored people about the frivolous bullshit, but if you knew him very well you could tell when he was placating parishioners about their diehard papal conspiracy theories. She felt sorry for the man, because he genuinely wanted to be God's servant, but ended up as God's babysitter.

Still, Hillary had not seen him in years. Even while she was Baptist in college she had not regularly attended a Baptist church. Now, instead of not going to a Baptist church, she didn't go to a Lutheran one. She was thus apprehensive about visiting her former family preacher.

"Do you know who the first person to phone Becky was?" Helen asked.

"The paramedics?"

"After them."

"I don't know."

"Tom Marcky," Helen replied crisply. She clamped her jaw shut and raised her eyebrows. The fact that ousted pastor Tom Marcky knew about the accident so fast was pretty clear circumstantial evidence that he had tampered with Reverend Thunderpop's brakes.

Helen pulled the minivan into Mercy Hospital's parking lot. The Norbitzes left the car with their pie. With surprising efficiency, they located Reverend Thunderpop's room and rapped lightly on the door.

"Yup," Thunderpop grunted genially from within. The two women entered as he struggled to sit up in bed. He wore a hospital gown shrewdly recycled out of some kind of paper towel collection, and had a couple of plastic bands digging into the pudgy flesh around his wrists. Five o'clock shadow, the most facial hair he had ever dared, covered his chin and cheeks. His rakish comb-over had suffered horribly from the car crash and hung limply on the wrong side of his scalp.

Helen gasped when she spied the preacher this way, then buried her face in her hands. Thunderpop rolled his eyes and waived at Hillary. "Hey, Hil," he said.

"Reverend Thunderpop."

He watched Helen get a grip on herself and sighed. "Helen, I'm perfectly fine. Just bruises, mostly, and of coursed a snapped clavicle. They wanted to keep me here for observation on account of my heart's rhythm, but I'll be back home by tonight and at the pulpit next Sunday."

His parishioner nodded and smiled. "We brought you a pie!" said Helen.

"Good, good," Thunderpop said, rubbing his hands together. "Thank you very much. Becky says 'Hi,' by the way."

"*And*," Helen said, grinning ear to ear, "we brought you *this!*" She withdrew the teddy bear from her purse and waived it in the air to make the limbs flail in a cute, un-grizzly-like manner. The little bear had a tie on and a small black book glued to its hand.

"Ah," Thunderpop said, attempting to summon the same attitude roused earlier by the pie. "Yes. Good. Thank you."

Hillary looked around the room and saw a plethora of teddy bears. Some were wearing t-shirts, some were holding tiny balloons, some were just sitting there emitting waves of cuddly warmth.

The teddy bear phenomenon was the ongoing effect of a good-natured prank started by Tom Marcky years earlier. On April Fool's Day, after the third or fourth time the preachers stole away to Guthrie for covert responsible beer drinking, Marcky had a friend deliver a stuffed bear to his office with a note reading "Dear Rev. Thunderpop—I know how much you love stuffed bears, so I thought you'd appreciate this."

It created the exact effect Marcky intended. The church's receptionist noticed the bear's explanation and told other people, who brought him teddy bears on his birthday. Even more parishioners noticed this second wave of bears, and resigned themselves to give accordingly come Christmas. Thereafter, the reverend received multiple bears on even the remotest of celebratory occasions. Marcky thought it was hilarious, and expected the prank to go on for years until Thunderpop finally convinced himself he actually *did* like stuffed bears.

In fact, when Marcky mentioned the joke to Thunderpop a year later in Guthrie, Thunderpop nearly slugged him in the jaw. Had it not been for the mellowing nature of the light beers they were nursing, he would have. Ever since, Thunderpop grudgingly accepted the stupid bear fetish everyone assumed he had, receiving them graciously but never encouraging people to continue the practice. Each Christmas he gave them to underprivileged children. Other times he went to a friend's farm and used them for target practice.

"What happened, exactly?" Hillary asked.

Thunderpop shrugged and pressed the nurse button to see if he could flirt some more Jell-O out of her. "Some idiot cab driver slammed into me and we went over the median and into three lanes of oncoming traffic before crashing on the other side."

"Where was this?" Helen asked, her fists clinched in fear.

"I-235."

"Ooh!" Helen exclaimed, as if this particular stretch of asphalt made the injuries even more gruesome.

"Listen," Thunderpop said, looking at Helen. "I'm concerned about your son."

"We all are," grumbled Hillary.

"He came into my office a couple of days ago and said some pretty weird things."

"Like what?" Helen asked, concerned.

"Well, he said he thought he'd been an alcoholic, but he'd quit. Then he started talking about how angels periodically kidnap him and release him in other states. He seemed pretty shaken up about it, and I think he might need to talk to somebody, a psychologist, maybe."

Helen collapsed into a chair next to the television, exhausted. "Frank is . . . Frank is trying to hold himself together after his father's death."

"Now Helen," Thunderpop said, kindly but firmly, "we don't know that Arthur is *dead*."

Hillary, who had no desire to join in on this conversation, excused herself. She went to the bathroom and filled up a small, hotel-style cup with water. She returned to her mother and former preacher, but the water break did little to augment any desire in talking about her brother's problems.

"—doesn't mean that he's *crazy*, Helen. Just that he ought to sort these things out with a professional."

"Oh, right, and *then* try to get a job!"

"It's all done confidentially, and therapy isn't the same as—"

Hillary set the water down and exited the hospital room. She decided she needed some semblance of a destination to explain her absence, if only to herself. If Mars Bars still existed, she would find them. If they did not, she didn't know what she would buy, but she could deal with Hershey's or Reese's Pieces if and when it came to that fateful moment. Behind her, Helen loudly argued that the Bible was the answer to all problems, and Thunderpop pointed out that the Bible was utterly fantastic but he was pretty sure his morphine drip had not been siphoned out of the Book of Nehemiah.

If Mars Bars still existed, they did all of their existing outside of Mercy Hospital. Hillary checked three floors of vending machines before deciding to give in and buy herself a Snickers. The vending machine made a satisfying whirring noise and pushed the little Snickers bar out of its shelving via a dark black spring.

As Hillary watched the treat drop into the collection tray below, a familiar reflection walked behind her own. She fished out her Snickers bar and turned to see the retreating man. James.

No, she corrected herself. Not James. It was the James-with-stubble look-a-like she had met on the bus a few days ago. He was even wearing the same outfit, or something like it.

She stuffed the chocolate bar into her purse and quietly stalked him down the hall. He turned left into a room but did not completely shut the door behind him. She tiptoed up to it and peered through the crack. Lying in a hospital gown was James, with a head bandage, nodding and occasionally taking a sip of orange juice from a plastic cup. "Thank you for your concern," he said. "No, the wounds are quite superficial. I had a mild concussion, but it cleared up some time ago. I'll be out of here in a couple of hours. I have a project I need to get to tonight anyway, so I can't be lying around in a hospital bed."

"James!" she exclaimed, jerking the door open.

"What?" James asked from a chair at the back of the room.

The James in bed tried to arch an eyebrow, but could not because of his bandage. The man she had followed sat next to James, aghast, and a fourth

James doppelganger with a mustache and flashy blazer stood next to the window. The mustachio suddenly gasped and looked around at the other men in the room. "Ye gods!" he exclaimed. "You all look exactly like me!"

Hillary scrutinized each man in total confusion. "James?" she asked again. James, recognizable only by his khaki pants and tweed blazer, raised his hand in a meek "hello" gesture. "What's going on, James?"

"Why," the mustachio by the window blurted out, "we must all have been separated at birth! This is astounding!"

"You!" Hillary said, pointing at him. "I saw you at the bus station!" The man stroked his mustache and concentrated deeply. "You were picking him up," she said, pointing to the scruffy James look-a-like with laughably pretentious glasses.

"Oh, well of course," the man by the window said. "He's my twin brother. I meant that myself and my brother must have been separated from these other two gentlemen, so that, you see, we are quadruplets, whereas previously myself and my brother had thought we were merely twins. Uncanny," he added. He looked to the others and nodded vigorously, as if asking for their agreement at the astonishing turn of events.

Hillary did not want to play mind games or argue with the man she distinctly remembered chasing in Oklahoma City. She wanted answers. "James, what's going on?"

James cast a quick glance at his companions. "I'm as flabbergasted as you are." He turned his head a little to the side and squinted at her, cautiously watching to see if she bought this or not.

She didn't.

"Tell me the truth," she ordered. "I want to know what's going on."

James's three doppelgangers gave him a "do we need to kill this woman?" look, and he put his hands up defensively. "Do we come clean?" James asked.

"Yes, of course," Monty said, thinking up a plausible explanation to tell her.

Vincent rose and shut the door. He positioned himself between Hillary and any potential exit.

"Seriously?" James asked, looking from double to double. "Are we going to let her in on this?"

"Hold on," Monty said. He turned to face her. "We really are brothers separated at birth." Hillary did not seem convinced. He sighed. "Fine, fine. Go ahead, James. Tell her."

"Wait," Karl ordered from the bed. He turned his head and sized up Hillary. Then he turned to his comrades and completely ignored the interloper. "This woman has nothing on us other than an interesting coincidence. We have no reason to tell her anything. Let her think what she wants."

Hillary glared at him. "I'll report you!"

"To whom?" Karl asked. "Listen, miss, you seem like a nice woman, and I don't want to be impolite here, but this is exactly the sort of situation the phrase 'none of your business' was invented for. The matter doesn't concern you. And I can promise you, if you knew what was going on, you would wish you did not. Why not keep life simple?"

Monty and Vincent nodded in assent. Reading detective novels at an early age had conditioned them to think you must admit to everything once you get caught, and they were glad Karl had stopped them. "He has a point," Vincent said. "Sorry, miss."

James nodded to his doubles and walked to the door. He apologetically opened it for her. "Hillary, I'm sorry, but this is something important and it has to be kept quiet. I'm going to ask you, as my friend, to forget you saw this."

"What?" Hillary demanded. "As your *friend*? If we're such good friends, why can't you tell me?"

James put a hand on her elbow and tried to escort her out the door. She refused to budge, so he pulled her through the frame. Vincent stood sentry next to the door.

"I'm sorry, Hillary."

She could see that he wanted to tell her but could not, and felt bad keeping her in the dark. She decided to use his guilt as a soft spot to plunge a mental probe into.

"You're a bastard," she seethed, intentionally being overdramatic.

"Maybe," James said. He slipped halfway through the door, then stopped. "Sorry I had to leave from dinner so early the other night," he said. "I had a lovely time. You look wonderful, by the way." Hillary glared at him. "How long are you in town for? Do you want to get drinks?" Before she could turn him down, Vincent grabbed him by the collar and yanked him back into the room.

CHAPTER 18

The Rectum Thief shut the door to the house behind him, as he was unsure whether or not the dog was allowed to leave the premises. It was a schnauzer, and barked like mad. Its mutilated owner lay unmoving inside. The man had let himself in through the back.

He walked casually to his car and got in. He took his leather gloves off and put them in the glove compartment, making him the only person he knew who actually used the glove compartment for its stated purpose. He set down his kit and thermos on the floorboards below. A series of papers clipped together rested in the passenger's seat. They were from a website called "Para-Watch," which monitored various aspects of paranormal activity in the United States, although their crop circle coverage in particular was "award winning." No doubt whichever esteemed journalistic foundation bestowed honors for crop circle coverage vigorously vetted all contenders.

He sifted through the stack of pages, noting each photograph's corresponding location. He found one suitably close to his current position and peered at the intricate geometric design. It was a crummy picture. Probably taken by an amateur on a crop duster, or someone with a cell phone camera and a helicopter. One would think if you could afford to get in the air, you could afford a decent camera. He sighed.

The grainy and pixilated quality of the photo

obscured some of the finer details. He could decipher the coded location and a few other minutiae, but only part of the encrypted name. The last name, specifically. The picture had been cropped, or had not encompassed the entire crop circle to begin with, so part of the surname was omitted.

The man continued to scrutinize the picture and considered choosing another target at a more distant location. No, he decided, he had enough information to get by on. He had done it before on less data than this. The surprising thing was not so much that he couldn't make out the full name, but that so many targets appeared to be in the same area. *It will certainly save on gas money*, he thought. Mostly he was just happy to have his car out of the shop— yesterday's events had soured him to the prospects of hiring taxis.

He dropped the papers onto the seat beside him and started the engine. His car cruised out of the neighborhood and onto the highway.

"Norbitz," he muttered. The name sounded familiar.

CHAPTER 19

Hillary rose from the kitchen table and the trashy novel she had been reading in order to turn the television off. Not only did Helen watch television too much, she left it on at all times. When she was home, she enjoyed the background babble about weight loss programs or used car ads, and walked out of the house every night to go to work with the machine chattering away, unattended. Hillary, who liked things quiet, found it endlessly irritating, like a great furnace of noise pumping distractions throughout the house.

She hit the power button and stood upright as the doorbell rang. She walked to the front door and looked out through the keyhole. James stood on the porch.

"Here to apologize?" she asked, opening the door. She put her hands on her hips and stared at him.

James seemed startled, as if he had expected someone entirely different. "Miss Norbitz?" he asked.

"Uh, yeah," she said, suitably conveying what an amazingly stupid question that was. "What's this 'miss' crap?"

"Is anyone else home?" He stood motionless on the front porch, boring into her with calm blue eyes. He rubbed the bandage over his right brow.

"No, Mom's at Wal-Mart until four. What happened to your head?"

Karl, who Hillary still incorrectly identified as

James, frowned. He had not at all anticipated this development. Aside from startlement at having to kill someone he'd previously met, James had the hots for this girl. It was going to make their next reunion awkward, no doubt about that.

"I'm feeling woozy," Karl said. "May I come in?"

"Yes," she said slowly. "James, is everything okay?"

Karl smiled, but it was an eerie and mechanical smile, like he had pushed a button labeled "grin" and strings had accordingly pulled his lips back like drapes. She beckoned him into the house and locked the door behind her. "Would you like something to drink?"

"Yes," he said, setting a satchel down on the coffee table. "I would like some ice water."

"Okay," she said stiffly, conveying that he was acting creepy and he needed to stop. She entered the kitchen and went through the cabinet to select a suitably clean glass. Technically they were all clean, but the dishwasher was old, and left disgusting but harmless watermarks on the assortment of old jelly and mason jars Helen kept as casual drinkware. She found a relatively clear one, wiped it with the sleeve of her shirt, and filled it up with tap water. Then, remembering the ice, she walked toward the refrigerator. Her phone rang. *James.*

She picked the phone up with her left hand but held it to the right side of her face, from force of habit. "What the hell are you doing? Just come to the kitchen." She hung up. She opened and shut the freezer as the phone rang again. *James.*

"What?" she demanded.

"What?" he asked over the phone, confused.

"What do you want?" she returned, irritated.

"I . . . wait, you want me to come to your kitchen? I called to invite you to get coffee tomorrow."

"Dammit, James, if you *really* want you can just yell from the couch."

James paused. "Hillary, I'm confused. I'm at *my* house right now. Are you inviting me over for dinner?"

"No, you're—" An idea, a very strange one, tiptoed into her head. She leaned away from the refrigerator until she could see Karl seated on the couch, quietly observing the den. Not talking on the phone.

"I'm what?" James asked, on the phone.

"Who's on my couch?" she whispered.

"Hillary, are you drunk?"

"A man who looks *just like you* is sitting on my couch!"

"I—what?"

"Is this James?" she asked. Maybe that was the problem. If someone was calling her from James's phone, it would explain a lot.

"Yes, this is James," he replied. "Hillary, what's going on? Who's on the couch?"

"You tell me!" she hissed. "One of your secret clones appears to be sitting in the den!"

"What does he look like?"

"What do you mean 'what does he look like'!? He looks like you, you moron!"

"No," James offered quickly, "I mean, does he have facial hair? Or glasses?"

"No!" she hissed in exasperation. "He looks

112

just," she paused after each word, "like," longer, for emphasis, "you!"

"Hillary," he said, alarmed, "I want you to get out of the house. Slip out a back door and go to a safe place. Find a neighbor or something."

"Why? What's going on? *Why won't you just tell me what's going on?*"

"I don't know, Hillary. I think . . . I don't know, he didn't tell me he was going to visit you. I think he might consider you a security risk or something."

"A security risk?"

"Is this your brother?" the man asked, walking into the kitchen, holding a picture frame. It showed Frank and Hillary in pajamas bounding down the stairs the fateful Christmas morning that their tree had spontaneously combusted because Arthur had failed to water it.

"Yes," she offered.

"Oh," he said, nodding. He studied the picture like a math problem. "Same age as you?"

"Frank is thirteen months older than me."

"I see." He let the frame hang at his side. That complicated things—Karl might have come after the wrong sibling. Narrowing down his victims by decoding intricate patterns smashed into corn fields and then uploaded to crummy cameras and posted on conspiracy websites was, he admitted, a less than ideal business practice. Oh well. He had already made the drive. "Who are you talking to?" he asked.

"Get out of there!" James hissed over the phone.

"Who are you?" she demanded.

"Oh," the man said regretfully, as if she just ruined a surprise birthday party. "No, you don't want to do that."

113

"Who the hell are you?" she asked again, backing away from the refrigerator.

"James," he said, following her.

"No," she slipped the phone into her pocket, "James is on the phone." Her hand fell on a knife on top of the kitchen counter. She thrust it out in front of her defensively. "Who are you?"

He continued walking toward her. "Miss Norbitz, I don't want to make this difficult."

She served the glass of requested ice water in a fastball pitch to his forehead. It shattered on impact. The intruder swore loudly, covering his face with his hand. She ran past him to the front door and yanked on it, forgetting she had locked it earlier. The force jerked her against the wood.

The James look-alike barreled into the room, composure gone, gripping a syringe. Hillary ran in the opposite direction, down the hall and up the stairs. She knew it was a bad idea to run up the stairs when being pursued, but she could not come up with a better idea on the fly.

Karl charged after her, arm outstretched with needle in hand, but stumbled as his shoe caught under one of three overlapping, stain-concealing rugs. After returning to his feet, he bounded up the stairs after her. She sped down the hall to her room, slamming the door behind her. He careened into it with a loud thump.

She locked the door but, lacking a bolt, it wouldn't buy her much time. She grabbed the chair from her desk and jammed it against the knob. It shook as the man hurled himself against the door.

About this time she realized that she still had the knife in her right hand. She looked at it for a few moments before deciding to continue fleeing from the psychopath. She had never fought with a knife before, and he might be able to lunge and get it. Instead she went over to her bed and located the rope tied to one of its legs. It was an emergency rope Arthur had attached in one of his few forward-thinking moments, for the likely event that he might one day set the house on fire.

She opened the window and threw the rope out. Gripping the knife between her teeth like a pirate, she shimmied down. As her feet touched grass she looked up. The man poked his head out the window, spotted her, and frowned. He started to climb out. "If you climb down I'll stab you, creep!" she yelled, thrusting the knife up. "Keep climbing and I'll put this up your ass!"

The man thought about her threat for only a moment before disappearing back into the room. Hillary did not wait around to see what he would do next. She ran away from Helen's house and down the street as fast as her legs could carry her. After she passed the first stop sign she looked back; the man was in hot pursuit. She had a decent lead and he had a noticeable limp, but these facts did not give her much reassurance.

A sedan turned into the neighborhood and headed toward her. Instead of instinctively getting out of its way, she ran straight at it, screaming and flailing her arms, one of which still clutched a knife. The car swerved to avoid hitting her, making a wide arc and nearly hitting a mailbox. It stopped as the driver within considered that a knife-wielding maniac had just run toward him, but that the maniac in question looked familiar. He rolled his window down. "Hillary Norbitz!" Jim Thunderpop yelled. "What on Earth are you doing?!"

She tried to open the door to the passenger's side, but it was locked. She reached in over the window to unlock it, then scrambled into the vehicle. "Drive!" Thunderpop nodded and hit the gas.

She hyperventilated for a couple of minutes, then remembered the phone still in her pocket. "Are you still there?" she asked.

"Yes," James said. "You're okay?"

"For now."

"I'm getting out of the city," she said. "I'm going to go stay with Frank. There are fewer people that look like you wandering around, and more guns."

"That's fair," said James. "Let me drive you—I owe you some explanations."

CHAPTER 20

Frank's trailer and surrounding lawn blew apart any existing theories that smaller property is more manageable and therefore better kempt. In fact, the only thing about the site which indicated care of home or lawn were the playful marigolds growing out of the top and bowl of a decommissioned toilet near the front door.

The ground around his trailer featured large and unexplained bare spots, but the tangled patches of grass near them grew wild and long, so that it looked like his home rested on the back of a large shaggy dog undergoing chemotherapy. If one had to guess as to how the dog came to such a sorry state, they needed to look no further than the scattered mulch of cigarette butts bleeding cancer into the ground.

The trailer itself was attached to an old pickup truck which could not now pick itself up without a jack. It had no tires, and probably hadn't for years, resting instead on four greasy cinder blocks. Somehow, for unknown reasons, a bicycle wheel was attached to the front left axle.

The guts of the truck were strewn throughout the mangy weeds, as if the vehicle had sputtered around the yard hemorrhaging mufflers and sparkplugs before finally dying and succumbing to rust. Frank had never actually owned the truck, but he had attached his trailer to it when he moved in to present himself as a more mobile, wealthy man than he actually was. Gus, a one-eyed tomcat who enjoyed mating with other felines at painful decibel ranges, lived in the truck before Frank ever hitched his home to it, and refused to relinquish the territory.

Frank's trailer was old and blocky, and looked like a brick enshrouded in tinfoil. It made funny creaking noises as Sephus walked up the two steps that marked the gulf between door and ground. The tattered screen door opened easily, followed by the actual door. He charged inside and stopped dead in his tracks when he observed Frank's listless figure drooped in the recliner, clutching a beer, trying to watch television. "Move," he ordered boredly.

Sephus, jaw agape, stepped away from the TV set. "Frank? You okay?"

Frank said absolutely nothing until commercial break. He took a sip of his Nattie Light and flicked a peanut off of his tattered undershirt. "What?" He gestured for Sephus to sit down on the thin layer of Cheetos covering the couch.

The farmer sat, angling himself toward Frank's slack figure. "I asked if you're alright, Frank."

Frank took a sip of beer and shrugged. "Yup."

"You sounded hysterical on the phone last night."

His friend smiled bashfully and belched. "Sorry about that, you know drunk talk."

"What?" Sephus asked. He leaned forward. "Frank, you weren't drunk. You were scared out of your gourd. You were screaming and crying and then you disappeared."

"Passed out," he corrected.

"No," Sephus affirmed, "disappeared. I got to your house about ten minutes after you quit talking, and you weren't here."

"Probably out peeing."

118

"I doubt it. Your couch was propped up against the door and all of your windows were locked from the inside. If not for my extra key, I wouldn't have been able to get in."

"No shit?" Frank asked. He got up to fetch himself another beer.

"Frank," Sephus said firmly, "something happened last night. Something that terrified you. You sounded horrified, not hammered."

"Well, I must've been drunk."

Sephus shook his head. "Listen, I know you hate the idea of being abducted, but I think you're blocking your memories because they're traumatic."

"I got drunk, *Sephus*. I didn't come home from Vietnam."

The farmer ran a hand through his hair and bit his lip in thought. He withdrew a pen from his breast pocket and a donut receipt from his wallet. He doodled something on the back before handing it to Frank. "Do you recognize this?"

Frank glanced at the drawing and froze. For all intents and purposes it looked like a slice of pie with a rounder crust. It had a couple of dots where a nose would go, a thin line in place of a mouth, and two vast, black eyes. Somewhere in the back of Frank's mind an errant memory finally chewed through its gag and fell out of a closet screaming. The picture was cartoonish and crude, but it meant something. Something frightening. He handed the receipt back to Sephus with shaky hands.

"I need another beer."

"Frank, do you recognize it?"

"Yes!" he barked. "Yes, I recognize that stupid thing!" He sagged back into his recliner and took a

119

deep breath. He looked at his friend with pleading eyes. "Sephus, what's happening to me?"

The farmer reached over to pat his wrist. "Basically, some extraterrestrials are screwing with you."

"Make them stop," Frank whimpered, burying his face in his hands.

The two men were in serious danger of having an emotional moment, but a fortunate knock at the door interrupted them. "Come in," Frank yelled, pulling himself together. Hillary stepped inside and looked around disapprovingly. "Sis?" he asked.

"Hi, Frank." Her voice was calm but tired. "Hey Sephus, how are you?"

"Yes," Sephus said, poorly answering the question.

Fortunately, Hillary had already quit paying attention to him. "Frank, I need to stay with you for a few days while I figure things out."

"No," Sephus interjected. "Frank is going to be staying with *me* for a few days while *he* figures things out."

"You can guard my trailer," Frank offered helpfully.

"Or you can stay in my guest room and Frank can take the couch," Sephus suggested. He pointed to James, who had come in behind her. "Who's this?"

"I'm James," he answered.

"Oh, right," Frank said. "How have you been, man?"

"Good. How are you Frank?"

"Frank is good," Hillary answered for him. "Can I speak to you outside for a moment?"

"Sure," James said, following her out of Frank's

home.

She stepped away from the trailer and opened the door to the attached rusting pickup. Gus, sunning on the dashboard, stretched and yawned. He blinked a couple of times as Hillary shuffled over to the passenger's seat with James behind her. Two humans were just too much for Gus, so he leapt out of a glassless window and did whatever it is that cats do.

Hillary bored into him through tinted blue contacts. "You said you owe me an explanation. So hand it over. Or I call the cops."

James weighed these options. "Okay . . . " he said slowly. "Let me think about this." He did, for thirty seconds or so, and decided against involving law enforcement. "Alright, I'll clue you in. But this stays between you and me, understood?" She nodded. "Okay . . ." He took a deep breath. "I . . . and the men you saw in the hospital room . . . used to be an extraterrestrial."

Hillary stared at him as if he had begun the sentence in English but finished in Esperanto. "That doesn't make sense for multiple reasons."

James shrugged. "No one ever said the universe makes sense."

"So you're an alien?"

"No," James said, shaking his head. "We *used* to be an alien." Hillary stared at him like he was a broken optical illusion. He took another breath. "My species goes through three stages of life. We're born on our home planet as a single creature. That's stage one. Then, when we reach," he searched for the right word, "*puberty*, I guess, we leave the homeworld. We go to another planet and assume life as natives."

121

"So you're an alien?" Hillary repeated.

He shook his head again, frustrated. "No, I mean we really become natives. I'm not an extraterrestrial parading around in a human suit. I, or we, acquired a human embryo, cloned it three times, and," he searched for another word, *"downloaded* ourself into them. They were implanted in women already trying to get pregnant. Biologically, physiologically, and mentally, we're human."

"You mean you're an alien in a human body."

He thought about this. "I wouldn't put it that way. I was born as a human being, on Earth. I grew up as a human, think like a human. So far as my home planet's law is concerned, I *am* a human. I am a United States citizen who could run for president or get married or do any other number of things without questions of ethics or interstellar law. In theory, I could be Earth's ambassador to my homeworld as a visiting terrestrial."

"Why go to such a hassle? Why not just visit other planets?"

He shrugged. "It's complicated. It's necessary for us to become another species before we can mature into the final product. On an intellectual level, we feel it's helpful to our world. Human beings *think* in a manner completely different than the beings of other planets. When we return to the homeworld for maturation, we bring with us lifetimes of experience. Each of us matures into the third stage of life and leaves its assumed species behind, retaining the experiences and perspectives of an alien world. While we're whatever species we've become, we engage in life fully on the new planet, and return home with the acquired knowledge and experience. As a result, our planet is the most intellectually diverse in the galaxy, and has intimate connections to a host of alien worlds. In a sense, the galaxy itself is represented on our little globe."

Hillary mentally chewed on this. Her first impulse was to declare it insane, the most extreme story he had yet supplied. But what else was left to explain the peculiar happenings of James? Only an over-the-top supernatural account could explain anything at this point. "And so this man who tried to kill me—"

"We don't know he was going to kill you," James said defensively.

"Alright, this man who came after me—he's another pubescent extraterrestrial running around in a body genetically identical to your own?"

"No," James said. "He's not *another* 'extraterrestrial.' And I'm not an 'extraterrestrial,' by the way. Please quit calling me that, because I've lived on this planet several months longer than you have, and I watched cartoons and went to school just like you. If you want to get technical you can refer to me as a 'metaterrestrial.'"

Hillary sighed. "Okay, this person, this 'metaterrestrial' who came after me—he's . . . how does that work?"

"We're the same being, we're just in different bodies."

Hillary slapped her forehead. "That does not make any sense!"

"No, it does," James assured her, touching her elbow. "Look, when I came to Earth I didn't become a human as a single organism. Our brains have four

123

lobes, and only one lobe can download into a body. There's just too much *me* to go around. I, or we, depending on how you look at it, branched into four separate, identical bodies. But we started out as one extraterrestrial. And, when we return home for maturation, we'll re-join as a single organism. Until then we're, or I'm, one being walking around in four bodies."

"So then why the hell did you come after me with a syringe?!" she demanded.

"I didn't! Or, rather . . . Gosh, this is complicated. There just aren't sufficient pronouns for this kind of discussion. Karl (he's the one that came after you, I think) has his own brain, just like me and the other two, although they're all genetically identical to facilitate a subconscious bond. We all tap into a singular dream when we sleep, and when something traumatic happens to one of us we all feel it. But I don't know and won't know what Karl is consciously thinking until we come together to leave the planet."

Hillary slumped into the passenger's seat, dumbstruck. She felt like a primetime character who had somehow stumbled into a Sci-Fi miniseries. "Should we call the police?" she asked.

"No," James said firmly. "I don't want to be stuck with strange needles any more than you do, and if the government gets wind of this, that's exactly what will happen."

"Am I safe here?"

"I don't know," James said, looking at the shattered windshield. "If Karl is coming after you I don't know how he would find you at Sephus's house. You should remain safe there."

"Okay." Her eyes softened. "Thank you for coming clean." They hardened again. "After several years of knowing you."

James refused to be apologetic. "You're welcome. I imagine you understand why I've been so reserved about the matter. In any event, I'm going to find out what Karl is up to. Don't worry about that."

"Good. Thank you." She squinted through spiderweb designs in the windshield to the distant alfalfa stalks and grain silo beyond. "You should have told me you were an alien in college. Not because we were close friends, but because you might have gotten into my pants."

"Regrets," said James. "I have a few."

CHAPTER 21

Sephus and Frank sat in lawn chairs precariously positioned on the roof of the farmhouse. Bright pink clouds skittered across the prairie sky, slowly stalked by billowy maroon ones. Above them, the firstborn stars of the evening punctured through the dimming blue canopy like pins popping through black construction paper one by one. The sun had nearly disappeared, but left a pleasant orange aftertaste all over the horizon.

In the kitchen two floors beneath them, Hillary cleaned up the evening's dishes. Sephus had insisted on doing it himself, as she and Frank were his guests, but Hillary insisted even more adamantly that she contribute to the meal's cleanup, as she had not contributed to its preparation. Frank, who frequented Sephus's home enough to bypass the nuanced protocols of "guest" status, felt no compulsive urge to assist either of them.

Frank finished the last of his beer and rolled it down the beer trail. The "beer trail" was a clever recycling system he and Sephus designed through trial and error and three six-packs one evening before they both fell off the roof and completely surprised themselves by surviving. They had rolled several empties off the shingling until one had finally made a "tink" noise as it landed in Sephus's aluminum recycling bin. Once they determined the exact spot to release a beer, ensuring its trajectory to a responsible location, they drove two nails into the roof next to where each end of the can should be. So long as the

126

top and bottom roughly corresponded to the nails, the aluminum cylinder would wobble down the shingles, arc slightly, bounce off of the gutter, and land in the recycling bin below.

"Thanks for putting us up, man," Frank said, lighting a menthol.

"Hey, no problem." Sephus took a long sip of his beer. "I'm happy to have you both here. It makes the house more cozy."

As is customary when drinking beer at sunset, neither man said anything for another minute. "I'm a little worried about all this alien business," Frank admitted. This was a profound statement for Frank, whose greatest fear for a decade had been that one of his contact lenses would float to the back of his eyeball and remain lodged in his skull forever.

"I'm sure we'll sort it out," Sephus said, as if the matter could somehow be solved through proper filing.

Frank nodded. "Sephus?"

The farmer grunted.

"Why are these aliens so interested in me?"

Sephus did not have to think about this for long. "They're after your seed."

"What, seriously?"

"At least your genetic material, anyway."

"Why do they want that?" Frank asked. Once, in high school, a girl who thought she was his girlfriend because they kept having sex had told him she suspected she was pregnant. A second pregnancy test disagreed with the first, and a third sided with "not pregnant," but by the time Frank found this out he was halfway to Iowa. If he did not want to impregnate a cheerleader there was no *way* he wanted to impregnate some skinny, gray, space monster.

"Their species is a lot older than ours, and with each successive generation more and more 'junk DNA' creeps into their collective genome," Sephus lectured. He had heard the subject often enough on *Midnight Chat* to be an adjunct professor on the subject. "Eventually the junk DNA will become so massive and cumbersome that it will render all of their males sterile. They've probably tried cloning, but that will only slow down the process, because with each clone generation a few errors creep in, like making copies of copies."

"Okay," Frank said slowly.

"They're only a few generations away from extinction, so they've come to Earth in search of new genetic material. They're hoping to create a hybrid species using human DNA to avoid extinction. *Midnight Chat*," he added, as a scholarly reference.

"I see," Frank said. "Why *me?*"

Sephus took a sip of beer. Then another. That was an excellent question. Why, of all the humans on the planet, would they pick Frank? He was a good friend, and a decent guy, but he was more space-pet material than an alien super-race component. Why weren't they going after scientists or politicians? Or Sephus?

"I'm not sure," he admitted.

The stratified light on the horizon darkened so that the sky, with no obstruction for miles, started cobalt at the horizon and melted into ebony above. Far away, where the sun receded only moments earlier, a star winked. Then another.

Frank stared intently. "Sephus!" he whispered,

nodding toward the blinking line of stars.

"I see it."

More stars winked at them as something silently lumbered through the night sky. After a minute or so they could just barely discern an object drifting toward them. A huge black something, big as a warehouse, floated through the sky like driftwood. "Sephus, you have to hide me!" cried Frank. He stood up from the lawn chair.

"No," Sephus said. "We're going to do this together, Frank. I'm right here with you. We're going to confront them."

"I don't want to confront them again!" Frank said. "You don't know what it's like! They . . ." he shuddered, letting the remainder of the sentence roll down the beer drop.

The black triangle sailed toward them, floating over Sephus's farm like a manta ray. Sephus stood up. "Frank, I want you to imagine a warm, white field enveloping you. Then think 'No!' strongly. Can you do that, Frank?"

"What?!" his friend demanded. "If they cared what I was thinking they wouldn't kidnap me out of my trailer. Go get your gun!"

"Frank, stay calm," he commanded. The ship hung directly over the farm house. A blinding searchlight encompassed them. Sephus raised his arms and looked above. He closed his eyes and smiled, letting the warmth bathe over him.

"*Sephus!*" Frank yelled. The farmer opened his eyes, only to see Frank floating upward toward the ship.

"Wait!" Sephus yelled, pumping his arms up and down, jumping jacks-style. "Take me with you!"

"Help me!" Frank pleaded. A hatch opened above the man as he drifted skywards. "Get a ladder!" He stretched his limbs out in a large X, pushing against the rim of the hatch. "And some rope! Sephus! *Go get a rope!*"

"Hey!" Sephus yelled. "Hey, I'm right here! Take me, too!"

Frank's limbs shook from exertion, then relaxed. The beam sucked him into the ship and the hatch shut behind him. The craft rotated slightly. "You bastards!" Sephus yelled. He threw his beer at the craft, and actually hit it, but the impact did little more than dribble foam. Even more improbably, the beer can deflected off of the intergalactic spaceship's hull and landed perfectly in the recycling bin dozens of feet below.

Without reorienting its bow, the ship shot away, rapidly ascending into the night sky. "You heartless bastards!" Sephus screamed, jumping up and down. He stumbled and nearly fell off the roof. "What's wrong with me?!" he yelled at the stars. "What's wrong with *me?*"

CHAPTER 22

It is an entirely eerie sensation to regain consciousness in such a way that you do not recall ever having lost it.

Frank had done it once before, three years ago. He had been reading a moderately dirty magazine in his trailer and then, sometime later, found himself talking on the phone. The space in between—putting the magazine down, walking to the phone, picking it up—he remembered none of. It had been a little unsettling, and he ultimately blamed it on lack of sleep.

This particular evening he regained consciousness in front of the door to Sephus's farm house. He stood on top of a soiled rug so encrusted with dirt that its role as a sole cleaner was purely ceremonial. His left hand was balled in a loose fist, halfway between his sternum and naval, poised to knock.

Frank was right-handed, so it was unlikely this was of his own design. He stood in front of the door, blinking, stupefied. The minds of humans do not work like light switches. There is no clean-cut "on" and "off" mode. Rather, they function like ovens, going through a mandatory period of preheating before they cook anything. Frank had suddenly jumped to "full broil" status, and it was peculiar and startling.

Even if he was left-handed, he would not have knocked. This was Sephus's home, after all, and he was staying there. He found the door locked, but kept a copy of the master key with his own for occasions just like this, or when he needed to borrow something like groceries or power tools and Sephus wasn't home. Once Sephus had gone out of town to visit his aunt and asked Frank to feed Roswell, which he had, right after he made a copy of the key.

He let himself in and walked to the kitchen. He was dehydrated and his head hurt, like he had sucked on a cigar packed too tight. He poured himself a glass of water, downed it, and poured another. A few dots of bright red sprung to life on the white porcelain below, alerting Frank to a minor nose bleed.

He turned around in search of paper towels and jumped as he noticed Sephus seated at the kitchen table, motionlessly staring at him.

"Have fun with your friends?" Sephus asked, with the tone of a wife confronting an adulterous husband.

"Oh, Sephus, you startled me," Frank said. He found a paper towel and held it against his left nostril while the blood clotted. "I have a splitting headache, do you have any aspirin?"

"Sure, Frank," he said in an overtly passive-aggressive way.

Fortunately, being male, Frank understood subtext about as well as beagles grasp sign language.

The farmer walked across the kitchen and rifled through a cabinet containing various vitamin supplements, wheat grass juice, St. John's Wort, and ginseng tablets. He found a Wal-Mart knockoff of aspirin in a bulk bottle the size of his head.

Everyone in Hoople had a similar bottle of non-name-brand pain relievers, because they had all read the back of aspirin bottles two decades ago and realized that the cheaper kind is chemically identical. Leland McCorvick was an exception, but only because he owned no medical supplies unassociated with arterial bleeding, as he felt popping pills for headaches was a task best left to menopausal women.

"So how was your evening?" Sephus asked, unscrewing the lid without breaking eye contact.

"Well, I don't rightly know," Frank said. "Actually, I just sort of woke up at your doorstep, just standing there." He scratched his head, trying to reassemble the evening. It came together painfully and pathetically, like a puzzle whose missing pieces had been replaced with cheese crackers. "What happened?" he asked.

"What happened?" Sephus mimicked. The lid popped off and dropped to the floor. "How would *I* know what happened?" he demanded. His face screwed up in pain and he slung the bottle like the hilt of a sword, spraying non-name-brand pain relievers across the linoleum tiling. He slammed the capless bottle on the counter, which belched out a few more capsules, and exited the room. Elsewhere a bedroom door slammed shut.

Roswell wandered into the kitchen and surveyed the scene. She did not like Frank, because he was new, and therefore threatening. She did not like the odd-smelling pieces of gravel now littered across the usually spotless tile. "Don't eat those!" Frank commanded. He vaguely recalled that if cats eat aspirin they explode, which is not altogether true, but is close enough to merit avoiding their use as cat treats.

Roswell sized him up and decided that she now hated him because he had yelled at her and had somehow tried to impute his will upon her, and that was the sort of crap she wasn't going to put up with. She resigned herself to do the exact opposite of whatever he had exhorted her to do, but was not sure what it was. Either he desperately wanted her to eat the gravel or he did not want her to touch the gravel. She couldn't be sure, so she politely excused herself to the guest room where she found one of Frank's boots to vomit in.

As the cat left, Frank found a broom and dustpan and cleaned up the spilt medication with surprising speed considering how categorically lazy he was. Once swept, he made a crude funnel from some newspaper and emptied the contents back into the pill bottle before screwing the lid on.

CHAPTER 23

Hardened salt and sand crunched beneath Karl's feet as he limped from his car onto the vast plain. Underneath the starlight the powdered brine glistened like snow, stretching into the inky distance. The ashen sheet pulled over the desert contrasted with the miles and miles of wheat and prairie Karl had driven through to get there. It looked peaceful.

Karl continued walking away from his car, into the deflated dunes, navigating between the silent sandcastles of the day's schoolchildren and discarded selenite crystals of the Great Salt Plains State Park. Karl suspected that this place looked like Carthage shortly after the Romans burned everything to the ground and flooded it with sea water to keep the future Tunisians from ever again growing petunias or ferns or rising against Rome.

The park had not been man-made, however. Eons before the Romans or even mankind itself, the area had been underwater. As the ocean receded, it left behind an expansive puddle, trapping orphaned saltwater, which eventually evaporated entirely. Now the basin was a salt desert.

Back in its heyday as an inland salt sea, dinosaurs had roamed its shores. Huge lurking reptiles that ate each other and probably roared a lot and maybe evolved into things like emus and toucans had all dwelt there. Further out in the sand and salt, different and more modern reptiles trudged toward Karl.

They were still too far away to see much detail.

He could see the starlight glancing off of their scales, their jerky bodies pivoting forwards and backwards like praying mantises. Their corsair rested near a hill half a mile away, and looked like a large top, glowing orange.

He met them half a mile from his own vehicle. There were four this time. They ranged in height from five to nine feet tall. The tallest was mocha-colored, the other three various shades of rust and algae. Lean and powerful, they had elliptical white eyes and red serpentine pupils.

Karl set his backpack down in the sand and took two steps back. The taller one stepped forward, opened it, and examined the contents. "Only two thermoses!" it hissed.

"I made a mistake," Karl said quietly. "The newspaper printed a circle backwards, and as a result I identified the wrong human. The rest of the shipment is complete."

"We have orders," the short tawny one said, gripping an electric thermos.

"I know," Karl said, with an edge, "and I'm doing my best to accommodate them. This was an unforeseen circumstance."

"Quota," growled the tall one.

"Yes, yes. Again, the rest of the shipment is there—you're only two vials short."

"There is no egscuze," the green one said, making a stab at a word the Reptoids had no equivalent for. The closest approximation to "excuse" in Reptoid tongue was "fail less bad."

Karl picked up the empty pack. "Take it or leave it."

The Reptoids looked to the short tawny one for

direction. "One week," it hissed. "You have one week."

"Fine," Karl said, hiding his relief at the prospects of at least postponed torture and death. He cleared his throat and looked down sheepishly. "I was promised lenses."

The tawny Reptoid snorted. It pulled a contact lens case out of a pouch and tossed it onto the sand in front of Karl. Karl snatched it from the ground and slipped it into his pocket, resisting the urge to jam on a contact right there in the salt fields.

The taller Reptoid gestured for the backpack. Without saying anything else, they collectively turned to lumber back to their ship.

CHAPTER 24

Sephus's farmhouse was built during the seventies and had experienced no major renovations in taste since then. The outside was everything a modest two-story farmhouse should be, but faux wood paneling and odd shades of orange and green ringed the inside. A sunken fire pit dominated the living room, complete with shag carpeting. The ceiling appeared to be composed of hardened cottage cheese, and the kitchen and bathrooms were the only places in the entire house with acceptable central lighting.

Sephus and his guests, Frank, Hillary, and Leland McCorvick, all sat at the dining table. The Norbitzes were present on the night Sephus and Leland routinely dedicated to sharing a six-pack and watching the History Channel, but McCorvick had magnanimously overlooked the departure from the norm and was going out of his way to make the two comfortable. He occasionally and forcibly smiled, which only unnerved both visitors.

Leland McCorvick ran into Frank on occasion and accepted him as a naturalized, but inferior, ruralite. He liked him well enough, but ever since finding Frank's car in the middle of his field, enjoyed staring at him until the man became unnerved. Hillary was from The City and was therefore not to be trusted, but being a typical country gentleman he would never mention this to anyone unless he had reasonable suspicion that she was involved in criminal acts or raising taxes.

Roswell rubbed against McCorvick's leg because, despite his total lack of response, the cat enjoyed capriciously choosing humans to love and disdain, and for whatever reason, loved Leland McCorvick unconditionally. The old bachelor extended his own brand of affection in the form of not kicking it away.

Several hamburgers sat on the table, the labor of every dinner participant. Leland McCorvick had brought the beef over, which four days prior had been grazing on his land and periodically relieving itself and doing whatever remaining worthwhile activities cows engage themselves in. For some reason it dropped dead one afternoon, and had been butchered and disseminated to friends and relatives within another two days. This was the usual course of action for Leland McCorvick, who over the years had served a good deal of suspicious meat, which had come about through even less mysterious circumstances.

Hillary had prepared the ground beef in the kitchen, rolling it into patties and adding a dash of seasoning. Frank had sat in the corner drinking beer and occasionally offering helpful suggestions like "Put milk innit." Sephus cooked the meat on his back-porch grill before delivering it to the kitchen counter, warm and delicious.

Now at the dinner table, Hillary savored another bite of her hamburger and dabbed at the corner of her mouth with a folded paper towel. She took a sip of the sweetened iced tea which both Sephus and Leland McCorvick consumed more of than water and beer combined.

Both men took a swig of tea in unison,

prompting Hillary to reflect on their bizarre friendship. Leland McCorvick was a grizzled veteran who believed that upholding the U.S. customary measurements of feet and pounds in the face of the encroaching metric system potentially warranted nuclear warfare. He had once killed two coyotes with a pitchfork, and believed that football summed up all that is good and right in the world.

Sephus, by contrast, believed that magnetic bracelets and certain types of crystals have healing powers. Most of his political, religious, and economic theories were somehow tied to the Lost City of Atlantis. He owned books about ley lines.

Somehow the men crossed the chasm of differences between them at least once a week to eat dinner and watch documentaries about Hitler. Their relationship was a testament to the peculiar Red State belief that geographic proximity is as much a factor in friendship as shared interests or trust.

"How's work at the Co-op?" she asked her brother.

"It's okay," Frank mumbled, navigating his words through a glob of baked beans. Frank ran the grain elevator at the Dacoma Farmers Co-op near Hoople. It was an honest but simple job, with little variation since the advent of electricity. Work was always "okay" because nothing significantly worse or better could conceivably happen. On a scale of one to ten, Frank's day at work could never vary more than one point.

Leland poised himself to speak and then chewed eight more times before swallowing. "Herb Morris still workin' there?"

"Yes," Frank reported. A belch crawled up his

insides but lost its grip and slid into his stomach.

"Good man," Leland said. He gave a hearty nod to confirm his appraisal of the human being.

"Did they ever catch the guy that mutilated your cow?" Frank asked.

McCorvick shook his head. "Sombitch gottaway."

"Well of *course* he did," Sephus said, gesturing to the last hamburger. No one objected, so he reached for it. "You called law enforcement officials to investigate a government conspiracy. The government won't catch itself. Who do you think owns all those black helicopters?"

Laughter blew out of Hillary like unexpected projectile vomit. It took her by surprise, startling the men around her. Sephus, correctly assuming that he had triggered the psychotic hilarity, cringed in his chair. He flushed a deep scarlet of embarrassment. Hillary clasped a hand over her mouth but could not stop guffawing.

"I'm sorry!" she exclaimed, gasping for air. Frank, wide-eyed, watched her chortle and backed away from the table. McCorvick suspected a nervous breakdown.

In a sense it was. All at once, the ludicrous nature of Hillary's situation caught up with her. She had fled from Moore, her Elba, to Hoople, her St. Helena. She was hiding there with her brother, a chronic alien abductee, in order to protect herself from her potential boyfriend's deranged extraterrestrial clone. And, in this light, Sephus had suddenly *made sense.* He magically transformed from an agricultural weirdo into a glorious, endearing punch line.

She rose from the table and hugged him. "Thank you for letting us stay here," she said. "It's strange, but I haven't felt this good in months."

CHAPTER 25

James's house in Nichols Hills was the immaculate *Skymall* residence of a man who seldom lived there. Four twenty-two Harvard Court was not as much James's home as a two-story mailbox he received bills at and stashed mementos in from his adventures abroad.

He sat on a black kitchen stool inside of his large mailbox. Around him gleamed the green marble tops of his kitchen counters surrounding a sizeable island in the middle where various spices stood sentry. In front of him lay a sheet of paper, a pen, and a cup of coffee.

Scrawled on the paper was the name "Karl," followed by an inkblot noting where the pen had rested as James ponderously considered what next to write. "Janus" was sandwiched between this inkblot and a second one created by the same problem. Nothing else was on the page, save an errant drop of coffee.

James hoped that some fantastic ideas would spring from his pen onto the tempting white canvas. He took another sip of coffee. He had finally accepted the possibility that Karl was the infamous Rectum Thief, although it was only that, a possibility.

What was Karl up to?

Why had Karl not mentioned anything to him?

What *was* he up to?

So far, James had deduced nothing. His double seemed perfectly stable and normal whenever they spoke. Karl had no anger issues, nor a vendetta with

Hillary. He had never mentioned any desire to attack people or even poke them with anything.

James dialed Karl for the sixth time that week.

Karl picked up. "Hello?"

"Karl, it's James. I need to talk to you."

"About Hillary?"

"Yes."

Karl sighed. "I've told you again and again, James, you don't want to get wrapped up in that mess. It will all come together when we rejoin."

"That's not enough information."

"Fine, I'll say this: I visited Hillary by mistake. She has nothing to worry about, nor do you. Now please refrain from calling me on this subject. Don't expect me to answer your calls for the rest of the week." He hung up the phone. James immediately redialed, but to no avail.

He took another sip of coffee and decided on a whim to call Karl's firm. He dialed information and waited for them to connect him through to the office.

"Carver, Rabeed, and Associates," a perky voice answered.

"Good afternoon, can you please connect me to Karl Janus?"

"I'm sorry, Mr. Janus quit working at this office a month ago. Lucy Canden is handling his purview. Would you like me to connect you to her?"

"No thank you," James said, confused. "Why did Mr. Janus leave the firm?"

"He didn't say. He just quit. Is there anything else?"

"No, thank you for your time." James hung up the phone and stared at it as if scrutinizing an expiration date carved into the receiver. A month?

James had seen him only a matter of days ago. He did not blame Karl for quitting his job as an HR manager, but why would he conceal this from himselves?

He decided it was time to inform Monty and Vincent of Karl's suspicious and unexplained behavior. He moved to his living room and eased into a sleek black recliner he'd once ordered from *Skymall* on his way home from Toronto.

Montgomery picked his phone up on exactly the fourth ring. James had never known him to do otherwise. For years he had taken it for granted that Montgomery was always on the opposite end of his home or office from the phone, but he now supposed that the man intentionally waited until the last possible moment to heighten the suspense, making himself seem less obtainable, almost lucky to get ahold of at all.

"Hello, Jim," he said, smiling over the line. "What can I do for you?" His voice sounded the same as James's, only louder.

"I need to talk to you and Vincent about Karl. Hold on a second while I call him."

"Alright."

James hit the "hold" button on the phone and punched in Vincent's number. After two rings the man picked up. "Yes?" Vincent asked, already bored.

"Hello, Vincent, I have Monty on the other line and I need to speak with you both."

In his head, James could see Vincent looking at his watch to determine if he could wedge in a conversation. "Okay."

James hit the "connect" button on his phone and put the receiver back to his ear. "Can everyone hear

145

me?"

"Yes," a voice indistinguishable from his own said.

"Yes," replied a third.

"Good," James said. He brought them both up to speed on the Hillary assault and clandestine job termination.

"That is strange," said Monty. "Did he say anything to you, Vincent?"

"Not a word."

"Hmm. Jim, did you actually see him come after this Hillary girl?"

"No." His voice grew angry. "Are you implying that she lied?"

"That, or she has her facts wrong. She saw all four of us just a few days earlier. Perhaps her mind was playing tricks on her?"

"It wasn't. Karl admitted that he visited her, and I heard part of the encounter over the phone. He . . . it sounded like he was *attacking* her."

"Bah!" said Monty. "James, Karl is a *human resources manager*. He files paperwork. I can't imagine him committing acts of violence. You're clearly mistaken."

"I don't believe Karl would keep something from us, either," said Vincent. "He would have no reason to do so."

"Then why wouldn't he just tell me that?" asked James. "He's refusing to talk to me about the issue at all. He admitted something happened."

"Ah, right," Montgomery said. "Well, listen Jim, I'll talk to Karl and see what I can do, alright?"

"Okay," James agreed. The three men exchanged goodbyes and hung up.

James closed his eyes and leaned back in the recliner. He flipped on the vibration mechanism and winced as robotic nubs kneaded his shoulders. Gradually, the Karl-induced stress melted away. The image of Hillary, seated angelically in the defunct pickup truck from the day before, began to dominate his mind. He thought about how amazed and surprisingly accepting she had been about his metaterrestrial identity. About how good it felt to tell her.

His thoughts drifted from solving the problem in front of him to the old feelings he once hid away from his college heartthrob. The old feelings stirred.

CHAPTER 26

Frank lay in bed on his back trying to sleep. He had briefly achieved it, but a bizarre, frightening dream yanked him back into consciousness.

He liked to rest his head on a pillow, put one in between his knees, and then flop an elbow over a third. *Nuts to pillows, I need a woman,* he thought.

He wished he had one at the moment. Not for sexual purposes, although he wouldn't be up in arms if she proposed something to that effect. No, he simply wanted the company of another human being next to him. His mind was alert and rigid and trapped in an otherwise relaxed body. For the first time since childhood, he feared the dark.

Something shuffled on the other side of the room, prompting Frank's eyelids to flutter open before immediately squeezing shut. He forced his body to remain perfectly still. It was an old house, and old houses make noise.

Swelling and contracting from the shift from day to night, he thought, *making pops and squeaks.*

A book on a desk a few feet from his bed fell to the old, carpeted floor with a thud. Frank thought he heard the tiny hush of the book being lightly returned to the desk, but he was probably imagining things. Except for the book, of course. Which had fallen.

Part of him wanted to turn around or sit up in bed and see who was skulking around his room. The rest of him screamed "Are you crazy?!" at this curious part of him, and strongly encouraged Frank to pretend he was a corpse in the very unlikely event that a bear had wandered in and would lose interest if he quit moving.

An aged wooden plank creaked beneath the carpet next to the door. Very slowly and very quietly, his door clicked shut. Frank squeezed his eyelids together with passion and wished his bed sheets were thicker. Chills ran up and down his spine in frosty marathons.

It's only angels, he told himself. *They're just here to make sure you're not an alcoholic. They don't want to scare you so they're waiting until you fall asleep so they can smell your breath to see if there's Southern Comfort on it, then go protect blind people in traffic or something.*

He lay still and hoped for Sephus's voice. He wished that the farmer would flip the light switch on and mumble something about looking for his car keys and shuffle some papers on the desk before apologizing and heading downstairs.

The room remained quiet and dark for several minutes. Frank finally allowed himself to relax. He was being silly and childish. It was probably juvenile memories from his childhood bleeding into his psyche as his mind drifted to sleep. He took a deep breath and exhaled.

His bed sheet, which had shifted a little as he inhaled, kept moving. He remained perfectly still as the thin layer of cotton drifted toward his feet at a snail's pace, barely touching his skin as it crept.

Frank took a deep breath and flipped onto his back. He forced himself to look up.

Two enormous black eyes stared back.

CHAPTER 27

Hillary could not see her father's face in the dream. Only the back of Arthur's head was visible, bobbing away from her as she chased him through a neighborhood. Behind her, she knew, ran her mother. A casserole hung underneath her arm like a purse, its contents sliding down her side and clopping off her feet as she loped after matrimony.

"Arthur!" Hillary called out. "Arthur, please stop! We need you!" Her father ran onto a road so full of traffic it seemed more like a parking lot with no stationary cars. He effortlessly passed through the tiny reprieves of zipping automobiles. He jogged through motorized death, barely awake, uncaring.

Helen caught up with her daughter and stood at the sidewalk. She screamed in frustration and hurled the casserole onto cement, shattering it across the curb. She screamed at Arthur incoherently and stooped to pick up handfuls of steaming casserole, lobbing them into traffic. She did it again with the ferocity of a frustrated ape hurling excrement at spectators.

Arthur was gone—he had never looked back. Her mother squawked again and slapped her across the face. The blow reeled Hillary back into consciousness.

She came to in a guest bed on the second floor of Sephus's home. The air was frigid on account of Sephus's stubborn refusal to accept the eighty-degree temperature outside. She sat up in bed, shivering, and glanced around the room for a blanket. Seeing none, she checked the closet, but it only contained an assortment of fishing gear.

Not wanting to wake anyone, she decided to go downstairs and borrow the Mr. Spock quilt she noticed on the couch earlier. She opened the door to the room and took one step into the hallway. As she did so, a tall scary monster strode by her. A long anorexic finger brushed her hand.

Hillary screamed.

The slender gray monster hurled itself against the opposing wall, startled. Its toddler-sized mouth opened as if about to scream itself.

Hillary did not wait to see if it would. She ran past it, through the hall, and to the bottom of the stairs. She sprinted past the living room and tripped over Roswell, who frantically scurried into the kitchen and decided to one day kill Hillary in her sleep.

She continued through the bottom floor and swung the door to Sephus's room open. The bleary-eyed farmer reclined in a rocking chair in a tattered robe and a lap blanket, listening to the second hour of *Midnight Chat*. "Kill it!" Hillary shrieked, running to him.

Sephus attempted to process the information. He could only comprehend that one of his fantasies (a beautiful woman throwing the door to his room open at two o'clock in the morning) just came true. "Kill it! Kill it!" she reiterated, grabbing his hand and hoisting him up.

"What is it, a coyote?" Sephus asked as she dragged him down the hall. "Burglar?"

"There's a monster upstairs!" she stage-whispered, in case it heard her. Momentary panic set in as she realized it could have walked its long legs *downstairs.* "I saw a monster upstairs where's your gun?" she said, fusing two sentences together through sheer terror.

"Monster?" Sephus asked.

Hillary, like anyone who sees a ghoul in a hallway after midnight, was understandably disturbed. She was processing the monster's existence in much the same way she would deal with a particularly large tarantula, which was to locate the home's owner and fully expect him to bludgeon it to death.

She reached the top of the staircase just in time to see the hall monster frantically climb out a window and into thin air. Sephus, a moment behind her, bounded into the hall and past her. "Where is it?" he asked in a normal voice. The fact that he neither whispered nor yelled inadvertently filled both Sephus and Hillary with a level of assurance. It meant Sephus was in control of the situation; it was still his house.

"It just went out the window," she said, panting.

"What did it look like?"

"Tall and skinny. Big eyes and no hair."

"A Grey," Sephus said, turning back to the window. His shoulders sagged as he recognized a missed opportunity to see one. In early childhood his parents had woken him up one Christmas to see Santa Clause. They got to the chimney seconds before he did, and told him upon arrival that Santa had just darted up, and had he seen him? No. Nor had he seen the space aliens walking around his home eight tantalizing seconds earlier.

"Okay," he said, sighing. "It's probably gone,

then. No point in getting worked up about it." He walked down the hall and shut the window.

"What?" Hillary demanded. "You don't believe me," she whispered, hurt.

"Oh yes, I do," he said, passing her and heading down the stairs. "I very much believe you. But I doubt it will be back tonight. I'll see you at breakfast."

"I'm not going back to sleep up here!"

"Alright. Why don't you come downstairs and I'll make you some herbal tea."

Hillary agreed. She followed the farmer downstairs and sat on the counter of his kitchen, bleary-eyed, as he microwaved a mug of tap water and plunked a tea bag into the steam. He let the tea steep, removed the bag, added stevia, and handed it to her.

She sat on the counter in silence, sipping her hot drink. Her host stood by the window hoping beyond hope that he would catch a glimpse of an extraterrestrial scuttling across the Bermuda grass.

"I'm not sleeping in that room," she said firmly, clinking the empty mug against the counter. "Thank you for the tea."

"What do you want, then? Would you like me to put on a movie?"

"No, I'm too tired."

Sephus said nothing, but only because he could not adequately express his irritation with Hillary's mutually exclusive demands and utter lack of solution. "Would you like to sleep on the couch?"

"No," Hillary said. "I don't want to sleep out in the open."

Sephus wished to make some insightful

observation about the differences between men and women but decided not to. "I could sleep on the couch and you could sleep in my bed," he offered.

"No, that's not much better than the guest room. I don't see why I'd be any safer alone in your room than upstairs."

This, to Sephus, sounded like a pickup line. She was obviously implying she did not want to sleep alone, which meant her companion could only be Sephus, Frank, or a returning space alien.

Except that Hillary was not batting her eyes at him, he thought. She was shivering a little and looked angry. She made no offers, just lobbed a poorly worded desire completely independent of sex at him. Sephus took a deep breath and decided to be a good guy. "Why don't you sleep in my bed, and I'll read a book in my rocking chair."

"No," Hillary said, attempting to thwart the only helpful suggestion either of them had made in some time, "that would be unfair to you."

"It's fine," Sephus said. "I was going to be up for another hour anyway. If I get tired after that I'll just slump over in the chair. It's not a problem."

Hillary agreed, promptly falling asleep on his king-sized mattress. Sephus passively scanned over his book about astral projection and eventually gave up. He stared at the breathtaking woman in his bedroom. She occupied only a small portion of the bed in a cute and apologetic manner. Sephus, by contrast, took up as much of the mattress as possible when sleeping. He sometimes regained consciousness with his arms and legs outstretched, as if waking up in the process of making a nocturnal snow angel.

He continued to watch her as the minutes passed, neither fantasizing about sliding under the covers next to her, nor entertaining any other desires toward her delicate figure. He merely admired the beauty before him as beauty, as if he had returned to his bedroom to find rosebuds sprouting from the mattress.

Sephus stared at her like this for an hour, hovering on the verge of sleep. Without sleep, thoughts came to him slowly, like grapes sucked through a straw. The time passed without recognition or boredom. Just a slow and quiet appreciation.

It was a good thing, too, because if Sephus had not watched over Hillary as a bedroom sentry, his cat probably would have killed her. He wondered if the Grey had woken Frank up. He made a mental note to ask his guest at breakfast.

CHAPTER 28

Karl had never before smelled the tang of a three-dollar hooker, but on an instinctual level he knew this was what his motel room must stink like. It was an outside room at a crummy little Motel 8 in Enid, Oklahoma. Above him, a couple watched television on high volume, occasionally jumping up and down on the bed and giggling loudly.

He was at this particular motel for two reasons. First, he had been there before. Second, it was a good central location for the region in which he worked. There was nothing particularly special about Oklahoma to Karl, nor Texas, Kansas, or Arkansas for that matter. They were simply the locations the crop circles directed him to.

A photo of one such sign sat crinkled on his desk. In a very mathematical language, so devoid of expression and metaphor that any paragraph of it would make an English major weep, it said "Bovine, Female, No. 352," followed by specific global tracking coordinates. These specific coordinates happened to be about half a mile from the sign itself, scribbled on wheat in Leland McCorvick's farm.

Beneath it was another photo which read "Norbitz, Male," and global coordinates around Hoople, Oklahoma. If flipped horizontally, the photo coincidentally gave global coordinates for Moore, Oklahoma, followed by "Female, Norbitz." If then flipped vertically, the message read "589 Nixon?" If flipped horizontally from there it read "Bite the red tadpole."

Karl sat on his bed perusing the various UFO watch groups literature which occasionally discussed crop circles. He was looking for another circle, anywhere in the U.S., that referenced a bovine specimen instead of a human.

He very much hoped to locate one of these so that his last and final commission on planet Earth need only involve butchering a cow. Cows were stupid, made no attempts to call the police, and very rarely dated anyone Karl knew. In general, working on a cow would be easy.

No such crop circle appeared.

Which left Norbitz. The male, Karl concluded, not the female coincidentally located in Moore at the particular time he had read the code backwards.

Above him, the couple in the motel laughed like hyenas, breaking his concentration.

Karl sighed. Precious few days remained before the Reptoids came looking for him. He had to find Norbitz, Male.

The couple above him dropped what sounded like a bowling ball directly over his head. This resulted in uproarious laughter, followed by another bowling ball and even greater laughter. Karl sighed and stood up from the bed. He exited his room and walked up the stairs, stopping at the door of the room above his own.

He knocked on the dirty wood. A ruddy faced man in a very good mood opened it. "Yeah, man?"

"Please be a little quieter, sir," Karl said. "It's getting late."

The man nodded, embarrassed. "I'm so sorry! We'll be quieter! Have a good evening!" He shut the door, and Karl returned to his motel room.

He fumbled with the newly acquired contact lens case until its top popped off. He placed the lens against his cornea. Chemicals infused within the plastic leached into his eyeball. They spread from his cornea into his brain and nervous system, filling his body with spider web patterns of euphoria and relief. He saw glimpses of the future, of the various possibilities branching through the multiverse. He eschewed their prophetic nature and focused on the calming effects of his narcotic rush.

Sighing with contentment, he assembled his kit for the following day, when he would find and kill Norbitz.

CHAPTER 29

There are three types of tired people.

The first type is a happy and often tight-lipped person who was obviously having a whole lot of slumber-reducing fun the previous evening. They are bushed, but their spirits are peppy and alert. Any number of activities have worn them out, most likely drinking or sex or both, as they are often interrelated. Four hours of sleep against eight voluntary hours of fun is always easier to run on in the morning than four hours of sleep against three involuntary hours of work.

The second type is a temporary exhaustion brought on by some arduous task which extended well beyond dusk. It is a groggy and grinding drain resulting from care of a sick loved one or playing video games for eight successive weeks and then, well after midnight, beginning a midterm essay. College students spend most of their time flipping between these two states of sleep deprivation like a dime in a tornado.

The final is a painful energy-sucking state of burnout from weeks, months, or years of being stretched unbelievably thin. People with hard lives, three jobs, frequent alien abductions, or children experience this zombie-like state of existence. It carves lines into their faces with a dull blade.

On this particular Saturday morning Frank definitely suffered from the third type of exhaustion. His eyes were small and swollen, peering out from beneath sagging eyebrows. His jaw hung slack. He was slovenly and unshaven, although this was not abnormal.

Hillary slid a bowl of grits in front of his buttered toast. He mumbled something, possibly a thank you, and stared at his pulpy orange juice.

Sephus suffered from the second kind of tiredness; from staying awake via task. He downed a ginseng pill with his glass of juice and thanked Hillary for the grits. They weren't delicious, but they were necessary.

Hillary, oddly enough, was not particularly tired this morning. She had merely woken up in the middle of night, which did little for her sleep cycle other than make her remember her dream more vividly.

"I think they took me again last night," Frank said. "I don't remember them taking me, but I feel like hell. And I had a pretty bad nosebleed when I woke up this morning. My head hurts." His hindquarters felt pretty bad too, but Frank would never mention this to anyone, under any circumstance.

Sephus glared at him as he unnecessarily chewed grits. He gulped them down with bitter contempt. Why did they want *him*? Frank, the idiot. Frank, who knew nothing, *nothing*, of history, politics, current events, or government conspiracies. Sephus angrily considered asking Hillary out on a date just so he could keep a list of species which rejected him.

She picked this moment to sit down next to him and favor him with a smile. "Thank you for staying up last night," she said.

"No problem, no problem," Sephus mumbled.

"What?" Frank asked.

"I saw one of your space aliens upstairs last night," Hillary said. "Sephus let me sleep in his bed and stayed awake in case they came back."

"I—" Frank choked. "Why didn't you come get *me?*" he stammered.

"I didn't want to wake you up."

"But," Frank stirred his bowl in frustration, "but they took me up again. And did . . . stuff . . . to me."

"Probably before we saw them," Sephus growled, with no real evidence for this theory.

"Fine," Frank said. "Fine."

"Fine," Sephus echoed, staring at Frank.

CHAPTER 30

The stars above Karl glistened like a gargantuan sneeze against the interior of a black bowl. He parked his car directly in front of the automotive skeleton of a truck that served as the pillar of Frank's trailer. The parking job was so tight that it almost looked like the truck and Lincoln were Eskimo kissing. It would have been cute, had Karl not been gripping a syringe intended to shut down Frank's heart.

As Karl's foot crunched through the rusted shards of a Coors Light can, he wondered, as he often did, if the Greys employed any strategy whatsoever in picking out humans. He doubted they used any comprehensive policy for selecting cows. The only thing about a cow that concerned Greys was its temperature, which absolutely had to be between 100 degrees Fahrenheit and 101.5 degrees Fahrenheit. Beyond that, they tended to use Black Angus more than anything, but this was probably just a statistical anomaly.

So far as humans were concerned, he had no idea. He theorized that they flipped through a phonebook, picking out names completely at random. Maybe, if they selected someone with an important sounding title, like "Pope John Paul II," they did it over again.

One keen feline eye paired with a less keen but slightly wiser feline eye watched Karl with interest as he kicked a can of WD-40 out of his way. Gus was at the end of a long evening involving several fights with other tomcats for the hell of it, impregnating their sisters, and nearly being flattened by a Union Pacific freight train.

He watched Karl knock on the door, wait for it to open, and look around. Karl tried the door when no one answered, then shouldered it. It offered scant resistance. He did not flip the lights on because he did not want to draw attention to himself. Square foot by square foot, he searched the trailer with a keychain flashlight. He hoped to find some large piece of paper with the phrase "I, Frank, will return to this trailer within six hours," or "I, Mr. Norbitz, am staying with such and such until such time," or something like that. He found no such clue.

In fact, Karl found virtually nothing of use except for a paycheck stub from the Dacoma Co-op next to the empty six-pack and bottle of Southern Comfort it had immediately contributed to. The stub only confirmed Frank's vocation, which Karl already knew.

As it was Friday, Frank would not return to work until Monday, and that would be too late. In Reptoid, the closest equivalent to "forgiveness" is "sufficient toe loss."

Karl decided he would have to locate Norbitz, Male, using less secure means. He had to acquire information about Frank, and discern his whereabouts from there.

He picked up the trailer's phone and hit "redial."

CHAPTER 31

Hillary sat cross-legged in Sephus's recliner thumbing through the tomes of Kurt Vonnegut and Arthur C. Clarke novels perched on the night stand. The phone, an old plastic contraption with hearty dynamics, crescendoed on the wall near the kitchen. Neither Frank nor Sephus were present—only Roswell, who stared at Hillary from the kitchen counter with malice. The cat was trying to figure out how to get her mouth around Hillary's head.

Sephus had no answering machine. The whole concept made very little sense to him. He theorized that anyone who ever called lived close enough to leave a sticky note on his door. Hillary picked the phone up. "Fitzbaur residence."

James's voice greeted her. "Hello?"

"James!" she exclaimed. Somewhere, at the opposite end of the transceiver, was the man most likely to free her from Hoople and possibly result in spouse acquisition. "How are you?"

"Oh, I'm just great," he said. "And yourself?"

She sighed. "I'm good, but I'm getting cabin fever here. What's the news about Karl?"

"I still haven't figured that whole mess out yet, but I'm working on it. I actually have a question for Frank, is he around?"

"Frank?" she asked. "No, he's out getting groceries, or maybe just beer. What do you need to ask him?"

"Just a couple of questions. I could call him at his home later. When do you think he'll be back?"

"Not for several days; he's staying with Sephus until he determines how to repel space aliens."

"I see. And it's just the three of you there?"

"Except when Leland McCorvick comes over. Listen, I'm getting antsy here. Would you like to get dinner tomorrow night?"

"Dinner? Sure, that sounds great."

"I was thinking we could meet in Guthrie. That's about midpoint between us. I'll borrow Frank's car."

"That sounds fantastic."

"Does seven o'clock work?"

"Yes, that will be fine."

"Okay, where would you like to eat at?"

"Anywhere."

"You know Guthrie better than I do."

"Sure, but I'd rather play it by ear, do something spontaneous."

"Alright. Why don't we meet in front of the Masonic Lodge and make plans from there?"

"Sounds good, I'll see you tomorrow."

"Yes, goodbye."

"Bye!"

Sephus came in the front door, huffing, as she set the phone down. He sported the top of a bright crimson jogging suit with reflective stripes. The matching pants were missing, replaced with dark blue basketball shorts that revealed surprisingly sculpted calves and thighs. The alarming mismatch of bright red long sleeves and blue short shorts made him seem more masculine, but only so far as masculinity frequently lacks taste.

He gave a quick, friendly nod before trucking into the kitchen for iced tea. He poured the concoction into a plastic cup and chugged it down, letting a rivulet of sweetness dribble off of his chin and onto the counter. He slammed the cup down like a shot glass and cleared his throat. "Okay," he announced to no one in particular, before heading to his bathroom for a shower.

It impressed Hillary that he jogged. Exercise was foreign to her family; until she reached college the only form of weight control she had been exposed to was wishful thinking and cigarettes.

Sephus did not jog regularly, however. He occasionally practiced it for a week or two if a *Midnight Chat* guest spoke at length on health concerns, but this interest in physique inevitably waned. He could afford mild bodily neglect because he ate healthy and had a lean constitution by nature. The revisited habit had little to do with his slender house guest. Nor did the forty-eight pushups undertaken daily or the abdomen-crushing sit-up regimen. He was not making himself more attractive as a man so much as a specimen. To the aliens.

Feelings of inadequacy had staked their claims in the otherwise rollicking party that was Sephus's mind. *The aliens have chosen Frank because he is a better specimen than you,* they chided. There was also a large but silent fear that penis size somehow factored in—a fear sunken so deep in his psyche it made no ripples on the surface as it swam beneath.

Without probing the apprehension further, Sephus endeavored to transform himself into a handsome and ideal specimen of humanity through a rigorous program of jogging and ups of the push and sit persuasion. His body frame rendered him incapable of actually adding to his existing muscle mass, but the various exercises did mildly define the mostly theoretical muscles of his chest and abs.

Frank came in moments later through the front door. "Where can I get some handcuffs?" he asked. He planned to bind himself to the bed frame before sleeping. He had bought a machete earlier that day, now hidden under the mattress.

"I don't know," Hillary said, which was a lie. But they were talking about different sorts of handcuffs. "Can I borrow your car tomorrow? I'm having dinner with James."

"No," Frank replied. He started up the stairs.

"What? Why not?"

"Because tomorrow is Saturday night, and that means I'm going to be at a bar." He turned around to wink. "And *might* not come back home."

The conversation immediately turned into an argument, and soon after turned into mutual assessment of each other's failings, and then finally into a shouting match. It ended when Sephus emerged from the bathroom in a robe and pajamas, heard both sides of the dispute, and suggested that Frank merely drive his sister to Guthrie before excusing himself to a bar there.

CHAPTER 32

Frank watched his little sister disappear behind him through the back window. Her receding figure, smartly dressed, sat on a park bench in front of the Masonic Temple, which had closed two hours earlier. Part of him felt obligated to wait with her for James to show up, but most of him did not.

He drove to Bronco's, a questionable bar with ample parking, to find a lady and a beer. He stepped into the establishment and immediately considered retreating. Its relative silence for a Saturday night unsettled Frank. Not because he particularly liked noise, but because his strengths in trawling for ladies consisted of providing beer and smiling a lot, whereas his weaknesses included conversation skills and honesty. He was handsome, in a grungy sort of way, and he knew how to capitalize on it.

Just as he turned toward the door, he caught sight of a woman out of the corner of his eye. He cast a glance back in her direction and confirmed that he knew her. Susan Miller, of Westmoore High. She saw him too, which made her face light up, fade, and light up again in a brief strobe effect. She half-heartedly beckoned for him to join the table by the window with her and her friend.

This was more than enough to keep Frank rooted at Bronco's. Susan had been a willowy girl in high school, fairly attractive, still holding up marvelously. Her short-haired friend was attractive, too, but only if Frank loosed his attention from her defiant expression, body language, and offensive lack of makeup.

"Hey, Susan," he said.

"It's good to see you, Frank. What brings you to Guthrie?"

"A night on the town, you know?" He winked and made a "gettyup" noise.

Susan nodded and turned to her friend. "Stacy, this is Frank Norbitz, a friend from high school. Frank, this is Stacy Wilhelm, my partner."

"Pleased to meet you," Frank said, accepting her firm handshake. He assumed that this meant the two were lawyers, which, to Frank, meant only that they both owned pant suits.

"Can I buy you ladies drinks?"

"You don't need to do that," Susan responded.

"Sure," said Stacy, who actually was a lawyer, and a shrewd one.

Frank believed that all women like men to offer them direction at all times and consequently ordered three mugs of Shiner Bock without consulting them. "Meeting anyone?" Frank asked coyly, to see if any boyfriends lurked in the bathroom.

"No," Susan said, "just us. What are you up to nowadays, Frank?"

"I'm a fireman," he replied modestly. This statement had nothing to do with reality whatsoever. In fact, Frank once set forty acres ablaze through his response to boredom and a tennis ball soaked in gasoline. However, he believed that he appeared more successful and manly in the minds of women if pictured gripping a massive fire hose and battling infernos.

"How nice," Susan said. "That's just lovely that you help so many people."

169

In normal conversation it would be Frank's turn to lob the ball back, but Frank did not always grasp the subtleties of dialogue. "The Rectum Thief killed my father," he responded. This surprised everyone, including Frank. He had not previously believed his mother's opinions in this matter, and did not even after blurting out her assertions. Some knee-jerk neuron in his brain wholly independent of things like continuity or segue assumed that this was a good statement for acquiring sympathy, and sympathy was a tool for getting laid.

Both Susan and Stacy did not know how to handle the knowledge. Too many unrelated words triggered even more wildly unrelated thoughts. Susan hated and detested her father. The thought of a dead father seemed good, but then made her feel guilty, because she didn't want her father dead, even if he was an abusive alcoholic. Then sympathy kicked in because *Frank's* father was dead, not hers. The word "rectum" started a different process entirely. Each of these bits of thoughts popped in all at once.

"I'm so sorry," Susan said. "When did this happen?"

"Year and a half ago." He took a sip from his beer and stared at the table. The graffiti carved therein lacked aplomb. "I don't want to depress you ladies with any of that, though," he said. "Let's just say if I ever find that Rectum Thief I'm going to kill him. A lot."

Susan nodded. "Um," she said, attempting to stall as she thought of something to save the unwieldy conversation. "Do you ever talk to anyone else from high school?"

"Not too often. I live in Hoople now, so I don't really see any of the ol' gang anymore."

"I stay in contact with a couple of people," Susan said, "but most of my high school friends and I fell away. I guess that's how it always goes."

Frank flashed a smile and leaned in a little. "Well, it's never too late to catch up with old friends."

Stacy, rapidly assimilating Frank's blunt and clumsy manner of changing topics, resorted to brute honesty. "We're lesbians," she announced. "We are lesbians, together. Susan is a lesbian." She knew the intent behind Frank's obtuse ramblings and did not want to spend an otherwise quiet night out with her partner broadcasting signals of militant disinterest to some idiot firefighter.

Frank the pseudo-arsonist showed no reaction whatsoever. He did not view this as an obstacle; he viewed it as an opportunity. He was now drinking beer with two women, who were drinking *his* beer, who found each other sexually appealing. He found them both sexually appealing, too, and could foresee no impediment to all three mutual impulses careening into a glorious story he would tell to friends, family, and strangers every day for the rest of his life.

"That so?" he asked, raising an eyebrow. "How about some more beers then, ladies?"

The next ten minutes of conversation consisted of a volley of unrelated, awkward exchanges between Frank and Stacy. Whenever Frank felt his powers of persuasion ebb, he threw out a wholly independent concept, like "I think art is good," or "What's with all these Mexicans?" to try and subdue

171

lesbianism into the thrilling footstool of his libido.

Stacy, with equal resolve and vigor, countered every ninety-degree turn in conversation with her own. The only difference was that all of hers were related to lesbianism, to her dislike of male chauvinists, and to her resultant and specific dislike of Frank. Her comments became crass and uncomfortable enough that a nearby table of diner employees all agreed to run for the state legislature to save society from people like her.

Frank admitted defeat and excused himself from their table, leaving behind his hopes of a threesome. He saddled up to the bar and nodded back to their table. "Those ladies back there have offered to buy my drinks," he told the bartender.

CHAPTER 33

Karl pulled up to the driveway of Sephus's farmhouse and observed the two men out front. They continued playing horseshoes on the lawn, even after noticing the car, so that its driver would not feel uncomfortably scrutinized. Neither man was Frank Norbitz, which addled Karl considerably. From his conversation with Hillary he had determined that Norbitz, Male, resided with one Sephus Fitzbaur.

He knew Frank Norbitz primarily through his criminal record, accessed online, like Fitzbaur's address. It consisted of four arrests over a twelve-year period. One such arrest had landed him in the Hoople newspaper, providing Karl with a recent photo. The headline read "Norbitz Kills Tree." More cynical readers had assumed the title included a typographical error, and that Frank had actually committed a triple homicide. In reality, he snapped a maple sapling in half with his car on a return route from a bar. The paper reported that Frank "leaned out his window and confided to the police officer on hand that 'the tree had been drinking,' and should probably be arrested." Later he admitted that he'd "had one or two beers, maybe," but probably only *appeared* drunk because of his "new bourbon-flavored mouthwash."

Sephus and McCormick paused their game of horseshoes and walked up to Karl's car. "Can I help you?" Sephus asked. Both men squinted through the setting sun at Karl's features within.

"Yes," Karl said, smiling. "I'm looking for Mr.

Frank Norbitz. I've been told he's staying here?"

"What do you need Frank for?" Sephus asked.

"I have a delivery for him. Is he home?"

"He's not. I can take the package, though."

"No, I'm afraid he has to sign for it personally," said Karl. "Do you know when Mr. Norbitz will be getting back?"

"Hold on a sec," the older man said. He put a hand on top of the car and made deliberate eye contact with Karl. "If you're deliverin' a package, why aintcha in a FedEx vehicle or some such?"

"Oh," Karl said, laughing, "my van blew a tire earlier today. Since this is my last package I'm just using my own car instead, and having FedEx comp me for the gas." Leland McCorvick nodded absently and ambled to the back of the car. "That's why," Karl added amiably, "I'm here so late. On account of car trouble."

Sephus Fitzbaur held a hand up over his eyes to block the sun. "James?" he asked.

"FWN-185!" Leland McCorvick howled. "Blue Lincoln! FWN-185!"

CHAPTER 34

Frank sat down on a bar stool and deposited his mug on the counter with no cheer or grace. The bartender walked over and looked at the glass, as if a note might be inside describing what he wanted. "Coors," Frank said. Having admitted defeat in the field of converting lesbians, he was free to drink light and cheaper beer.

The bartender turned to the next drinker. "Same," the man said. Frank turned to look at the men to his left and paused. They wore trench coats and dark mustaches. The one closest to Frank looked incredibly familiar.

"Do I know you from somewhere?" Frank asked.

The man shifted uneasily on his stool and forced himself to look Frank in the eyes. "The name's *R. J. Kilroy*," he said, clearly annunciating each syllable. He sniffled a bit and held a hankie to his nose. "This here's *Phillip McPilkerton*," gesturing to his drinking buddy.

"Frank Norbitz," Frank responded. "Where do I know you from?"

"I just have a familiar face," the man known as R.J. said. "I get that all the time."

"Yeah, maybe."

McPilkerton stared at Frank, wide-eyed. When he caught Frank's attention he immediately returned to the counter and took a long sip of his lager. R.J. sneezed and wiped the bar with his hankie, which only evenly distributed the germs. He sniffled again and put the hankie to his nose, introducing fun immigrant communities of bacteria to the virus building a tiny civilization in his sinus cavities.

The bartender returned and set a mug of beer in front of each man. He had acquired his liquor license only a week earlier and was having a hard time catching onto the bartending profession. A struggling actor, the bartender finally yielded to a steady job after months of making ends meet between plays at the Guthrie Theatre and small, regular gigs as a Murder Mystery actor. He walked to the tap and forgot which mug belonged to whom, forgetting his boss's advice to associate the mug in his left hand with the man on his left, and the right mug with the man on his right. He further evidenced his idiocy by neglecting to get entirely new mugs, instead serving both men the same drink in the other's mug.

"Get out to Hoople much?" Frank said, still trying to determine where he knew the mustachio from.

"No, can't recall ever having been there," replied R.J. "Is that near Tulsa?"

"No," Frank said. He held his hand up and curled his middle, ring, and pinkie finger to create a small map of the state with his hand. He pointed his other index finger to the northwest quadrant of his palm. "About there. Between Jet and Nash."

"I see." The mustachio leaned toward his compatriot and spoke in a frenzied whisper. The man introduced as Phillip McPilkerton looked around R.J.'s head as he spoke to peek at Frank, who immediately realized they were talking about him.

The two men returned to their positions and

assumed states of mutual overdone nonchalance. McPilkerton sighed as evidence of his relaxed condition. R.J. Kilroy took in a breath to sigh, but then sneezed a violent and frightening blast, propelling his fake mustache and thousands of hardworking viral colonies onto the bar's counter.

He immediately snatched the mustache and attempted to reaffix it to his face, but its adhesive quality was no more. It floated to the counter and, like a dying squirrel, twitched slightly from a minute, unseen breeze. R.J. and his compatriot stared at the deceitful facial hair, panic stricken. "I'm going through chemotherapy," R.J., who Frank now recognized as Jim Thunderpop, stammered. "I've always had a mustache and my face feels naked without it."

"Right," Frank said. "That's understandable." He took three swigs of beer compressed into one long glug.

This is a gay bar! he thought. Why else would Jim Thunderpop be drinking incognito with another fake mustachio? Why else would two women shun him?

He fought all instincts to run, knock the barstool over, and jump through a window. Homophobic fears wailed in his mind like ambulance sirens in a conch shell. For some reason he felt it was imperative to remain calm and metered, as if running away might set off some predatory instinct in all the assembled gays.

He finished his beer and slapped a few bills on the table. "Keep the change," he declared loudly, so that the neophyte bartender could hear. "Well, I'm off," he announced to Thunderpop and his presumed gay lover. "Good to meet you gentlemen." He

177

nodded to both. "Mr. Kilroy, Mr. McPilkerton."

Before the door to Bronco's shut behind him, he ran away from the gay bar as fast as he could, desperately trying to blow off whatever residual homosexuality might be clinging to his clothes. Homophobia and adrenaline fueled his fifteen-minute sprint.

CHAPTER 35

Guthrie was the original seat of Oklahoma's capitol, less than a block from where Hillary sat. She was by no means a history buff, but recalled hearing once that an intrepid governor had realized that the state's capital was officially wherever the state seal was. Thus, one evening he and friends intent on moving the capital out of a Republican-controlled city broke into the marbled hall and absconded with the seal under cover of darkness. They relocated it to the fledgling cow town of Oklahoma City, the capital ever since. Upon reflection, she suspected that the actual story probably involved at the least *some* element of voting or lawful decisions, but she liked the idea of bandito legislators nonetheless.

In any case, the former state capital was now a wing of a huge Masonic Temple, rising like a marbled Greek cult from the prairie. She sat on a bench nearby checking her reflection in a small makeup kit. She pouted her lips and gave an obligatory brush to her hair, which required no change and changed nothing.

After a few minutes James pulled up. He shifted his car into park before getting out to open the passenger door for her. "Good evening," he said as she buckled herself in.

"Good evening," she returned, with sex appeal. "Where would you like to eat?"

"There's a restaurant downtown called Bathtub Gin's. It started out as a brothel in territorial days, then turned into a speakeasy during prohibition. I don't know whether it's named after a hygienic prostitute or a house special. In any event, now it's a bed and breakfast with a restaurant downstairs, and the food is delicious."

Hillary brightly assented, but inwardly wasn't sure how to interpret a date at a former whorehouse. Her fears were quickly allayed, however. Bathtub Gin's was quaint and wry, like a grandma with a joy buzzer. They sat by a window overlooking the old downtown, a sloping boulevard dotted with a procession of wrought iron lamps. A waitress re-lit their table's vanilla-scented candles and offered them menus. Outside, a horse-drawn carriage clopped down the street, prowling for tourists.

"It's so nice to get out of the house," Hillary said. "It's getting beyond cabin fever there—I have cabin Ebola virus." James chuckled. "Strangely enough, I'd rather be there than at my mother's. It's more entertaining because Sephus is so . . .so *weird*." James cocked an eyebrow inquisitively. "I mean, he has a framed, autographed picture of William Shatner hanging next to a framed picture of Stonewall Jackson. Who does that?"

James shrugged. "A confederate Star Trek fan?"

Hillary shrugged too, allowing her diminutive breasts to hop. "Anyway, what have you been up to?"

"Mostly wracking my brain, trying to figure out what Karl is up to. I've spoken with the others, but they haven't come up with many ideas."

Hillary was not sure where to take the conversation from there. It seemed the evening could transform from a date to a meeting if the banter leaned toward her attacker's motivations. She wanted to be on a date, but she also wanted to find this information out. "What have you determined?" she asked, letting common sense trump menial chit-chat.

"Not a whole lot," he admitted. "Karl quit his job a month ago, and no one at his apartment in Chicago has seen him for weeks. He's gone AWOL. I don't know why. He won't return my calls, and he refuses to discuss anything pertinent with Monty or Vincent."

"Your other . . . selves?" Hillary asked.

James nodded. "You saw them briefly at the hospital."

Hillary perused her menu. It featured a number of items with cute names derived from the restaurant's past, mostly tarts. She ordered brisket; James had planned to order brisket but did not want to look like he was caving into peer pressure, so he ordered a steak instead.

The conundrum of Karl could only grip his thoughts for so long before James ventured a quick look at Hillary's perky blouse. Her top was not particularly revealing, and her breasts were not even that big, but they contained a vibrant, unexplained energy which captivated him. The shift from homicide to boobtography improved James's mood and allowed him to shuffle through rote, more shallow thoughts.

They started talking about movies or something; he wasn't keeping track. He gazed at Hillary, observing her moist lips and enlarged pupils with silent relish. He felt handsome, desirable. He had a healthy bank account, a fun job, a nice house. The situation was no longer one of compulsive, dismal longing. He sat across from Hillary as an equal who could lose interest without any major detriment to himself. He liked it.

Hillary, conversely, found herself staring at the prototype of the man trying to kill her. Try as she may, she could not now dislodge the image of him reaching across the table and poking her eye out with a syringe.

Several minutes of chit-chat passed. Both were happy they could keep the conversation rolling without awkward, married-for-three-decades pauses. At last the brisket and steak arrived. "I'm curious," James said after his fifth bite of tenderloin. "Why did you text message me instead of calling?"

Hillary cocked her head. "What?"

"It's not important," James said. "I'm just curious."

Hillary's pupils slid back and forth, nudging the corners of her eyes. "I didn't send you any text message."

"Yes, you did," James countered, nodding. "I got it from you yesterday. You asked to me to meet you at the Masonic Temple."

"Oh," Hillary responded. "No, you called me, remember? We worked that out over the phone."

"I didn't call you yesterday."

"Then—"

The two stared at each other with confusion and then alarm. "If Karl tricked both of us into meeting here," he said slowly, "it's because he wanted to distract us from something else."

"Frank!" yelled Hillary. She jumped up from the table and dashed towards the door. "C'mon!"

James shoved his chair back and stared achingly

at his half-eaten steak, then slid it between the pages of a glossy magazine he had walked in with. He tucked the magazine under his arm, tossed a handful of bills onto the table, then raced out the door after his date.

CHAPTER 36

Leland McCorvick grabbed Karl by the neck and attempted to hoist him out of the driver's side window like a negligent babysitter moving a one-hundred-and-fifty-pound toddler. His efforts were largely impeded by a seatbelt designed specifically to keep its wearer from flying out of the car in the event of accidents or muggings.

"Is this the evil twin?!" Sephus demanded. "I think it's the evil twin!" he said again, watching McCorvick try to wrench the man from his seat.

"Whoever it is, this is the *same car* I saw the night someone mutilated my cow!"

"Dammit!" Sephus said angrily, joining in the heat of the moment. He jumped around to the passenger's side, let himself in, and released the seatbelt. McCorvick heaved Karl out the window and slung him against the ground. "Should we call the cops?" Sephus asked.

"Nah, they'll only ask questions about all the blood." Karl tried to stand up, prompting McCorvick to boot kick him in the shoulder before firmly applying a heel to the man's neck. "Go get a pitchfork!" he commanded. A dark stain formed over Karl's breast pocket where his syringe had just cracked.

"What?" Sephus asked, shocked. "Leland, you can't kill this guy with a pitchfork!" McCorvick said nothing. The farmer's nostrils flared in syncopation with his twitching, vengeful eyes. "I'll be right back," Sephus said, running to the house. "Don't kill him!"

he yelled behind him as he flung open the door.

He returned a few moments later with duct tape. Karl struggled, but a few more boot kicks rendered him docile enough to be bound hand and foot. "Let's put him in the storm cellar until the police come," Sephus said.

Leland said nothing, as he did not want to assent to the idea of calling law enforcement officials. Nonetheless, he helpfully dragged Karl by the collar to the bare stretch of grass between Sephus's back door and the ensuing acres of alfalfa. Sephus opened the door to his storm cellar and McCorvick cut Karl's hands loose with the pocketknife he kept on him at all times except when bathing. He did this so that Karl would have something to break his fall with when he was thrown into the cellar like a forgotten Christmas decoration. The thick steel door slammed shut above him, followed by the click and clang of a butch padlock.

CHAPTER 37

"He's going to kill Frank!" Hillary screamed for the third time.

James glanced behind him and gunned out of the parking lot. "No, he's not." He shifted into drive and revved the gas, reeling out onto the road.

She buckled her seatbelt and glanced at the passing succession of bistros and barbeques. "He's not after me anymore. He called wanting *Frank*. To see if *Frank* was home. He only set up this date to get me away from him!"

"Why would he have let me know, then?" James asked. "Maybe he's just trying to make up for nearly injecting you the other night. You know, play matchmaker."

"Maybe he's going to kill me *and* Frank!" She gripped James's collar. "*We have to find Frank!*"

"Listen, Frank's not even *in* Hoople right now," James said, irritated. "Stay cool, okay? He's in Guthrie. Even if Karl is after Frank, he'd think Frank is in Hoople, alright?"

"I'm just worried about my brother," she said softly.

James turned his head to face her. "Hillary. We're going to find him. Nothing is going to happen to Frank."

Frank slammed into the hood of the car.

"Shit!" James yelled, jamming the brake pedal and lurching forward. Hillary screamed as the figure of a man bounced onto nearby grass and continued rolling. "Shit! Oh shit oh shit oh shit!"

Hillary put her hands against the dashboard and tried to gasp. "Did we hit a deer?"

"He came out of *nowhere!*" James yelled, unfastening his seatbelt. He flung his door open. "What kind of idiot runs across the street without looking?"

"Is he okay?" Hillary asked, starting to cry.

"I'm checking!" James said, running to the body. He bent over to check for a pulse and then stopped. "Oh. Shit." He stood up, ogling the bleeding, panting figure in the grass. "Hillary?"

"Is he all right?" she yelled from inside the car. James surveyed the bruised individual then looked back at the car, agape. "Is he breathing? I'm calling 911."

He stooped down to make sure the pulse was steady. "Uh, Hil?" he called again.

"*What?!*" she demanded, putting her hand over the cell phone's receiver.

"You know how we were just talking about . . . Well, hey. I . . ."

"James, hold *on*! I'm calling an ambulance!" she shouted, wiping tears off her cheeks.

He stood up and faced the car. "Uh, yeah, we definitely just hit Frank."

Hillary stared forward, unblinking. "We hit *what*?"

James bent down. "Frank, can you hear me?"

Frank moaned.

Hillary exited the car, screamed.

"Listen, Frank, paramedics are on the way. Do you think your back is broken?"

"Frank!" Hillary bawled, running to his sprawled body. She knelt beside him and sobbed uncontrollably.

"*Ergggmmm.*" Frank whimpered, rolling onto his side. He sneezed. He mumbled something under his breath. He passed out.

CHAPTER 38

If hitting Frank with a car had not improved James and Hillary's date, it at least prolonged it. Frank had suffered what the emergency room doctor had called "cosmetic damages," meaning extensive bruises and two broken legs. It made James curious as to what other ills the doctor dismissed as superficial. Given the impact of the automobile and the sturdy suspension system of that particular vehicle, the ER staff had described Frank's lack of permanent injuries as a "medical miracle," but had still required him to remain overnight for observation and astronomical medical bills.

Sephus and Hillary unloaded Frank from the car like an antique mannequin. James hovered behind them in a seemingly helpful but ultimately useless manner. Wisps of guilt trailed his movements like smoke. They deposited Frank's inert form, passed out on pain killers, into Sephus's bed.

The three adults retired to the kitchen. James and Hillary sat at the counter while Sephus fetched them orange juice from the fridge. "How bad is it?" the farmer asked.

"Pretty good, considering," said Hillary.

"Well, thank God for that," Sephus said. "Full recovery and everything?"

"They think so. He won't be able to tap dance for a while, but he'll walk again in a few weeks."

"Good, good," Sephus said. "Oh!" he turned to James. "I'm glad you're here—we caught your evil twin."

"You *what?*" James asked.

"Last night, when you were busy plowing into Frank's shins, your evil twin stopped by to look for him." He glanced out the window toward the storm cellar. "I suppose I should've called . . ."

"Karl?" Hillary asked, facing James.

James shook his head, bewildered. "Where is he?"

"Leland and I locked him in the storm cellar. He's been in for about a day now, but don't worry, there's plenty of food and water."

"Why didn't you call the police?" Hillary asked.

"Oh, I wanted to," said Sephus. "But Leland insisted we kill him. He seems to think this is the guy who mutilated his cow. Anyway, we agreed to keep him locked up until y'all got back. I'm calling the cops tomorrow."

"And where is Leland?" James inquired.

"He goes to bed promptly at nine o'clock every evening. You'll see him tomorrow. Can I make a suggestion?" James nodded. "You've both had a long night. You're tired. Now's not the time to worry about the guy we've trapped underground. Why don't both get a good night sleep? James, you can sack out on the couch, and Hillary, you keep the guest room. So why not take a snooze and worry about this mess tomorrow when the sheriff drops by?" James and Hillary nodded reluctantly. "Okay," Sephus said, signaling the end of the conversation by clasping his hands together. "Think I'm gonna head to bed. G'night." He trotted off to the bathroom.

James sat down on a kitchen stool and sighed. "You know, I really thought our date would end with us sliding your inert brother into bed. But instead it turns out my alien double is about to be turned over to the police."

"I'm sure it will all work out fine," Hillary said, placing a hand on his shoulder.

"I doubt it. I think at the very least things will get horribly, horribly complicated. At the worst . . . federal agents, prison . . . secret military bases."

"Maybe he *should* be holed up in one of those places," Hillary offered.

"Hillary, I have *no idea* what Karl has been up to. Say he's done something illegal and winds up in prison. Myselves and I can't leave without him. And I don't mean ethically. He's literally a part of us. It wouldn't work if he stayed behind on Earth."

"Couldn't you, I don't know, beam him out of jail or something?"

James shrugged. "We'd try to think of something . . . But, as I said: complicated."

She leaned down to hug him and kissed him on the cheek. "Go to bed. Come say goodbye to me before you leave the house tomorrow. We'll figure everything out, okay?"

He nodded. "Good night, Hillary. Once again, I'm really sorry about hitting your brother with my car."

"It really wasn't your fault, James. And in any event, he's going to be fine. So don't beat yourself up about it." She started walking out of the kitchen, but turned her head around. "James, try and relax, okay?" He nodded. "Okay, good night."

He sat there for several moments until he was confident that Hillary was safely locked in the bathroom dismantling her makeup. He unseated himself to pace around the kitchen. Within a couple of minutes, he stepped outside into the breathy summer air, ambling past alfalfa stalks. Thoughts stretched inside his brain like a laundry line overloaded with soggy bathmats. He did not know where to begin.

He noticed a slab of cement poking out of the backyard like a large filed tooth, and assumed it was the storm cellar the farmers had stashed Karl in. An impressive steel door capped it off, fastened with an equally imposing padlock. A doormat caught his attention, which struck him as an odd accessory to a tornado shelter. He kicked it over with his foot and, without surprise, found a key.

He picked it up and stared at it far longer than is necessary to appreciate a brass double-sided key. His deliberation erred on the side of stupidity, prompting him to unlock the mighty padlock. He opened the door a crack and slipped in, as if Karl was a small terrier who might scurry out if the door opened too wide.

The storm cellar was the oldest building on Sephus Fitzbaur's property. It had been built with the original farmhouse in the 1920s for the family to cower in when tornados tossed livestock around like beanbags. Sephus's father, Argus, more than doubled the storm cellar's size in 1968 when he converted it into a fallout shelter. Possessing a hearty pioneer spirit and no concept of self-pity, Argus had planned to haul his family into the refuge, abode there for half a year, then emerge to rebuild civilization from the ground up in the wake of a Soviet nuclear holocaust. The incredibly thick, strong door was one of his contributions, along with extra locks in case the neighbors, maddened with communist radiation poison, attempted to break in and steal the family's toilet paper.

The bombs never fell, however, so the storm cellar principally served as a storage facility throughout the seventies and eighties. Sephus restored it to the state of an apocalyptic haven in 1999 to prepare for the Y2K bug, which threatened all of civilization through cheap computer programming.

He had spent his New Year's Eve sitting in a lawn chair underground, surrounded by two years' worth of food and dozens of Star Trek novels. He remained there an additional two days until Leland McCorvick, through the use of a CB radio, convinced him that civilization had survived and the threat of mobs trying to bum rush him for stockpiled canned olives was no higher than usual.

Karl sat in this same lawn chair in the same location it had been since civilization survived the doomsday calendar shift. *I am not Spock*, by Leonard Nimoy, lay across his lap. A toilet dominated the rear corner of the room, connected to a septic tank no one knew the location or origin of. "Karl," James started, but the captive held up a finger to signify the near completion of a paragraph. He slipped a receipt into the book and closed it before looking up.

"Hello, James. Here to rescue me?"

"Probably not," he replied grimly.

"I thought so. Thank you for coming, anyway. I appreciate it."

"Are there any other chairs?" James asked, looking around.

"No, just the cot. Take a seat." He gestured to a bunk on the opposite wall. As James sat down, Karl flung the book he had been reading across the room. It slammed against the wall and fell onto a pile of Star Trek literature with multiple severe spinal injuries. "I hate Star Trek," Karl said. "Why would this miserable hayseed have so many stupid Star Trek books?"

"I don't know," said James. "One would think he'd have Star Wars as well."

Karl nodded and tossed a *Star Trek: Deep Space Nine* novel (which, to be fair, Karl had not even opened yet) to the existing corpus of science fiction texts. "I take it you won't let them kill me?"

"Of course not," James said. "But I don't think they're planning on it. Sephus is calling the police tomorrow after his neighbor comes over."

"I thought as much. I don't suppose you'd think it practical to let me go? Getting the police involved is only going to make things messy. All of our heads in jars of formaldehyde, and so forth," he looped his hand in the air dismissively, as if signing "et cetera."

"If you'd like to clue me in on this secret life of yours and it seems like a good idea, I will. But right now, I'm just as inclined to turn you over to the authorities."

Karl sighed. "I'm going to get some beans. Would you like any beans?"

"No, I've already had dinner."

"Are you sure? There is at least a year's worth of canned goods down here. I've actually eaten fairly well today."

"I'm full, thanks."

He dithered around a can-laden storage rack. "How was your date?"

"Pretty bad. I hit Hillary's brother with my car."

Karl cringed. "Really? Is he alive?"

"Oh, sure," James assured him. "He's fine, just . . . incapacitated. Broken legs, but nothing permanent. About the date. Did you set that up?"

"Yes," Karl said, selecting a can of baked beans. "But I wouldn't have if I'd known you were going to maim your date's brother."

"*Why* did you set it up, Karl?"

The detainee glanced around the room idly for the can opener. "Simple stuff, James. I already spoke to Hillary on your behalf, and I didn't want you to inadvertently stand her up."

"Yes, but—"

"James," he said, holding a hand up, "we can deal with that in a moment. I was thinking, though—let's get off of this planet. I'm going to call Monty and Vincent. I think we should leave. Soon."

"Really? Why?" James asked, momentarily dropping the unresolved date. "Your impending jail time notwithstanding."

"It's dangerous here. We're mortal as long as we stick around, and that frightens me."

"Does it have to do with you running around stabbing people with syringes?"

"No, not really," Karl said, sitting back down in the lawn chair. "Actually, by next week that whole thing will be resolved, one way or another." He located the can opener and turned to face James. "Listen, James, I really am very sorry about all this. It's never been my intention to inconvenience you." He set the can opener down on the bed. "I hope they realize what's happened before the police come. You'll find some aspirin in the first aid kit next to the lamp. Once again, sorry."

James arched an eyebrow, curious as to what Karl meant about the aspirin, when Karl beaned him in the head with a can of baked beans. James flopped over on the cot. A large knot, one worthy of Eagle Scouts, formed on his forehead. Karl blinked and swallowed as James's fleeting consciousness addled his own. He walked over to check his double's pulse and breathing. It seemed fine, but Karl suspected he would wake up in an hour or two with an angry migraine.

He undressed James and himself, then switched outfits with the unconscious man, leaving keys and wallets with their original owners. It was one thing to incapacitate a man; it was quite another to steal his wallet. He did, however, borrow twenty dollars for gas. Karl scribbled a quick I.O.U. onto a piece of paper and placed it in James's breast pocket before exiting the shelter. He locked the door behind him.

It did not take him long to locate Frank. Karl turned the bedroom light on and nudged the sleeping man until he grumbled. "Frank," he said, "the doctor just called. I need to take you back to the hospital for more X-rays. They think you might have a concussion."

Frank grumbled something else and rolled over. Karl peeled off the covers and did his best to heave the man's quasi-conscious body onto his back. Frank was heavy, and the casts made him bulky. The former human resources manager considered making a quick surgery at the farmhouse itself, but decided against it for fear Hillary would come in to check on her brother.

Outside, he buckled Frank into the passenger's seat of his car. Strapping himself in, he looked through his small black dot kit for another needle, but found none. He sighed. That meant things were going to get messy. As he waited for the engine to warm up he noticed Frank shiver a little. "Cold?" he asked. Frank nodded, then slumped over against the window. Karl turned the heater on, but at a low setting, as it didn't feel chilly to him.

The automobile rolled away from the farmhouse and onto the county road.

In the passenger's seat, Frank sneezed loudly.

CHAPTER 39

Hillary woke with an urgent need to visit the restroom. She slid out of bed like Lenin's thawed and re-animated corpse, picking up a tennis racket by the door before wandering down the hall to the upstairs bathroom. She had spied the racket in a closet two days earlier, and now kept it with her at night while everyone slept. Firmly gripping its handle made her feel safer and more comfortable, as if she could savagely beat any hall monster into submission with an instrument she probably couldn't swat a racquetball with. She knew that if a seven-foot-tall skinny gray apparition appeared, it was about as likely to be frightened of a tennis racket as it was to whip out its own and volley with her, but she gripped hers nonetheless.

By the time she left the upstairs bathroom, her state of consciousness had bumped up to "alert Lenin." In this heightened state of awareness she decided to check on her brother and make sure he was sleeping soundly.

Frank was gone. In his place Roswell lay stretched out, comatose. The moment after Frank left, the cat had leapt onto the bed and curled up in the residual warmth. Hillary's footsteps alerted Roswell to her presence, who in turn extended all available claws to indicate feline dibs on the mattress.

Hillary left the bedroom and unsuccessfully searched for James. She at last went to Frank's old room upstairs, where she assumed Sephus would be. She cracked the door open and stepped in. The farmer had fallen asleep in a chair, his tattered robe billowing around his figure like a cape. His head was tipped back and his jaw slack, leaning to the left. A hand was tucked under the elastic band of his pajama pants, lightly cupping himself. (Men invariably position themselves in this manner if they fall asleep sitting up. On a subconscious level they are afraid someone will try to steal their testes while they sleep.)

Next to him on the floor sat a small radio with a cord running to the wall. A tail of foil jutted out of it like an aluminum tumor, in place of the original antenna. It was quietly babbling out the last few minutes of *Midnight Chat.* "—but haven't seen any results of remote viewing," Charles Gander said. "It's an intriguing concept, but if it really works, why aren't these remote viewers ever telling us something practical? When's the last time they've told us about an impending natural disaster, or located buried treasure? What we ought to have psychics focus on—"

"Sephus," Hillary whispered.

The farmer's eyes fluttered open. "Yes?"

"I can't find Frank or James."

He yawned. "Have you checked downstairs?"

"Yes, they're not there. Frank isn't in bed."

Sephus rose from his chair and turned off the radio. He followed her downstairs to observe everything she had already told him. The notion that aliens had taken Frank (but not Sephus) occurred to him, and his mood soured. "I'm sure his *friends* will drop him off before morning. Hell, maybe they'll fix him up."

"You think the aliens got him?"

"Of course. They take Frank every few days. You're fortunate to have such a fascinating specimen of a brother." Sarcasm dripped from his uvula.

"What about James?"

Sephus's nostrils flared. He had not considered this. "I suppose," he said, through clenched teeth, "that James is *also* a fascinating human to look at." He balled his fists and started lumbering up the stairs. "Maybe they'll come get you tomorrow, too. I'll make you all a picnic basket so you can have a nice meal with the aliens."

"Okay, goodnight," said Hillary, exasperated. She shut the door and walked downstairs, then looked out through the front door. James's car was still there, but his double's was not. She ran back upstairs and knocked.

"Hello?" Sephus said excitedly. "Come in!" She pushed the door open, but appeared to disappoint the farmer. "Yes?" he asked, clearly hoping for a different species.

"Karl's car is gone."

"Who? The evil twin?"

"Yes. I think he has Frank."

"I doubt it. I secured the storm shelter with a very sturdy lock."

"I'm just telling you they're not around. Will you come with me to make sure Karl is still in the cellar?"

Sephus nodded, knotting his robe around his waist. He walked Hillary out to the shelter and inspected the lock, which was completely intact and impregnable, but had its key sticking out the bottom. "That's strange," Sephus said. "I'm certain I slipped it under the mat."

"Well, let's open it."

"No," said Sephus, "he could bust out and kill us."

"How else will we know if he's still in there?"

Sephus squinted at the lock, nodding slowly. "I'll go get my gun. You hold it as I open the door. If he tries to come out, shoot him."

"No!" Hillary protested. "You shoot him!"

"I have to go in to turn the lights on."

"Oh," Hillary said. Hers was the sweeter deal. "Okay."

Sephus disappeared into the house and returned moments later with a shotgun. "Basically you just pull the trigger," he instructed Hillary, handing it to her.

"Right," she replied, holding it like a baby.

Sephus unlocked the door and entered the cellar. He braced himself for a kidney punch, but none came. After flipping the lights on he saw the prisoner sleeping on the cot. "He's still here." The prisoner stirred from sleep and groaned. He put a hand against his forehead as if to keep it from leaping off of his neck and scuttling into an air vent. "Oh no," Sephus warned, "none of that. You have a bathroom and plenty of food and water. This is going to be nicer than jail, so don't complain."

The prisoner groaned again and applied his other hand to his forehead. "My head!" he moaned.

"There's some aspirin around here somewhere," Sephus said helpfully. "You can look for it when you wake up. It will be a fun activity, like a treasure hunt."

The man sat up in bed and stared wide-eyed at Sephus. "He's escaped!" he yelled.

The farmer backed out the doorway. "Nope. Not buying it."

"Sephus! I found the key under your mat and let myself in! Karl threw something at my head and knocked me out!"

Sephus froze. He could now plainly see a red welt on his prisoner's forehead, a large and purple swelling that looked like it might be the beginnings of a third eye. "Or," he said, "you smacked yourself in the head with a can of creamed corn, to evidence your story."

"Sephus!" the man said in exasperation. "I don't care if you think I'm James or not! But can you please at least locate the man who looks like me? Lock us both down here, just make sure you get him. Okay?"

The farmer's eyes narrowed to slits of distrust. He shut the door behind him and snapped the padlock into place. He turned to Hillary. "That . . . may or may not be him."

CHAPTER 40

Leland McCorvick's panther-like reflexes both woke him and placed his hand on the phone next to his bed before it actually rang. When the tiny bell clanged inside of the old plastic receiver he jerked it to his head and sat up. "Yes?" he asked, businesslike.

"I'm sorry to bother you at this hour, Leland," said Sephus. "Hillary just woke me up and Frank is missing. And maybe our guest."

"He escaped from the storm cellar?" Barely awake, his voice sounded like a cello with gravel in it.

"Maybe. I'm not sure. The man's car is gone. There's still a guy in the cellar, but he has a knot on his forehead and claims he found the key under the mat and was knocked out by his evil twin."

"Hmph."

"Exactly. Listen, I'm going to call the cops. I just wanted to—"

"Shh," Leland ordered.

"I—"

"Shh!" he commanded again. Both men paused. "That's him."

"What, the guy? He's at your house?"

"No, just drove by."

"How do you know?"

McCorvick did not bother explaining that he remembered the sound of the Lincoln and that the likelihood of a different vehicle of the same make driving by his home at three o'clock in the morning was not just slim, but bulimic. He hung up the phone and leapt out of bed, halfway into his jumpsuit before his feet touched carpet. Ten seconds later and his boots were on. Soon after that, he tucked a thick chain and a pistol into his waist belt.

Nary two minutes passed after hanging up the phone before Leland McCorvick, armed with chain and pistol, coasted his truck out of the driveway and into the inky morning. His eyes locked onto the tail lights of the distant Lincoln.

CHAPTER 41

"How about some music?" Karl asked. Frank sneezed in a somewhat positive manner. "Alright then." He put in a selection of Chopin.

Outside of the sedan, Oklahoma whizzed by at sixty miles per hour. High beams from behind suddenly pierced his rear window and glanced off the mirror to burnish his pupils.

The blue-black veil of early morning concealed everything but the two glowing orbs rapidly approaching from behind. Behind him, Leland McCorvick flashed his brights off and then back on politely, then fired a pistol at Karl.

The bullet exploded through his back window with enough remaining pith to clear the front windshield as well. Karl jammed his foot against the accelerator and frantically thought of a way to evade the trailing gunman. "I just got that windshield fixed," he muttered.

Leland McCorvick pulled his pistol into the truck and rolled the canister. He put it back out the window and fired, blowing out the Lincoln's back left tire. He had aimed for the base of Karl's neck, but it was still a good shot for using his left hand, and without taking a steady bead on his target. In any case, it was louder thank honking.

Karl turned his emergency lights on and began to slow down. He ducked, but no additional bullets punctured his automobile. Karl made a left turn onto a dusty private road. He turned again as he parked, blocking it. Leland McCorvick stopped his truck a few feet away and exited his vehicle.

Karl dropped to the ground, shutting the door to his car as he heard McCorvick shut his own. He rolled underneath the Lincoln, inching his back toward the passenger's side. As McCorvick walked past the bumper and to the driver's window, Karl lifted himself up on the opposite side of the car and crept behind the trunk. When McCorvick fumbled with the door handle, Karl jumped out from behind and pegged him squarely in the back of the skull with a thick metal flashlight normally kept under his seat. The farmer crumpled to the ground.

Karl loomed over him with the weapon, breathing heavily. He debated whether or not to strike again, beating the meddlesome farmer to death. After a moment of debate he shook his head back and forth. He was an opportunist, not a murderer. He might kill this man out of necessity, but he would not do it out of anger. Granted, that was a strange ethical position for an acknowledged killer to take, but Karl applauded himself for maintaining it.

He picked up the pistol and set it on the car's armrest. After removing the farmer's keys, he hoisted him into the trunk and shut it. With the tire out, he would have to use the truck to get away. His work on Frank would be gruesome but fast, and there was no reason he could not leave McCorvick alive and inside the trunk so long as he remained unconscious.

Karl got back into his car and shut the door. Taking a deep breath, he removed his kit from the glove compartment and fished out a scalpel. He pulled Frank into an upright position and buckled his seat belt to keep him stationary. "This will hurt

Mr. Norbitz, but only for a moment."

He placed the scalpel lightly against Frank's neck just below the jaw. The blade hesitated. He put the back of his other hand against Frank's forehead. "Oh dammit!" he moaned. "You have a fever."

He returned the scalpel to its place in the kit and rested his head in his hands. He felt Frank's forehead again to make sure he wasn't imagining anything. It was hot. The substance he had just nearly gutted Frank for like a fish was undoubtedly lost. Out of its two-degree temperature range, it would degrade and dissipate within half an hour. Frank, through a common cold, had obliterated Karl's only hope of appeasing the Reptoids.

He fought the impulse to give up. Several hours remained before the Reptoids would come looking for him and his unfulfilled order. In the precious, small amount of time he had left, he needed to assemble the others and get them all off of the planet and as far away as possible.

Light stirred him from his panicked thoughts. Around him a dim white beam encompassed the car, gradually increasing to a level of blinding luminosity. He squinted to try and discern the three blurry figures wading toward him through the heavy glow.

Karl grabbed the farmer's pistol with shaky hands. The beings came close enough for him to make out the slender, elongated shapes of Greys.

Karl put the barrel of the gun squarely against Frank's temple. "I'd like to talk to you," he said loudly. "There are a couple of things I wish to discuss."

No talk, they said, piping their answer into his

mind. *Put it down.*

"No," he said firmly. "I want to make an exchange."

No exchange.

"I, and three of my friends, need passage off of this planet. Our ship is docked very close to this location. Drop me and my friends off, and you can have your mule back."

You are in no position to make demands, human. The three figures backed out of the light.

"Don't screw with me!" Karl yelled. He jammed the gun against Frank's temple, shoving his head into the window. "Let's talk!" Every hair on his body stood on end, waving back and forth like sea anemones. The car squeaked and rocked slightly, then steadied.

He looked out the window and toward the shadowy ground sinking away below. In the four seconds before it vanished altogether he sent one desperate text message to James:

GREYS

CHAPTER 42

Frank lay suspended within what appeared to be a giant rectangular jellyfish. It felt like the inside of a waterbed, filled with warm, pink olive oil. He woke within the peculiar amniotic sack and tried to look around. His eyelids could open and close without much effort, but the liquid around him obscured everything. The fluid did not hurt his eyes, although its warmth made them feel funny, like steam from hot coffee sliding across his cornea. He discerned miniscule blue shrimp creatures swimming around him, swarming in particular around his legs.

He panicked, but did not attempt to scream until several moments later when he realized he could not breathe. He kicked and flailed his arms, opening and closing his mouth. The action accomplished little more than disturbing the school of shrimp aboding with him in the thick amniotic soup. It also made his legs hurt like crazy. All of the aches from ricocheting off the hood of James's car went berserk, as if Icy Hot had been injected directly into his bone marrow.

Frank, a voice said in his mind. Frank moved his mouth, but, with no air, made no noise. Even if he had, anything burbled in the goo would have been indiscernible. Above him a gray blob, humanoid in shape, looked down.

Frank, you are in a recuperation pouch. You have been damaged and we are repairing you. Resistance will only delay the process. Please try not to irritate the healer prawns.

Frank tried to scream "I can't breathe!"

You may be concerned that you cannot respire; this is an instinctual response, but do not worry. Oxygen is being provided to your body through other means.

The alien monitoring Frank was named Kuzar. He stood at five feet, eight and a half inches tall. He was gray; about the same color as porridge. Frank did not remember Kuzar, but had interacted with the technician every time he had boarded this particular ship, exactly half of his abductions.

Kuzar stepped away from the gunk sack and checked on the other two Terran creatures in the lab. On a table not far from Frank's ooze pocket laid an Alaskan woman in her late thirties named Milly. Her nervous system had been zapped by a paralysis beam, leaving her completely immobile for at least another hour. Her lids remained open but Kuzar could not tell if she retained consciousness or not. Nor did he particularly care; the woman's emotional status was not his concern.

Mr. Zno, he thought-said, summoning his assistant. Mr. Zno walked to him and stood attentively. He was five foot eight and a half inches tall, with pasty gray skin. He slouched imperceptibly when no one was looking, which caused Kuzar to refer to him as "that slacker Zno" outside of the lab.

Sir? Mr. Zno inquired.

Are we finished with this woman?

Yes, sir.

Nod, thought Kuzar, which he could have theoretically done instead of thought-projecting. Mr. Zno noticed this but said nothing. Kuzar took various instruments out, checked the woman's vital signs, then scrutinized her various orifices to make sure everything was in working order. *Her ovaries are slightly inflamed,* he commented.

Yes, sir, Mr. Zno answered.

She should be fine, but make a note to avoid stressing them further next time.

Yes, sir.

There is no need to lessen her injections, just relocate some to other spaces. I believe we can use her sinus cavities.

Acknowledged.

Kuzar turned to the next creature, a milk cow named Sissy. Sissy lived in her eudemonic state on a dairy farm in Wisconsin. She arrived there as an organic gift from a farmer to his nephew who happened to be working for him one summer. Her life consisted of eating, pooping, and lactating, the proceeds from which eventually turned into ice cream consumed by school children.

We're finished with the quadruped, Mr. Zno informed.

Very good, Kuzar projected. *Clear its memory.* "Clear" was not the most accurate term, as parts of the experience remained, buried in the subconscious. The process was like shattering the memory of an event like a Christmas tree ornament, then sweeping it under a rug. A rug that happened to be located in a person or cow's brain.

Clear it, sir? Mr. Zno asked.

Yes, Kuzar confirmed.

But it's . . . This is a "cow," sir. It's a domesticated lactating ungulate; an oblivious animal. There is no need to clear its mind.

Kuzar stared at Mr. Zno. Had Frank seen the exchange clearly, it would have appeared to be an

211

emotionless exchange. But to an average Grey, Kuzar was definitely glowering at his assistant. *Protocol dictates that we clear the mind of anything we take before returning it, Mr. Zno. You will follow protocol and you will do your job.*

Yes, sir, Mr. Zno projected. He took out the necessary instrument to render Sissy the milk cow unconscious and to scramble her traumatic memories. (Ironically, when Sissy woke up in a field three hours later, she had the *exact same thought* she had been dwelling on while onboard the ship: "Grass!")

Kuzar left Mr. Zno to his various menial duties and walked out of the larger lab into the more intimate, poorly lit one next door. In it, Karl lay on an examination table, paralyzed and unblinking. Joopah, a Grey of equal rank but a specialist in human neurology, looked up from his instruments. His healthy gray frame stood five feet and eight and half inches tall. Large ebony eyes, referenced by many as "dreamy," dominated his pale eggplant head, chiseled by the gods themselves.

Kuzar, he projected.

Joopah, Kuzar curtly returned. He hated Joopah, because Joopah was, by general ship consensus, the most handsome crew member around. It made him smug and cocky, and Kuzar was jealous of the attention it gave his colleague. *What have you determined about this one?*

He is biologically normal. His genetic code is that of an average Homo sapien.

Perhaps he went mad with fear? The ship's crew had been perplexed by the flinty little man's response to abduction. When the ship hovered over

212

the car and turned the floodlights on, he had not panicked or prayed: he held a gun to his passenger's head and threatened to kill him.

In similar situations, with two humans in a car and their searchlight engulfing multiple passengers, no human had ever taken the other hostage before. Why would they? How would they discern any sort of bargaining leverage? Kuzar, upon hearing of the incident, supposed that the man knew Frank was a frequent abductee, and thus believed by holding a gun to his head he could hold some sort of transactional clout.

A second odd thing about the man was the communiqué sent shortly before the ship swallowed his car: *GREYS*. It added to the strange familiarity he displayed when they approached his vehicle. Most humans reacted with sheer, witless terror, not hostage scenarios.

Finally, and most intriguing of all, the human had demanded that they take him to his spaceship. This lead the captain to believe that the man, Karl Janus, was actually an extraterrestrial posing as a human being. The captain subsequently ordered a biopsy to determine the man's species.

So he is human? Kuzar asked.

Genetically, Joopah thought-said. *The interesting thing is that this part of his brain,* he pointed to a graphic of Karl's neural map tacked to the wall, *is far more active than any other human's we have studied.*

Which part is that?

Because this region of the brain is so unused, we are uncertain. In other Earth animals it is typically associated with telepathic herd instincts, such as a flock of birds flying in unison.

Interesting, Kuzar projected.

Very.

At this time Captain Cosmowobsy entered. He was five foot eight and a half feet tall, although his commanding presence made him appear five foot eight and three-fourths, or perhaps even five foot nine. His cool black eyes regarded both Greys in front of him and the human paralyzed on the table. *Well?*

He appears to be human, Joopah projected. He did not interject "sir," as he ought to by virtue of his lower rank. Kuzar reflected on what a cocky asshole Joopah was. *But he has deviant brain activity I have not before encountered, at least not on anything but the most miniscule of levels.*

Keep him for observation, the captain ordered. *When the paralysis wears off, inform me, so that I may inquire about his alleged "spaceship." He has piqued my curiosity.*

Yes, I will, Joopah said.

Yes, SIR, Kuzar corrected.

CHAPTER 43

"And we're back," Charles Gander told the world. "Joining me tonight is Dr. Albert Frenden, PhD, who will be discussing his theory that the world is actually hollow."

Helen sighed and nestled into her armchair. The radio host had a deep, articulate voice which curdled the post-menopausal ex-housewife. He sounded out every vowel so perfectly it felt as though he were cleaning the inside of a bowl with words.

"Dr. Frenden will be joining us next hour. Until then, we'll run through the news before opening the lines up for your thoughts and questions." Helen let her mind wander as the radio host rattled off a story about some no-goodniks setting cars on fire in Paris, a seal-clubbing report from Canada, and a Bigfoot sighting.

She pictured him in her mind: a powerfully-built man with a granite jaw and eyes the color of glacial friction. His necktie hung loose to one side, as if he'd just said "Dammit, we have to let the American people *know* about this!" and rolled up his sleeves. She liked that image. His sleeves rolled up, a gray blazer slung over a chair. With five o'clock shadow from working all night.

"Fascinating stuff, folks," Gander commented, finishing up a brief update on the whereabouts of the Lost City of Atlantis. "I think we'll find definitive proof of the city within the year."

Keeping with his own staggering charisma, Charles Gander seemed to turn and face a different direction to signify a break in thought. It was the exact same effect news reporters use when they switch cameras, except that it was done both silently and without any visual aid. "At this point we'll take a few calls. You can phone in about the news reports or musings on our last show, whatever you'd like. If you wish to speak to Dr. Frenden, however, you need to wait until the end of the show. Okay, first time caller line: Hello, you're on *Midnight Chat*."

"Hello?" a voice asked, quiet and awed, as if speaking before Oz.

"Yes, hello."

"I've . . . I've turned off my radio," the man said. The caller had a pleasant honey-roasted baritone quality, though he was obviously overcome by the prospects of speaking on the program.

"That's good, thank you," Gander replied. "I'll remind future callers to do the same. There's a delay of several seconds, so you *will not* be able to hear yourself over the radio. Who am I speaking with?"

"Sephus," the man offered, almost asked.

"Where are you calling from, Sephus?"

"Hoople, Oklahoma."

"And what's on your mind tonight?"

The man took a deep breath, audible over the radio. "First let me say, Mr. Gander, that it is an honor, perhaps my greatest honor, to speak with you. I've been listening to your show for . . . well for *years* now, and this is the first time I've ever called. Such . . . such a *privilege*."

Gander chuckled, humbly brushing the compliment off of his shoulders. "Thank you, Sephus. I appreciate that."

"And I wouldn't call you, Mr. Gander, unless I

had a very good reason to do so. I understand how valuable your time is."

"Yes," Gander said, "Thank you. Noting that, why exactly *are* you calling?"

"Mr. Gander,"

"Charles."

"Yes, *Charles*," Sephus said, although he used the name reverently, like a peasant holding the king's crown. "My neighbor and my friend, and another man who kidnapped them, have been abducted by extraterrestrials and haven't been returned. It happened early this morning," he checked his watch, "or yesterday morning, actually, so it's almost been twenty-four hours, which is much longer than they've ever kept Frank before."

"Really?" Gander asked, leaning forward over the air. "Please go on."

"My friend Frank has been abducted regularly over the last few weeks, probably seven or eight times now."

"I see."

"Okay, that's the first bit. His sister was recently attacked by the evil twin of one of her college friends."

"And . . . how does that . . ."

"It'll all come together momentarily. This evil twin broke into her home and tried to inject her with something. She escaped, and went to live with her brother until she could sort things out. He, in turn, decided to live with me, because he's very shaken up from getting abducted so often."

"Uh-huh."

"Right. So the other night she went out on a date in another town, and while she was gone, the evil twin showed up at my house."

"To inject her?"

"No!" Sephus corrected excitedly. "He actually *arranged* for her to be out of town! And, when he showed up at my house, he asked for Frank, not Hillary. (Hillary is Frank's sister.)"

"Okay."

"But, as luck would have it, her brother *drove* her to her date. So he was gone. When my neighbor and I realized who the man was, we locked him in my storm cellar."

"Right," Gander said slowly, dragging the word out.

"The catch is, he escaped: his twin, the good one, accidentally let him out. So he kidnapped Frank and drove away. My neighbor followed him and apparently shot at his car, but they've *all three* disappeared! I found my neighbor's truck an hour ago, but not the evil twin's car."

"Sephus, if what you're saying is true, it's very serious. You need to call the police immediately."

"The catch is," Sephus repeated, "the car couldn't have driven away. My neighbor's truck was blocking it in. There are tire marks from the Taurus in front of it, but it couldn't have gotten out of the little road. There are fences and it dead ends."

"Well, before the truck was parked—"

"And the evil twin sent a text message to the good twin, who was then at my house: it read 'Greys.' With an 'e,' as in the aliens. Which are, coincidentally, the same group that keeps abducting Frank!"

Charles Gander remained calm on the other end, thinking. "This is a very outrageous story, Sephus."

218

"I know, but it's all true. Oh, and another thing: I'm pretty sure that the evil twin is the Rectum Thief."

"The Rectum Thief?" Gander's voice dropped an octave. He had previously been placating the man; now he seemed concerned.

"Mr. Gander, how . . . *what* can I do? (Charles, sorry.)"

"Well, nothing, really. Think about this for a moment, Sephus. If your friend really has been kidnapped by the Rectum Thief, and they're both now in turn being held prisoner by extraterrestrials, what *can* you do? It's not like you could rig up a stepladder to go get him. I think it's much more likely, however, that your friend has been kidnapped, not necessarily by the Rectum Thief, and not necessarily by aliens. If that's the case, the police actually *can* help. You need to call *them*."

"But I—"

"Thanks for listening, Sephus," Gander said. The first-time caller line silently shut off and another opened. "International line! You're on the air—"

Helen shut the radio off and stood up, shaking. She looked around the room, agog. She picked up her phone and called Jim Thunderpop.

"Zhello?" the preacher mumbled into the phone. "Izzisanmergency?"

"Reverend Thunderpop?" Helen quavered.

"Helen?" he asked, sitting up in bed. "Is everything okay?"

"The Rectum Thief has my baby!"

"What?" Thunderpop asked. This was a whole lot of crazy to take in after eleven.

"He killed my husband and now he's kidnapped

219

my son!" she wailed. "He's taking my family!" The word "family" broke into multiple syllables by her sobs, so that it came out "fa-a-a-a-mi-ly-y!"

Thunderpop sighed deeply. "Hold on, I'll come over."

CHAPTER 44

Sephus sat in a lotus position on a flea market Turkish rug in his farmhouse. Cheap votive candles rested on top of surfaces around him; the armchair, the couch, the coffee table, the two empty bottles of Peppermint Schnapps. Dusk approached outside, but curtains blotted out the fading light. The interior of the house was a despairing midnight.

Various dog-eared books lay scattered around him, ranging from advice on close encounters of the kinds first through third, to models of UFO's, to astronomy, accounts of abductees, and a *Victoria's Secret* catalogue. Strewn in between these effects lay the shattered pieces of his life.

Charles Gander had failed him.

The charismatic giant of *Midnight Chat*, a man who had single-handedly spoken with more abductees and UFOlogists on air than anyone else in North America, turned out to be, when pressed for advice, a blowhard. It was the single greatest letdown of Sephus Fitzbaur's life. It was like discovering that Santa Claus existed, but that he wouldn't be bringing any gifts to Christmas on account of syphilis.

Charles Gander, radio father figure, was a flop.

The emasculating comedown that extraterrestrials did not remotely care about Sephus remained as well. They had chosen Frank. *Frank.* If whatever beings ascending and descending from the stratosphere like yo-yos wanted a human being, why not pick Sephus? He was in good health, had a keen mind, and knew enough about paranormal activity and crypto-history to discuss topics most Americans could reach only by sitting inside of a flaming marijuana warehouse.

To Sephus, this utter neglect had a kind of religious abandonment to it. He derived a purpose in life from being "in the know" on the matters of cosmic importance nudging his planet. Most people in Grant county relied on God for fulfillment, but Sephus relied on conspiracy theories and the knowledge that he was part of a small cadre of Homo sapiens who actually knew what the hell was going on.

This knowledge allowed him to peer through the mundane life he otherwise plodded in to something vital and invigorating. It transformed the tedious mediocrity around him into the transparent backdrop of an unfolding galactic drama. It did not matter that he hadn't gone to college or married or left his hometown, because whatever goals he failed to accomplish were ultimately unimportant; they were just more props in a cosmic play very few people knew the script for. Now this super-reality had passed him by. It had picked up his friends like a wave and carried them away. He was left behind, flotsam in an otherwise dull and meaningless existence.

Roswell padded into the room. She surveyed the after-dinner séance environment and decided she disliked it, because she did not like change in general. The cat lightly tread over the books in a mildly curious expedition to determine what her "master" was focusing on, so she could redirect his attention to her. She detected no specific diversions near Sephus, so she assumed that this was the normal, unfocused lack of attention the farmer occasionally slumped into when eating or sleeping, which completely screwed up his priorities in life.

The cat crawled into his lap and rolled onto her back until he finally extended a hand to absently stroke her belly. Roswell was keen enough to know she was being placated, which was simply unacceptable. Physical affection was incidental; she merely wanted to confirm that everything living in the house was thinking about her. She kneaded his stomach with her paws until he finally looked down at her.

"Meow," she said.

"What's wrong with me?" Sephus asked, with the same inflection a man might use after discovering his wife left him for a comatose lesbian. To Roswell it was obvious: he spent several hours a day doing things completely unrelated to her.

Sephus looked up as he heard a knock at the front door. He scooped up the cat as he stood and set her down on the couch. Bits and pieces of his will to live trailed behind him on the sad trek to the door. He unlocked and opened it, squinting at the silhouetted figure obscuring the setting sun.

The visitor was a head shorter than him and possessed a medium-sized gut which extended an inch past his belt buckle, amply filling a Grateful Dead t-shirt. He had the longish hair of a man who is not entirely convinced the 1970s are actually over.

"Sephus Fitzbaur?" he asked.

"Y-yes," Sephus said, blinking.

The man extended his hand. "I'm Charles Gander. I'm here to save your friend."

CHAPTER 45

Both Sephus Fitzbaur and Helen Norbitz had pictured Charles Gander driving a stately Jaguar or BMW. In reality he drove a clunky van which had at some point been a shade of baby blue before rust and mud obscured it. The van made an odd clicking noise whenever Gander tapped the brakes. Six bumper stickers peeled away on the back, ranging from "Free Tibet!" to "Save the ugly animals, too!"

Gander drove his van toward the setting sun at fifty-one miles an hour, well below the speed limit. Sephus sat in the passenger's seat. He stared at Charles Gander, who was cleaning his aviator sunglasses in between glances at the road. Diminishing sunlight glinted off of his salt-and-pepper-and-allspice beard. He turned the air conditioning off and the CD player on. The last half of Paul Simon's "Diamonds on the Soles of Her Shoes" resumed halfway through.

"Are you a Paul Simon fan, Mr. Fitzbaur?"

"Sephus," he said. "I like him okay."

Gander nodded. "*Graceland* happens to be the most popular Earth album amongst interstellar folk."

"Oh."

"Not that most extraterrestrials have any idea where Earth is. But the ones that actually come here are usually pretty familiar with Paul Simon."

"I'll keep that in mind."

Gander signaled and turned onto the highway. He took a sip out of the bottle of ginseng tea he had picked up when they stopped for gas. He owed

Sephus thirty dollars. "Can I level with you, Sephus?" he asked.

"Of course."

The driver screwed a cap onto the bottle and put his sunglasses back on. "Normally I keep people in the dark on these kinds of things, but I need you to identify the Rectum Thief when we find him. Things will go smoother if we're on the same page. Everything I tell you from this point on is strictly and utterly confidential, understood?"

"Sure," Sephus said.

"I'm quite serious, Sephus." Gander glanced at him. "Stephen Hornswild is not my first co-host," he said ominously. "So whatever I tell you . . . you take it to the grave either way, yeah?"

Sephus gulped. "Alright. To the grave."

"Good." He threw the empty tea bottle into the backseat. "Sephus, I'm an extraterrestrial."

Sephus lurched forward, grabbing the dashboard for support as his entire world spun out of control. "You're an—" He couldn't even finish the sentence. The confession hit him like a waffle iron.

"Yes, Sephus, an alien. The real Charles Gander died in 1972. Killed himself. One of our operatives found out about his death before the authorities did, and we downloaded me into the body before it went cold. The following day 'Charles Gander' picked himself up, packed his suitcase, and started a new life in Nevada."

"Why would you pretend to be a human?" Sephus squeaked. He took his hands off the dashboard, but the universe continued wheeling like a drunken, one-legged ballerina.

"I'm affiliated with the galaxy's equivalent of

226

the Coast Guard, stationed here incognito. I need everyone, human and extraterrestrial, to think I'm a native. Otherwise my cover is blown." Sephus's jaw went slack. "The radio show affords me a perfect opportunity to monitor extraterrestrial activity on the planet. If something really weird happens, someone generally calls in to tell me."

"But then . . ." Sephus's mind could not quite wrap around the concept. It stretched and dislocated a couple of joints but failed to encircle the notion that Charles Gander, who had provided the American public with hundreds of stories about extraterrestrials, might actually *be* one. "Are you . . ." He took a deep breath and focused on finishing a question. "Has your show been accurate?"

Gander laughed. "Hardly!" Sephus gasped and clung to his seat belt. "Sephus, the public can't know everything that's going on." Sephus nearly cried; Gander had delivered multiple fiery soliloquies built on the premise that Americans had the right to know what's happening and the capacity to handle it. "It's for their own good. If they knew the truth, they'd only be powerless to alter it. Better to leave them oblivious than frightened and ineffectual."

He caught a glimpse of his passenger and dropped his smile. "More importantly, extraterrestrials don't give heed to my show *because* of the amount of crackpot guests and silly theories I pump into it. I have to keep it that way."

The car fell silent for several moments as Sephus came to terms with the revelation. His face locked in a grimace that turned more and more gargoyle-like as daylight bled away from the horizon. "The Rectum Thief," Gander asked, "does he look to be about twenty-eight?"

Sephus closed his eyes and thought. "He looks thirty or older, but that's probably just his demeanor. His twin brother, James, looks roughly twenty-eight."

"Do they have any other twins?"

"I don't know. Why?"

"A number of the Rectum Thief's victims suffered from what appears to be suppressed abduction experiences. In some cases they actually reported being abducted, or at least mentioned it to friends or families."

"So . . . The Rectum Thief is seeking out abductees? Like with Frank?"

"Exactly," said Gander. He took his sunglasses off and set them on the dashboard. "But how would he know who's been abducted? Most of his victims never publicly reported anything of the kind. I only know myself because of confiscated aliens' records."

"I suppose . . . he somehow has access to a list of abductees?"

"Right. But there is no exhaustive 'list,' at least not with human authorities. In fact, most people who *think* they've been abducted are really just suffering from a particular kind of seizure. So, I theorize, either the Rectum Thief is being aided by extraterrestrials, or—"

"He *is* one!" exclaimed Sephus.

Gander nodded. "And I think the whole 'evil twin' bit is too weird to be coincidental. I looked into immigration logs, and twenty-eight years ago, an anthropologist from Zeta Reticuli came to Earth. He registered himself and is here legally in four identical human bodies."

Sephus screwed his eyebrows up. "*Four* bodies?"

"Yes, it's still one entity, but it lives in four different bodies."

"So *James* is an alien?" Sephus asked, aghast. He suddenly grew angry. "Is *everybody* an alien all of a sudden?!" He folded his arms.

"Calm down, Sephus. My Zeta Reticulan hypothesis seems to be the most probable explanation at this point."

Sephus absorbed this knowledge. James's alien identity went down far smoother than Charles Gander's off-Earth origins. "So the real question, other than where Frank, Leland, and The Rectum Thief are—"

"Leland?"

"Leland McCorvick is my neighbor. He's been abducted too."

"I see. Go on."

"The question is: why is the Rectum Thief killing all these abductees?" He put a hand on his chin to aid his pondering.

"Oh, we already know that," said Gander.

"Really? Why?"

"For the drugs."

Paul Simon missed a beat as the CD player skipped.

"For the drugs?"

"Yes." Gander turned off of the highway onto a gravel road. "What exactly do you think most abductions are about, anyway?"

"Well, testing . . . and reproductive experiments."

"Ha!"

"They're not?"

"No, they're about drugs."

Sephus's eyes narrowed. "I don't understand."

"Listen, Sephus, no offense to your planet, but why the hell would anyone ever want to come here? It's an unadvanced, warlike little ball a billion miles from anything important."

Sephus drew a blank. "Uh . . . well, I suppose if not for testing purposes, I would have supposed aliens would come to plunder vital resources?"

Gander swiveled his head to frown at him. "Please. Anyone capable of building a spaceship and travelling thousands of light-years can figure out how to extract minerals from asteroids or combine molecules to make water. Coming here for resources would be as economical as you guys trying to drill for oil on Mars."

"So . . . the Greys are making drugs . . . out of people?"

Gander laughed. "No, the Greys are utilizing how obscure this planet is in order to smuggle drugs. Illegal narcotics are manufactured in the Outer Rim, and the Greys come here and cram the stuff into various orifices on random humans, and then *other* Greys come and pick them up. Earth is so unfrequented by anyone else in the galaxy that there isn't a big chance of getting caught, but there would be if they transported shipments directly from their manufacturing centers to the galactic hub."

"But that doesn't make any sense!" Sephus exclaimed.

"Really? Do you think it makes a lot of sense that aliens suck human beings out of their homes, scare the piss out of them and prod them with

230

instruments, then put them *back?* If I were experimenting on human beings, *I* wouldn't bother returning them. High school students don't throw dissected frogs back into the wild, chum."

"Yes," countered Sephus, "but they've clearly been doing experiments. Anal probing—"

"Why is it," Gander interrupted, "that human beings are so fixated on anal probing as a scientific application? What would anyone *learn* from that? Honestly, do you guys think aliens can surpass the speed of light but have yet to surpass the technology of anal thermometers? *Really?* No, the reason Greys are so obsessed with your bungholes is because they're stashing drugs up in your junk."

Sephus folded his arms. "So . . . the aliens aren't conspiring to conquer Earth or make human-alien hybrids?"

Gander harrumphed. "Hardly. Earth is important to them precisely *because* it's unimportant."

"So you're telling me that human beings are just . . . intergalactic drug mules?"

"The ones who are abducted are."

"I see." Sephus looked out his window at a herd of cows. "What about cattle mutilations?"

"Same story, different drug. The Greys smuggle in two types of illegal narcotics, both of which have to be stored at precise temperatures. If they kept them in warehouses on Earth or the Moon we would've detected them by now. But, as luck would have it, humans are the right temperature for the one, and cows are the right temperature for the other."

"Why don't you just confiscate the drugs from

abductees?"

"We do, when we actually locate some. But there are upwards of six billion people on the planet and our resources are limited."

Sephus nodded and leaned back in his chair. "And the Rectum Thief is intercepting these drug shipments?"

"Yes. Most likely some rival cartel pays him to, stealing and selling the drugs for themselves. A competing Grey syndicate could provide him with instructions of how to decode the crop circles."

"Right. Crop circles. So those are made by extraterrestrials after all?"

Gander chuckled. "In effect. Greys abduct college students and math enthusiasts and brainwash them into thinking it would be a funny prank to make crop circles and blame it on aliens."

Sephus shook his head in awe. "Genius."

"Yes, they're quite sharp. Of course they suppress the crop circle makers' memories of the encounter, but they imprint particular images into their minds so that when the circles are made the correct image is left on the field."

"And the circles coordinate drug cartel efforts?"

"We think so. They're simple but cryptic. We believe they're associated with the narcotic shipments. We could otherwise scan for tracking devices left in abductees. Coded messages broadcasted over space would give away their positions."

The conversation hit a momentary lull during "Crazy love, Volume II."

"Where exactly are we driving to, by the way?" asked Sephus.

"We're not driving anywhere. I've just been waiting for it to get dark. Are you buckled in?"

"Yes . . ."

Gander checked the rearview mirror. "There aren't any cars behind us?"

"No . . ."

"Good." He turned the van's lights off and jerked the emergency break. Rather than skidding to a halt, the Ford Windstar shot off of the road at a sharp incline.

From there, it sailed into space.

CHAPTER 46

"Would you look for my phone?" James asked, frisking his pockets in the driver's seat. Hillary turned the dome light on before poking around the car's interior and handing James his phone.

He dialed Vincent's number as they drove through the city of Moore and into Norman. "Vincent? James. Call Monty and tell him to meet us at Griffin's parking lot. Okay. Bye." He set the phone down on his lap.

"Who's Griffin?" Hillary asked.

"It's not a person, it's a place. We're parking at Griffin Memorial Hospital."

"The mental institution?" Hillary asked.

"Uh-huh."

"Why?"

James ventured a brief glance at her. "We parked the ship there under the theory that anyone who sees us use it will be dismissed as insane."

After a few minutes they passed a sign for the mental health facility and insane asylum. James turned into the site. Vincent and Monty waited in separate rental cars in one of the parking lots. They exited as James and Hillary got out of their own vehicle. "Hey guys," said James.

Monty smiled and nodded to him. He extended a hand to Hillary, and instead of shaking it, planted a kiss. "I assume you're in the know now, my dear?"

"I think so," said Hillary.

"Good," Monty said. He faced James. "So, as I understand it, Karl has officially wigged out and is now being held captive by the Greys?"

"That's the conclusion I've drawn."

Monty walked toward the northeast end of the campus with the others in tow. "We don't have any method of contacting the Greys so long as we're down here. Once we're in space we'll send out hailing frequencies and try to secure Karl's release."

"And Frank's," noted Hillary.

"Yes, and Frank's."

"Do you think they're going to attack you?" Hillary asked.

Vincent nodded. "There's a good chance. The Greys aren't particularly sociable or law abiding."

"Could you call your home planet for help? Have them send a battleship or something?"

Monty shook his head. "After reaching maturation, our people are extremely reticent to leave the safety of their home planet, Hillary. No one has died on Zeta Reticuli—from accident, disease, or aging—in over six hundred years. Leaving the planet means leaving the security of immortality. It's difficult to motivate people to risk that."

James stopped and looked around. "Dammit, where did we park?"

Monty pointed toward the tallest building of the complex, an old brick edifice, somewhat gothic and resembling a church. "It should be up there."

"How are you going to get in at night?" asked Hillary.

Monty lead the way toward the tall, dark building. "They haven't used the place in years. Flood damage." He gestured toward the boarded-up windows. "We'll break in, find the ship, then leave."

James attempted to open the front door, but the

lock wouldn't budge. He threw a brick through one of the small rectangular panes of glass, then reached his hand through to unlock it from the inside. "Quick," he said, checking to see if anyone had heard.

He led the way to and up the stairs using his cell phone as a flashlight. They reached the fourth floor and stumbled into things for a couple of minutes before finally locating the utility ladder to the roof. The top of the building afforded a decent view of Norman, warm wind, and an uncomfortable height.

"Alright," Montgomery said slowly.

"There," Vincent said, pointing to the west edge of the building. He walked over and slapped his hand out, nearly falling over the side. "Where is it?" he mumbled, ambling along the edge, waving his hand through the air. He leaned over and peered around, agitated. He lifted his head up and loudly banged it against apparently nothing. He cursed and stepped backwards, rubbing the back of his skull. "Ah, here it is. It's all coming back to me." He felt along the air a foot away from the building until he mimed a handle of some sort and twisted. A space craft suddenly blinked into existence, hovering off the side of the roof.

It was slightly larger than a Volkswagen van. Curved but flattened, it looked like a synthesis between a coffin and a chicken egg. It had no holes, windows, seams, bolts, or lines: just a uniform glossy surface the color of orange sherbet. It neither moved nor made noise, but hung motionlessly without support or suspension two feet from the roof's shingling.

Vincent leaned over the edge to rest his hand on

its shiny exterior. He moved his palm another foot to the left, leaving an orange phosphorescent hand print in its place, which slowly faded away. He kept resting his hand on different locations of the ship until a bright green square lit up directly beneath his palm, which produced the sound of a raindrop hitting a bucket. After a few seconds the square made a higher-pitched drip noise and turned green.

A slit developed near the bottom of the ship, then shot up like a pull-style window blind, providing an entrance to the craft. Hillary followed the three men on board, hoping to avoid a wrong step and subsequently falling down the side of the building. The door slammed shut behind her, disappearing entirely.

The ceiling was low enough to necessitate a slight crouch. It had a soft white light throughout, from no discernible bulbs. Four chairs in the middle of the ship sat in a plus configuration facing outwards. The chairs, walls, floor, and ceiling all had a pale cream color, broken only by a six-inch panel which came out from the wall and extended around the interior in a large oval. On the panel, colored schematics and lights blinked on a black background. Due to the low ceiling and unobtrusive color scheme, Hillary felt more like she was in a peculiar limousine than an extraterrestrial spacecraft.

James and Hillary sat in chairs at the aft of the ship, with Vincent and Monty at the bow. "Everyone ready?" Montgomery asked.

"Yes," James and Vincent returned. Montgomery nodded and rapidly pressed doodads on the panel in front of him like a keyboard.

The ship made the sound of a clucking noise,

prompting several of the previously dormant panels around the interior to light up. A circular portion of the wall in front of Hillary, about four feet in diameter, suddenly turned transparent to reveal the skyline outside. The distinction between opaque white and utter clearness blurred, like typing paper smeared with grease. When she glanced at the front of the ship it suddenly jumped to the center of her focus, enlarging. Quickly looking around the interior of the ship, she realized that the walls, floor, and ceiling turned transparent wherever her focus was, while the interior in her peripheral vision remained opaque.

Peering through the selective clear wall, she saw Norman rapidly disappear as the ship hurled upward to surge forward at a blinding speed. She looked beneath her feet and could see North America falling away. She did not feel any movement. No sense of inertia, speed, or change in direction presented itself. Had her eyes been shut she would not have realized they had cleared the roof.

Vincent squinted through his meaningless glasses into the depths of space, although from Hillary's viewpoint he appeared to be scrutinizing the smooth, creamy wall of the ship. "So now we find the Greys," he said.

"We'll send out a message over the standard frequencies," announced Montgomery, tickling the panel in front of him.

James fumbled around his pockets nervously. "I think I might have left my keys in the car."

CHAPTER 47

Sephus could see the diminishing Earth from the van's rearview window. It was upside down, or at least appeared that way. Technically there is no "up" in space, but every picture of the Earth shown in Western Civilization features the northern hemisphere on top. Sephus could not quite get over the sensation that either he or the entire planet hung inverted, which fortunately distracted him from the many other oddities surrounding him.

For instance, he knew that less than an inch of glass, or at least what appeared to be glass, separated him from the silent scream of cosmic void. Another oddity was the strange feeling of zero-g gravity, though he and Charles Gander remained secured by their safety belts. This did not apply to the ginseng bottle previously rolling around in the back, nor a handful of crumbs floating in front of his face, nor the three stray empty bags of Doritos drifting around the interior.

"Dammit!" Charles Gander exclaimed as one got in front of him. "Hold on, this will hurt a little." He opened the driver's side door, sucking the air and floating debris out into the vacuum of space. He slammed the door shut with a grunt, then locked it. "Are you alright?" he asked.

Sephus nodded, although he felt winded, cold, and light-headed. "Couldn't that have killed us?"

"Yes, if I'd kept it open much longer. Fortunately the airconditioning system is superb, and it replaced the missing air almost instantly."

"You realize that . . ." he tried to articulate what little he knew about biology and the vacuum of space, "wasn't *possible*."

"Technology," Gander piped happily, patting the dashboard.

"May I turn on the heater?" asked Sephus.

"Oh, right. Go for it."

"What are we looking for, exactly?" Sephus asked. He glanced out his window toward the brilliant diamonds of the Milky Way.

"Unregistered ships," Gander replied, peering out through the windshield into the brilliant incandescent cosmos. Stars twinkled brightly in the skies of Hoople but nothing, absolutely nothing, compared to their brilliance from the Earth's orbit. Gander shifted the windshield wiper stick up. Green lines and words appeared all over the windows. He touched various symbols with his middle finger, which lit up as he did so, changing the windshield's display. "Alright," he said to himself, "and now to adjust for satellites . . ."

He pressed a few more symbols and the majority of the illuminated figures disappeared. In their place, tiny green labels for every star and star system appeared. Sephus turned behind him to see the Earth similarly labeled. "Most instruments won't be able to pick up a concealed ship, but we ought to be able to see them. If the Windstar detects one, it will make a beeping noise and a yellow dot will signify where the movement is. If you see something, tell me."

"Copy," said Sephus. He looked out at the millions of white dots but could see no lurking spaceships. "How likely are we to see anything?"

"From here? Not very. I—" He leaned forward and stared out toward the Betelgeuse system. "Wait a sec . . ." He put his thumb against the top left corner of the windshield and then touched his other hand's index finger to whatever he was staring at. The windshield instantly magnified, then did so again three times as he tapped the glass. The magnification was so perfect in its display that it seemed the van leaped forward by miles with each tap, although the other windows remained the same. After six taps Gander peered at floating space debris. "Junk," he pronounced. He released his thumb from the windshield and the original, un-magnified view of space instantaneously reappeared.

"How far can you zoom in with this thing?"

"It's just about equal with the Hubble, but your thumb gets tired."

"Really?" Sephus asked. "That's astounding."

"And this is only the Windstar," he said. He turned the van around so that the Earth loomed directly above them. He set the cruise control, keeping the Windstar in the same orbit pattern at a steady ten miles per second. For the next few minutes Sephus leaned forward to peer out above the van at the gigantic, brilliant planet he hailed from. "Where's the Great Wall of China?"

Gander made a "pfff" noise and batted a hand. "You can't see it from space. At least not outer space. I don't know who keeps saying that."

"Astronauts, I think."

"What?" Gander glanced down at the Earth. "The Great Wall is about as wide as a highway. Can you see I-35 from space?" Sephus nodded in agreement, but kept scanning for it anyway.

After five minutes Gander clicked off the cruise control. He pressed the top of the steering wheel forward, causing the Windstar to dip downwards until the Earth hung directly behind it. In front loomed the Earth's moon, huge and blindingly silver.

Gander reset the cruise control for seventy-five miles per second. Despite this, it still took forty minutes or so to approach the Earth's satellite. It grew larger and larger until the glowing circle extended beyond the perimeters of the windshield. Gander guided the Windstar toward a gray blur on the moon labeled Mare Humorum in the window. When the spheroid became close enough that it was visibly hurtling at them, he applied the brakes and eased up a little.

He maneuvered the van to the correct point in the Mare Humorum and righted the vehicle so that its wheels faced the moon's surface. After a few more minutes of skimming over the moon, he brought it down, gently touching the surface within a large basin.

The lunar terrain was flat and bright. The effect of light was like nothing Sephus had ever seen; a weird, incandescent glow, a combination of no atmosphere and the reflection of solar and terrestrial light off of lunar soil. He found it more thrilling than the just completed 250,000-mile space flight.

In his adolescence, he experienced a giddy feeling whenever he drove a pickup through a field. It felt alien piloting a vehicle normally limited to constrictive roads through huge, open expanses. The fact that the truck could go in any direction, with no people around, had felt liberating. It was like jumping a train from the tracks and directing it purely at the conductor's discretion. Driving a van on the moon was all this and more. It was surreal, ultimate freedom.

The empty, smooth basin extended far ahead of them. On either side of the Windstar Sephus could see the edges of the crater towering up, high as mountains. He noticed a tiny speck ahead, which grew into a dot, then a fat dot. After a few moments it turned into a motor home.

It sat on the huge, open plain of lunar dust as nonchalantly as a retired couple's motor home parked for lunch in the deserts of Arizona. Its midsection had an extension which could be popped out from the coach for more interior space, and was. A small satellite dish perched on top near the back.

Sephus blinked a couple of times to make sure it was not some kind of lunar mirage. It wasn't. It was a normal motor home that happened to be parked on an otherwise lifeless, desolate, and untouched rock 250,000 miles away from the nearest grill or lawn chair.

Gander pulled the van up next to it, stopping when he felt the wheels make contact with a couple of acutely placed cinder blocks. "Here we are," he said, unbuckling his seatbelt. "If you'll open the glove compartment, you'll find what looks like a garage door opener." Sephus did so and found the specified device underneath a bottle of mouthwash and another bottle of scotch. "Go ahead and hit the button."

As Sephus did, neon purple graph lines extended out of the motor home's doorway to encompass the Windstar. "Force field?" Sephus asked.

"Yes," Gander replied. "Actually more of an atmosphere and temperature field. We'll need to wait a minute for the ground to cool down, otherwise our shoes will melt. And some air would be nice." He turned the car off and pocketed the keys. After humming along to Paul Simon's "Gumboots," he opened the door to the van. Air rushed passed him, but with none of the angry vacuum suckage of space. After Sephus exited, Gander not only shut but locked his door. The likelihood of anyone breaking into it at this location was very small indeed, but old habits die hard.

The air around Sephus felt hot and thin. He followed Gander to the motor home, noticing a number of footprints in the powdery lunar soil. A sneaker with the discernible Nike insignia imprinted the shiny gray moon dust. A large pawprint rested next to it. "You bring your dog to the moon?" he asked.

Gander fished the keys out of his pocket and unlocked the door to the motor home. "I used to, but not so much anymore. You'd be amazed how high a Jack Russell terrier can jump in one sixth of the Earth's gravity. Skippy usually is, anyway." He gestured for Sephus to enter and shut the door behind him.

The interior of the motor home was nothing out of the ordinary. The carpet, fabric, and walls involved inordinate amounts of gray and beige, but were offset by several framed photographs of colorful Italian cities. "I'm going to use the restroom," said Gander. "Please make yourself at home." As he excused himself, Sephus sat down in the motor home's diner-style dinette booth. Across from it rested a couch with a couple of *TV Guides* splayed across the cushions and a crocheted blanket.

Gander emerged from the bathroom a few moments later, drying his hands off on his blue jeans. "Do you want anything to drink?" he asked. Sephus shook his head. "Help yourself to the fridge if you change your mind. The kitchen's in the back."

The two men walked to the driver's compartment at the front of the motor home and sat down in swivel chairs. Gander hit a switch, prompting a label system similar to but more opaque than the Windstar's to sprawl out across the windshield and flanking windows. He pressed a few symbols and the passenger's side window registered dozens of small squares displaying alternate close-up views of the Earth.

"We're tapped into the Earth's satellite system," he said. He touched a few more symbols and the windshield filled with a dense cloud formation over the North Atlantic. "The surveillance equipment here is powerful enough to make voyeur amoeba movies. Space-faring trespassers usually have some tricks up their sleeves, but we may get lucky."

The extraterrestrial talk show host leaned back in his chair, scrutinizing cloud bank footage. "So," he said, fishing for conversation, "what's your favorite *Star Trek* movie?" This lead to a lengthy discussion which eventually unfolded into a deep conversation about each man's goals in life, personal reflections, regrets, and theories on female psychology. Within half an hour, Sephus consented to have a beer with his hero, and they sat in their swivel chairs, shooting the breeze, scanning the Earth's orbit for illegal aliens.

"Yeah," Sephus said, folding his arms, "I always thought I'd end up out of state, or at least in Tulsa, but things rarely go as you think they will. Right?"

"Right," Gander replied. "Forty years ago if you'd told me I'd end up on Earth, I would've been like 'Where's—'"

"Hold it!" Sephus said, leaning forward in his chair. He put his thumb against the window and touched part of the glass with his index finger. He magnified it three more times, until what looked like a large top, spinning across a storm system, dominated the window.

"There you are," Gander said, his eyes narrowing to slits. "A Reptoid corsair." He tapped some instructions into the driver's side window and read the ensuing text. "Not registered, either. Good eye, Sephus."

"Thank you. For the record, though, the text message said 'Greys.'"

"Who knows, the Reptoids might have typed the message in. Or he might have misidentified the ship. Either way, they're not supposed to be here." He typed more into the panel next to him and stood up. "The motor home is going to track their position and relay it to the Windstar. Let's go."

CHAPTER 48

A Grey cruiser's hull can withstand asteroid impacts and nuclear explosions. They are heavily armed and well armored. Because of the virtual impregnability of their external defenses, they require little internal security. They are not built expecting stray humans to pop up unnoticed in the lower decks. Homo sapiens are simply not an issue in terms of ship safety precautions, in much the same manner that submarine schematics do not take into account elk infestations.

It is for this reason that Karl Janus's car, safely tucked in a cargo hold, came to be completely unsupervised. No one saw the car rock slightly or heard a sudden thump and "Dammit!" from within the trunk.

The Lincoln rocked again, this time more forcefully. An agitated rhythm of fist impacts against the trunk's lid echoed throughout the cargo hold. A taillight exploded as a boot kicked through. After a minute of irritated, cuss-filled struggle, the trunk released and flew open. A grizzled and angry farmer sat up to scan his immediate vicinity for something to kill. Finding nothing, he climbed out, taking with him his chain and a tire iron previously laying underneath him.

The spaceship's cargo bay looked remarkably similar to a cargo bay on any other type of vessel; it was a large hoary room with scuffed-up, stained floors, and littered throughout with junk. Leland McCorvick did not know where he was. He assumed a garage. He circled Karl's car, taking in the layout of the room, and decided to vacate. A large garage door dominated the other side of the bay, but Leland could not locate the button necessary to open it. This was good, because had he done so, the ensuing vacuum would have wrenched him into space.

Instead he walked to a smaller rectangle near his car which looked to be a needlessly sophisticated door. Finding no knob, he kicked his foot toward it to see if it had an automatic sensor, but it didn't budge. He reached a hand toward the frame and the door slid open.

Once outside of the cargo hold it became readily apparent that he was not inside of a garage. The hall was sleek and metal, with a ceiling so rounded it was almost a long tube. Similar rectangular doors dotted the corridor, along with occasional computer screens and signs in a language he did not recognize. For this reason Leland assumed he was on a battleship, most likely Chinese.

A slender gray creature nearly crashed into him as he turned a corner at the end of a corridor. He immediately recognized it as an alien from a couple of questionable History Channel documentaries. He struck it across the face with the tire iron, dropping it to the floor, unconscious.

He poked the alien with the toe of his boot a couple of times and made a long, low whistle. Aliens. Apparently he was onboard an extraterrestrial spacecraft. Not captive, however. He accurately supposed that the car had been taken onboard without the knowledge that he lay unconscious inside the trunk. Leland tucked the tire iron and chain into his belt and dragged the alien by its heels back to the cargo bay. He deposited it in the trunk of the car, then set a heavy, unknown gadget on top.

Thinking quickly, he decided the best course of action was either to use the unconscious alien as hostage and bargain his way back to his farm, or, to single-handedly seize control of the spaceship, figure out how to fly an intergalactic craft, and land it at Ft. Sill in Lawton, Oklahoma.

He decided to use the hostage as a backup plan.

CHAPTER 49

It took another hour to return from the moon to their earlier position orbiting Earth. The Windstar caught the Reptoid corsair over the North American continent. It pulled up behind the flying top until both vehicles could readily view one another. Gander flipped his brights on and off. The top-like spacecraft continued, unaffected.

"There's a car phone under your seat," Gander told Sephus. "Please get it."

Sephus poked around until he located an old, clunky mobile phone. He handed it to Gander, who punched in a few numbers and put the receiver to his mouth. "*Windstar* to unidentified ship: you are not registered to visit this planet. Please accompany us out of the Earth's orbit for questioning." He tilted the trajectory of the van upward but brought it back to normal when the spaceship showed no sign of compliance.

"*Windstar* to unidentified ship," he said again. "You are ordered—" The ship shot upwards and away. Gander pulled the steering wheel back, shooting the van up and out of the Earth's orbit. "Hopefully they've decided to—" The van shuddered violently and an alarm sounded.

"Are they attacking us?" Sephus asked.

"Looks like it," Gander said, rapidly turning the steering wheel, hand over fist. The Reptoid corsair hung in front of them menacingly, spinning slowly. A light at the bottom of the ship flashed, simultaneously lighting up the windshield with a crackling red glow. Gander flipped a switch on the dashboard and pulled back on the windshield wiper stick, which doubled as a trigger. The Reptoid ship rocked back; brief flashes of blue danced across it like exploding pellets of neon.

"Notice how you can't hear anything outside?" Gander asked, his voice slightly louder over the Windstar's alarm.

"Yes?" Sephus said, double-checking his seatbelt.

"That's always something that's bothered me about science fiction movies." He spastically pulled back and forth on the windshield wiper stick. The corsair shuddered. "There isn't any air in space, so there's nothing to transmit sound waves. Hold on." He derogated from his criticism of sci-fi cinema in order to concentrate on the unfolding space battle. "Also," he said, launching a barrage of light across the Reptoid hull, "you can't *see* lasers flying through space! That's another problem with films."

It is to the loss of the Ford motor company that there is no documented footage of the firefight between the Windstar and Reptoid spaceship. In the Earth's orbit, the van possessed a predatory speed and agility. Photon packets shot out from its headlights, shaking the Reptoid craft apart. After five minutes of dramatic barrel-rolls and staggering 120-degree angle turns, Charles Gander floored the vehicle, slamming it into the Reptoid ship at the neck-splintering speed of twenty-eight miles per second.

Sephus's seatbelt caught him, but badly jarred his neck. He looked up in time to see the Reptoid vessel wobbling horribly, one flame rotating on its chassis like a punctured beer can spinning around in a pond. It continued its off-kilter descent, dropping toward the Earth at a steady and slow rate, maddening to the powerless crew within.

"Well alright then," Gander said, relaxing slightly.

"Were my friends in that ship?" asked Sephus.

"What?" Gander said, turning to look at him. "No, of course not. Maybe." He put his foot on the gas, but it prompted no acceleration. He tried to gun the ignition, but the motor didn't turn.

"It's broken?" Sephus asked.

Gander nodded, adjusting his seat to a more reclined position. "Looks like it. Fortunately our van wasn't knocked out of orbit, unlike our space-lizard friends."

Sephus released his seatbelt and floated into the air. "I don't suppose you can fix it from the inside?"

The driver shook his head. "Not without removing the air conditioning system, as well as several other charming and essential components."

"So what do we do?"

Gander flipped the emergency lights on. A tiny icon flashed rhythmically from the dashboard in the shape of a triangle. "We wait for a lift." He hit the "play" button on the CD player and bobbed his head as Paul Simon's voice filled the Windstar. "Don't worry, these things generally sort themselves out."

"And if they don't?"

Gander shrugged. "Then we die up here. Or," he gestured to the star field beyond, "out there, depending on our inclination."

The two men stared out at the endless cosmos. The Windstar floated at a slant, so that the Earth dominated the left half of the car's windows. "Say," Gander said. "Do you like whiskey?"

CHAPTER 50

James and the surrounding spaceship rocketed around the Earth at an orbit so blindingly fast they would complete a full revolution within an hour. "Detect anything?" James asked.

Montgomery tickled the panel in front of him. "Nothing out of the ordinary. A few extraterrestrial vessels, several satellites, some junk. No Grey ships, though."

"Probably cloaked," commented Vincent.

"Or gone," returned Monty.

"Open a general hailing frequency," said James. Montgomery tapped a few buttons and nodded. "Greys: We are aware that you've captured one Karl Janus and currently have him in your custody. His whereabouts and safety are important to us and Zeta Reticuli, and we would like to discuss terms for his release. We will monitor this frequency for your reply." He gestured to Montgomery to cut the signal and sat back in his chair.

"Very nice, James," Montgomery said. "You kept our position ambiguous, which is for the best considering we're in an unarmed skiff."

A few moments later a bleep sounded off near Vincent. "We're receiving a message." He hit a button and piped it into the ship's intercom.

"Unidentified vessel—who is this Karl Janus and why do you want him?"

"Do you have him?" James asked.

"Hold on," Montgomery said, "I'll patch you in." He nodded to James.

"Do you have him?" James repeated.

"*Yes,*" replied a voice.

"Well . . . please return him."

"*Is he a human being?*"

"They're tracing our signal," Vincent said quietly.

"Are you planning on returning him to Earth?"

We have not yet decided. Why?"

"He is under our protection," stated James.

"Quickly," Vincent pressed.

"We only want to make sure that he and anyone with him are returned safely to Earth."

"*We should discuss this matter further.*"

James looked at Montgomery for help; should they reveal Karl's identity or not? Montgomery prepared to mouth something but stopped to look at his panel. "They're here."

Hillary glanced around aimlessly until she spotted a dark behemoth directly behind them. "We're prepared to discuss things with you," James said.

"*That is good,*" the hulk responded.

"They've locked onto us with a tractor beam!" announced Vincent.

Montgomery and James both tackled their stations in a futile attempt to escape the looming Grey cruiser. Hillary watched the ship beyond as it approached their tiny vessel. She could not be sure of its size, but a battleship edging up to a kayak seemed like a fair comparison. A circular door opened behind them, then inched toward the craft, engulfing it. The field of stars disappeared inch by inch behind opaque black.

Beyond the bow of the skiff the circular door

shut. Although the moment of total eclipse was silent, Hillary imagined an ominous "clink."

CHAPTER 51

Kuzar sat at a conference table across from Captain Cosmowobsy. Mr. Zno slouched at his left, and his arch-nemesis, Joopah, sat on his right. Beuldine, the ship's first officer, perched next to the captain. The ship's second officer disappeared a few minutes earlier and had not yet returned.

They're genetically identical, Kuzar informed the ship's leadership. *The males,* he noted.

Furthermore, projected Joopah, *they all have the same unusual brain activity.*

And a ship, added the captain. *It is safe to assume they're not human.*

Genetically and biologically they are, down to the last detail, Kuzar stated.

Perhaps, mused Captain Cosmowobsy, *but they must have some connection outside of Earth. They could not have built the craft themselves.*

Could they be agents? Mr. Zno asked. *Here to crack down on the drug cartel?*

Captain Cosmowobsy thought about this. *No, I do not think so. If they were operating in an official capacity their craft would have had some kind of weapons system. They did not put up a fight at all.*

What does that leave? Joopah asked.

Someone has been stealing our shipments, the captain projected. *Whoever it is would have to know what we were doing, and who we were abducting. And, considering they kill our drug mules, they are probably keeping or selling the drugs for themselves. I think these beings might be responsible.*

Shall we terminate them? Beuldine asked.

In time, replied the captain. *First I will interrogate them individually. Mr. Joopah can run tests on whoever is waiting to speak with me.*

Kuzar scowled at the neurologist next to him; why hadn't the captain asked Kuzar to do it?

In the meantime, resumed the captain, *the next shipment—*

The door to the conference room opened and a Homo sapien literally jumped in, squatting slightly as he hit the deck plates. He stood up fully erect, sizing up the Greys in front of him. He gripped a metal blue "X" in one hand. The other rested at his side, clutching a large metal chain. It hung down the length of his pants and jingled menacingly like a rattlesnake.

Human! the captain projected. *Do not—*

Leland lunged forward and smacked the chain upside the captain's head with considerable force. Captain Cosmowobsy dropped to the table. His head bounced once, then lay across the surface, unconscious.

The door behind him opened. The ship's third officer, who happened to be named Jeff, surveyed the scene and turned to run. Before he completed a step, the human pelted him in the back of the head with the tire iron. Jeff toppled over like a camera's tripod stand. Leland dragged his bleeding form back into the room.

The human took a deep breath and turned to face the seated extraterrestrials. "Listen up," he said slowly, making long and deliberate eye contact with each and every alien. "I am now going to kick every single one of yer asses."

He let this sink in.

"This is not a negotiation. You sombitches have messed with my cattle and my farm, and yer gettin' an ass kick'n." Mr. Zno flinched suddenly, so McCorvick clobbered him in the face with the chain. Zno doubled over and made strangled bleating noses, trying to keep blue blood from squirting out his nostril holes.

"*After* the ass kick'n, yer gonna take me back to my farm and leave me the hell alone. If you do this, and you do a very good job of convincin' me yer not gonna SCREW AROUND," the aliens cringed as his volume jumped, "with my planet or my farm anymore, then I might not kill y'all. Do you extraterrestrial sombitches understand?"

Kuzar and Beuldine nodded vigorously. Joopah glared at the farmer. In response, McCorvick swung his chain at Joopah's torso, knocking him over before kicking him squarely in the groin. Joopah possessed no noticeable genitals, but seemed in sufficient pain, regardless.

"Which one of you pencil-necked bastards is in charge here?" McCorvick demanded. Kuzar pointed to the unconscious figure of the captain, who remained face down on the table, gurgling slightly. "Okay then," McCorvick said. He scanned the room, looking at the aliens, mentally counting them.

"Okay," he said again, glancing at Kuzar and Beuldine. "One of you grab yer commander, and the other one grab the chunky one on the floor." He said "chunky one" sarcastically, as every one of the Greys looked completely identical to him, but in fact from their perspective Jeff *was* getting a tad pudgy, and the farmer's hurtful comment would stick with the

259

third officer long after his bruises from the vengeful tire iron had healed.

"Go!" McCorvick barked. Kuzar slipped two bony arms underneath the captain's armpits and Beuldine helped Jeff to his feet. "You!" the farmer said, gesturing to Mr. Zno, who shrieked slightly and cowered beneath the table. "Help git smartass up off the floor." He pointed to Joopah, who was not unconscious but wished above everything else that he was. Mr. Zno stooped over to help Joopah to his feet.

McCorvick walked to the door and waited for it to automatically open. He popped his head into the hall to look for passing extraterrestrials. Finding none, he jerked a thumb over his shoulder. "Now y'all 'er gonna walk in fronta me, and quickly. If I say 'left,' you *damned well* turn left, y'understand?" The various bleeding aliens nodded. "Okay then. Git goin'. Exit and turn left, damn you."

The small procession of wounded and assisting extraterrestrials exited the conference room a few paces ahead of McCorvick. "Now I'll bet you sombitch aliens are think'n 'bout make'n a break for it, huh? You try it, and I will chase you down and whip the pulp out of you with my chain. Then I'll go back and tickle yer friends with my tire iron." He poked one in the back with the metal X. "Keep walkin' you scrawny gray bastards! Git!"

He led them back to the cargo hold and marched them to a wall. "All y'all stare forward," he commanded. He set the tire iron down lightly, so they could not hear him disarm, and removed the clunky unidentified scrap metal he had set on top of the Lincoln's trunk. "Forward!" he barked, as he caught sight of Joopah glancing behind.

He unlocked the trunk. The alien inside bolted upright, then immediately regretted it as McCorvick punched him in the face. A second blow struck the extraterrestrial's windpipe to ensure he lost consciousness. "Okay," he said, facing his captives. "On the left! That's you, fatty! C'mere!"

Jeff walked toward him warily and stood next to the car. As he turned to look at the ship's first officer laying in the trunk, Leland socked him in the jaw, dropping him to the floor. He stooped to pick up Jeff's unconscious body and chucked him into the trunk like a pile of firewood.

"Okay, next," he said. "Time to pile in the clown car." He repeated the process until the trunk brimmed with swollen, unconscious aliens. Confident he could not cram in anymore, he shut the trunk's lid and returned the massive space gizmo to its place on top of the trunk lid, then added additional heavy objects for good measure.

Kuzar and Mr. Zno stood shaking in front of the cargo hold's bay doors. They had not seen the efficient trunk stocking process, but they had a pretty good idea of what was happening based on the repeated sequence of "Next!" smack, thud, and grunt.

"You two stay there for a minute," McCorvick commanded. He jingled his chain to let them know he meant business. He poked around the cargo hold until he located some wire sitting in a corner. He picked up the spool and returned to the car. "Next," he said.

He opened the driver's side door for Mr. Zno and allowed him to take a seat. Then, he slammed the alien's head into the steering wheel. When Mr. Zno groggily returned to a relatively alert state he found himself expertly bound to the wheel and headrest with no mobility in his arms or legs.

McCorvick walked to Kuzar and stood a couple of feet behind him. "Don't turn around," he ordered, compelling Kuzar to nod his head vigorously and stare at the bay door. "I'm gonna give you an option, understand?" Kuzar nodded. "I can either kick yer ass now, *severely*, and tie you up in my painmobile with yer friend." He slapped the tire iron against his palm. "Or, you can take me to the other humans on board, and then the command center. Yer choice."

Kuzar thought about this. The right decision was probably to take the thrashing and let the human run loose on the ship, assuming the remaining crew would notice and apprehend him. But Kuzar did not want a thrashing. He decided the ship's compliment could probably handle the human, regardless of where Kuzar happened to be. *I'll show you to the lab and bridge,* he projected.

"Sir," McCorvick added.

Sir.

"That's better. Now if you try anything funny, like brain-yellin' at yer friends, or take'n off runnin', I'm gonna kill ya. I think I've only handed out painful concussions to yer friends, but I have no doubt I can end yer life with one good blow to the backa yer mushy grey skull. Understand?" Kuzar nodded. "Yes, *sir!*"

Yes, sir! Kuzar exclaimed, standing at attention.

"Alright, Twiggy. Lead the way."

CHAPTER 52

Nine hundred and sixty-two miles above the Earth, Sephus and Charles Gander floated inside of an interplanetary Ford Windstar, massacring The Beatles' "Good day Sunshine." After listening to the album Graceland twice, Gander had put in a mixed CD of Beatles medleys downloaded off of the Internet, but once legally purchased in the form of LP records.

The song's timing was perfect, beginning as the sun, swollen and blinding, exploded into view behind the planet Earth; an emerald and sapphire sphere eclipsing a golden orb. "And we lie, beneath a shady tree, I love—" Sephus stopped in mid-sentence. His jaw would have hung agape, but in anti-gravity it went slack in much the same position it had been. "It's . . . *beautiful*," he said. Sephus had seen the sunrise over his alfalfa field thousands of times, and had watched each iteration with piety. The same phenomenon, seen over the entire planet, blew him away.

The song finished as a wave of bullion dawn swept across the planet below. Sephus paused the CD as to witness the daybreak in reverent silence. High above the Earth, surrounded by vacuum, the Windstar was a temple of tranquility. For the first time in many years Sephus felt religious. He remained unsure about whether or not he believed in God, but he found himself hoping *some* deity existed. If not to create light and orbits and planets and beauty, to at least appreciate them.

A strand of pearly tears dribbled out his eyes and floated like tiny drops of glass, catching the morning light in their liquid prisms. They mingled with slightly larger blobs of scotch, the imbibed brothers of which contributed to Sephus's heightened spirituality and bloodstream.

"Charles?" he said, after a few moments.

"Mff?" Gander asked groggily from the backseat. A bottle of bourbon peeked out from his belt.

"I just wanted to say . . ." He looked out over the ball of his origin and the surrounding cosmos. "I want to say that if we die up here, it was worth it. It was worth every minute. Thank you."

"You're welcome," mumbled Gander. He grabbed the headrest in front of him and hoisted himself to the front seat. His lips smacked together loudly as he rubbed his eyes. "You've got a nice little planet, Sephus."

"Yeah," he said.

After a few more minutes of quietly watching the sunrise, or as from space, uneclipse, Gander squinted. "Sephus, do you see a little dot out there?"

Sephus strained his eyes. "Near the edge of the sun?"

"Yes."

A minute passed. "I think so. It looks like a tiny little triangle." It rapidly approached, growing into a small, medium, and finally gigantic triangle.

A chime sounded from the van's dashboard. Gander pressed a spot on his window. *"Unidentified . . . van,"* James's voice said over the sound system, *"Do you need assistance?"*

Gander fished out the mobile phone and held it

to his mouth. "Do you have any jumper cables?"

CHAPTER 53

With an attention span as short as Frank's, the ten hours of captivity within the jellyfish mattress felt like days. The blue shrimp-things had concluded their repair work on his legs two hours ago, and now meandered indiscriminately throughout the warm gel. He watched them idly, occasionally reaching out to surprise one with a finger.

He drifted between boredom and sleep, wondering if his alien kidnappers had somehow forgotten about him. If so, he might find himself trapped in the fluid indefinitely; he did not feel the least bit hungry. He suspected that between the amniotic goop around him and the healer-prawns whirling about, his dietary needs were externally catered to.

Frank punched his arm forward and spasmodically kicked his legs, trying to puncture the membrane around him. Nothing happened. Blows glanced off the rubbery casing harmlessly. The most he could accomplish was to make the glop pocket jiggle like a water balloon.

"Frank?" a voice mumbled from beyond the goo. He looked above him and saw two shadowy figures peering down. "Hold on, son," McCorvick said. "We're gettin' you outta this . . . thing."

Frank, Kuzar projected, *don't be alarmed. We're going to cut you loose. Try and expel any liquid in your lungs or mouth.*

The alien figure leaned over the top and injected a purple liquid into the pouch with a large syringe. It set off an immediate chemical reaction. The blue shrimp creatures scattered to the edges. The gel turned solid around his feet, rapidly surrounding the rest of him. All around his body the amniotic fluid congealed into squishy marbles until the whole of him was encased in a tub of translucent gristle balls.

Kuzar slid a scalpel along the top of the membrane. He pulled the rubbery flaps apart and lifted Frank out with the aid of Leland McCorvick. Frank coughed and doubled over, spilling little globules of bouncing gunk across the floor. A final, morbid hack dropped another gelatinous bubble to the stainless steel below.

He stood up and surveyed McCorvick and Kuzar. "Leland?" he asked. "What are *you* doing here?"

"Commanding this vessel," he said. "I captured the crew, renamed the ship the *USS Barry Goldwater,* and declared myself Commodore." He pointed above him to the command center on the next deck. "Sephus is my first officer. I left him upstairs with his radio buddy to steer the ship. C'mon."

Frank followed the farmer and attending space alien through a glossy corridor and up a staircase to the vessel's bridge. He immediately recognized the room as the set of a poorly imagined 1950s science fiction thriller. Not only did the command center's color scheme limit itself to steel, tin, and aluminum, it lacked any of the sleekness or curvation associated with modern technology. The whole place seemed clunky and box-like, and desperately in need of some Steve Jobs design upgrades.

Computer terminals lined every wall. James and two look-a-likes manned them. Sephus and Hillary stood at the center of the room, where a pot-bellied older guy reclined in a stainless steel lounge chair. "Frank!" Hillary exclaimed. She rushed across the gray deck plates and threw her arms around his neck. "You're all better!"

He nodded, returning the hug. "Yup. Howdy, all."

Sephus sauntered over and laid a hand on his shoulder. He was beaming. "Frank, I'm glad you're okay." He gestured to the spaceship surrounding them. "Pretty neat, huh?"

Frank nodded.

"We're here for another three hours until galactic law enforcement officials arrive to tow the vessel away and interrogate the Greys. Then it's back to Earth for us."

"Bullshit!" McCorvick exclaimed, drawing the curse word into four distinct syllables. "We're flying this mother straight to Pyongyang."

"What?" Gander asked, sitting up in the command recliner. "Why do you want to go to North Korea?"

McCorvick clenched his jaw and looked into the distance. "To finish what I started."

"With all due respect, *Commodore*, we're not going to use an interstellar cruiser to conquer North Korea."

"Liberate," McCorvick corrected. "And we'll do whatever I say. *I* captured the ship. It's mine."

Gander cast a sideways glance at Sephus. "I'll talk to him," the farmer mouthed. McCorvick sat down in a clunky metal chair to compose a list of communist countries in need of deliverance from socialism. Beginning with France.

Across the room James tapped his doubles. "Conference?" he asked.

CHAPTER 54

The brig which the three clones entered had been converted into a snack bar the previous week by Joopah and Mr. Zno. The two aliens had had no idea that the holding facility would ever be used again, let alone for their own detainment. Now the large cell they shared with the crew and Karl was flush with the scattered amenities of a Grey coffee nook. There were a couple of chairs about, but not enough to accommodate everyone. Most of the Greys sat on a bench on the far wall, sipping beverages from festive mugs, grumbling and rubbing their bruises.

Karl stood up as his three doubles entered and approached the sizzling lime-green force field which cordoned the cell off from the rest of the brig. "Finally," he said. "Let's get out of here."

"We're not here to bust you out," said James. "We're here to talk."

Karl darted his eyes between his duplicates in frustration. "You're joking, right? Galactic enforcement will be here in a matter of hours, and you want to *chat?*"

Monty held up a hand. "Karl, we can't just pop you out of brig confinement, okay? We need to know what's going on."

"Very well." Karl gestured for them to come closer. He checked behind him to make sure the Greys were still absorbed in thoughts of their impending reckoning with the law. "I've been intercepting drug shipments from the Greys and

270

selling them to the Reptoids at an exorbitant price." He forced a smile. "We'll return to Zeta Reticuli with a sizeable nest egg."

Vincent stroked his stubble neurotically. "Or we'll end up sitting in an asteroid penal complex for a few decades. What were you thinking?!"

"Don't worry, Vincent. Who will they be looking for? Karl Janus, Homo sapien. Not a newly matured Zeta Reticulan. Such a being has committed no crime."

"Are you sure about that?" asked Monty. "Gander seems to know our origins. I wouldn't put it past him to put two and two together."

"Are you quite through?" asked Karl. "If that's the case, then we need to leave *now*. Make a run for it and hope the authorities are content to mop up the Greys."

"Karl," James said slowly, "How did you 'intercept' these drug shipments?"

The captive sighed. "I killed them, James. Quickly and painlessly."

Monty and Vincent stepped back, aghast. "Karl?!" Monty demanded. "You *murdered* people?" he stared at James and Vincent in disbelief. "*We* murdered people?"

"Oh, don't be so dramatic," hissed Karl. "What are we returning to, hmm? Immortality. Once we get to Zeta Reticuli we say goodbye to death forever. Terminating *that* would be murder, Monty. I would never kill someone in such a position; destroying immortality is an atrocity. But that's not the situation with humans. They're already going to die. All of them. Every human you've met is going to die. I didn't kill them, I just ended them a decade or two before they might have otherwise expired."

"I don't think they would view it that way," said James, long-faced.

"No, they wouldn't," Karl agreed. "And their opinions and feelings about death are certainly understandable given their finite circumstances. But they can't see the big picture." He edged towards the force field, as close as he dared. "Humans act as if death is some kind of horrific lottery. As if the *normal* plan for existence is to live on, indefinitely. In their hearts," he said, pointing to his chest, "they feel that diseases and accidents are cosmic injustice. Do you see?" His voice rose. "I only altered variables. I didn't change the equation."

"Those were innocent people," seethed James.

"*Finite* people."

"Well, what are we going to do?" asked Vincent, deflated.

James frowned. "What do you mean?"

"They're already dead, James. It's awful, I know. But it's . . . well, we have to figure out how we respond to it, don't we? I mean, once we rejoin, does it matter if Karl did it, or I did? Do we turn ourselves in? Do we . . . "

"Run?" Monty offered.

"No!" James balked. "Absolutely not!"

"What will you do, James?" Karl yelled. "Turn me in? Leave me to rot on a prison asteroid for fifty years while the three of you risk death on a dangerous, ugly little ball?"

"That's better than getting away with murder, isn't it?" James faced his two free compatriots. "I think that's exactly what we should do. Turn Karl in. There's no galactic death penalty, just . . .

reconditioning. And while they," he glanced at Karl, "fix up our wayward fourth member, the three of us can continue on Earth. We can experience full lives there. Then, when the time is right, rejoin with Karl and return to Zeta Reticuli."

"Madness!" exclaimed Vincent. "What if I die of a stroke? What if Monty has a heart attack? All four of us have to rejoin to be a viable adult. One death will doom all of us! Doom us to mortality. Those are grave stakes."

"What if we turned Karl in," Monty suggested, "but *we* left. If we traveled near light-speed, we would hardly age. After what felt like a week to us, we could pick up Karl, and rejoin."

"If we hadn't wanted risk," James said slowly, "we shouldn't have come to Earth. There are a lot of other planets with better health plans and fewer wars. But the danger makes the experience rich, and I think we should see it through." He turned to Vincent. "Aging is part of it. So is fear of the unforeseen. So are untapped fields like marriage and children."

"Marriage?" asked Karl. "Is that it?" He looked at Vincent and Montgomery. "His mind is clouded by hormones and Hollywood precepts." He turned to James. "You'll risk everything just to copulate with some tart from Earth?"

James glowered. "Karl, if that's how you want to look at it, fine. Fine by me." He swung his gaze to Montgomery and Vincent. "We're here as anthropologists, not tourists. You can both hide on the ship for the next thirty years if you want, but *I'm* going back to Earth." He glared at Karl. "You've damned all of us, Karl." He tapped his head. "When we rejoin, we'll all be murderers. And we'll have to live with *that* forever."

CHAPTER 55

Karl shooed a Grey out of one of the snack-brig's lounge chairs and sunk into the vacant seat. The combined weight of his thoughts and predilections made the chair's frame creak. "Does anyone have any lenses?" he muttered. The Greys blinked at him. "Someone give me a lens!" he demanded, sitting up to glare at them. He balled his fists and prepared to stand, but Mr. Zno tossed a small contact lens case, in hopes of avoiding further horrendous violence. "Thanks."

Karl fished out the translucent plastic and lightly pressed it against his left eyeball. His pupil expanded to the size of a quarter as his retinas absorbed the drug and flooded his mind with the vitality of the cosmos. He slouched into the chair, head spinning. Senses engorged. His vision shifted to the ultraviolet range, where the Greys turned into primary colors no human eye has ever seen, and his ears rocked from the sounds of light zipping through space.

As his iris expanded to buttress his eyelashes, his thoughts scrambled and recollected again and again. He could glimpse into his past, see himself presently sitting in a chair, and thrust his mind out into the sea of probabilities that was the future. He could see himself drugged up in his eighth year of mandatory group therapy on a penal asteroid. He saw the group rejoining in a decade, returning to Zeta Reticuli.

He saw another timeline: Monty collapsing in

the middle of a racquetball game, severing the surviving duplicates from full maturation on Zeta Reticuli. He saw James dropping a child off at school, kissing Hillary at her office, writing books, playing golf. He saw them all grow older. He saw more: Monty dying, James dying, Vincent dying. He saw Hillary.

And as Hillary stared back at him from a thousand untapped probabilities, his mind fixated on her as the singular chain tethering James and the others to life on Earth.

The tiny speck of "here and now" around him summoned back his attention. The Greys, shining with the radiance of an unlabeled ultraviolet color, engulfed in three-foot neon auras, were agitated. They all crowded around the force field.

Kuzar stood beyond the crackling confines of the electric barrier, punching a gadget into a control panel near the door. With a final poke the force field flickered and died. The Greys swarmed out of the brig and into the corridor.

Karl stood up dizzily and tried to snap out of his trance. He willed his neurons to congeal back into their regular position and forced practical thoughts to come together. The ensuing chaos of a Grey insurrection was the perfect diversion. He had to escape. With the others. Alone.

CHAPTER 56

On the bridge, Vincent gawked at his monitor. "Captain?" he asked, referring to Charles Gander. Leland McCorvick had reluctantly bestowed the title on the only man capable of steering the cruiser.

"Yes?" responded Gander, ensconced in the captain's chair.

"The Greys are out!" he said, standing up in excitement. "They've broken out of the brig!"

"Dammit! Seal off all decks!"

Vincent's fingers flew across his console. "They've overridden the system."

Montgomery pointed toward his own monitor. "They're accessing the ship's armory."

Gander stood up. "Vincent, work on restoring control of the ship's systems. Monty, keep an eye on them through the security monitors. Everyone else stand by the doors and prepare to—"

The door to the bridge opened and three Greys dashed in. Gander reached into his belt, pulled out a Glock, and squeezed off four rounds in one fluid motion. The bullets had no effect. As soon as he pulled the trigger, thin neon spindles of graft lines rippled across the Greys, shattering the otherwise spot-on shots into metallic dust. "They've got force fields!" Gander shouted.

Humans! Captain Cosmowobsy bellowed. *We have—*

Charles Gander hurled his Glock at him, catching the Grey soundly on the forehead and dropping him to the floor. Before the other two aliens could react Leland McCorvick head-butted one, while Sephus simultaneously scissor-kicked the last, losing his balance and tumbling to the deck plates. McCorvick kicked the wounded alien in the head, knocking it out, then kicked it in the groin for good measure.

"More are coming," said Monty, looking at his monitor. "They have weapons."

"Abandon ship!" Gander ordered. "Everyone! Follow me to the shuttle bay!"

"What!?" roared McCorvick. "Where's my chain?! Someone get me my tire iron!"

Sephus grabbed him by the arm. "We've got to *go*, Leland. C'mon!"

"I've disabled the cruiser's shields and engines," James said. He grabbed Hillary and ran toward the door. "If we can get to our ships, they won't be able to follow."

Gander opened the exit to the corridor and rapidly rotated his arm in a gesture to propel the crew out. "Good, James. It's only—" He rocked back as the sound of an exploding spring factory echoed through the corridor amidst purple lights. "They're firing on us," he said, ducking and running away from the detonations. "Heads low! C'mon!"

The entirety of the humans on board the ship, save Karl, sprinted through the corridor, avoiding blasts of purple. They turned a corner and approached a fork. "Left!" Gander commanded. Everyone dashed down the new passageway as the deck plates rumbled from alien salvos.

"Not too far now!" Gander wheezed, loping behind the group. "It's just—" A lavender discharge ripped through the hall, tripping Sephus and hurling

Gander and Leland McCorvick across the deck plates.

Sephus picked himself up, then ducked as a flash of electric eggplant nearly took his head off. "Charles! Leland!" He scampered across the shuddering floor to the two fallen men.

Leland McCorvick lay on his back, limbs sprawled beneath him, his flannel shirt on fire. He shook his head groggily and slapped the flames on his torso into submission. Gander fared worse. His face was singed and bleeding. Chunks of stubble had been scorched away, revealing bright pink, blistering skin. Blood trickled from the corner of his mouth. His left eye was cut and obscured by blood.

"Charles?" Sephus whispered, hovering above him on hands and knees. "Mr. Gander, can you hear me?" A blizzard of purple fire whistled through the air above him.

Gander nodded, coughed. "Sephus," he said, fumbling a burnt hand into his pocket. He fished out the keys to his van and tried to hand them to Sephus, dropping them onto his chest. "Get these people to safety." He convulsed, then gasped sharply. "Use the windshield wipers to blast the bay doors open, then head to the—"

"I'm not leaving you," Sephus cried. "C'mon!" He slung an arm underneath the fallen radio host and tried to heave him up.

Gander coughed blood onto his scorched Grateful Dead t-shirt. "Leave me!" He struggled to wrench himself from the farmer. "I'll only slow you down. Get to the van! Get everyone off the ship!" He hacked again and slumped over, fainting.

Sephus flung the man across his back and

turned to Leland McCorvick. "Leland, can you walk?" Leland nodded. "Then follow me. We've got to get out of here." He trudged toward the shuttle bay, trembling with fear as another neon fuselage narrowly missed his skull.

Leland McCorvick stood up and brushed off the smoking tatters of his plaid shirt. "Well that's *it*," he growled. He drew himself to his full height and stared down the corridor into the eyes of the pursuing Greys. Shiny packets of death sailed past his limbs as volley after volley hurtled by, each inexplicably missing its mark. His steely eyes blazed with the silent terror of a trillion angry farmers' wrath. His mouth twitched.

Leland McCorvick let out a marrow-curdling war cry, and plunged into the Greys.

*

"That's the shuttle bay ahead," panted James.

"Where did the Greys go?" asked Vincent. They could hear discharges roaring away down the corridor, but none approached their current location.

"They must be mopping up with Gander," Monty said. He touched the door to the shuttle bay and gestured for everyone to go inside. "Everybody pile into our skiff." Vincent ran to the craft and opened its door. He jumped in, followed by Frank and James.

"Where's Sephus?" Hillary asked Montgomery.

He glanced back towards the corridor and grimaced. "We'll just have to wish him the best. C'mon."

Hillary gripped his arm. "They're still firing

back there! That means someone is still alive! We have to help them!"

Montgomery jerked her towards the skiff. "We don't have any weapons, Hillary!" He pulled her into the vehicle. "The best we can do is wait here, and hope someone makes it. If not . . ."

Hillary jerked free. "I'll be right back," she said, jumping out of the vehicle. The door snapped shut in front of her. She sprinted toward the exit to the corridor.

"Hillary!" piped James over the skiff's external speaker system. *"What are you doing?"*

"Sephus!" she mouthed back.

"Don't even—" James stopped as something caught his eye. The door of the blue Lincoln, parked next to Gander's van, swung open. Karl climbed out, scalpel in hand. *"Karl!"*

Karl took no notice. He scanned the room evenly, then darted towards Hillary. Hillary screamed. She made a hard left, racing towards the opposite end of the room from Karl.

"Karl!" yelled James. *"Don't do it, Karl!"* Karl weaved between hunks of machinery, brandishing the scalpel above his head. *"I'm warning you!"* Inside the craft, James's hands danced across the control panel.

"What are you doing, James?" asked Monty. He tapped Vincent on the shoulder and pointed toward the "anti-space debris laser" insignia on James's control.

"James?" Vincent said slowly. "Tell Hillary to run to the skiff. We can restrain Karl onboard."

The craft's passengers watched as Hillary arrived at a wall and furiously searched for another path of retreat. She stepped over a large probe and turned to see Karl bounding toward her.

"Karl," James said. *"Karl, quit chasing her."* The man erupted into a full gallop, slashing the scalpel back and forth. James's finger paused over a pink button.

"If we're all incapacitated," whispered Montgomery, "no one will be able to pilot the skiff. Think about what you're doing."

James nodded. "I am." He pressed down.

In the shuttle bay beyond, Karl doubled over. An invisible laser lanced into his shoulder, piercing through to the next. The beam sliced his upper torso as he fell, cutting his neck, and almost severing his head. He flopped to the deck plates, unquestionably dead.

Inside the skiff, James's forehead slammed against his computer terminal. Montgomery and Vincent toppled over.

*

"Just . . . just *leave* me!" Gander wheezed, his arm around Sephus, painfully limping.

Sephus sighed, exasperated. His face and arms were slick with sweat. "If you would put the same effort into *trying to escape* that you do bitching, maybe we'd be in the van by now."

Spasms rocked Gander's body. "I don't think I'm going to make—"

"Yes, yes!" Sephus snapped. "You've been saying that now for the last four minutes!" He grunted as more of the radio host's body weight slumped against him. He half dragged the man across the corridor, finally arriving at the entrance to the shuttle bay. "Alright, now—" A lavender blast exploded nearby, toppling both men over. Sephus crawled forward, opening the door. "C'mon!" he called, heaving himself inside.

Gander remained sprawled on his back, sucking in labored, shallow breaths. Sephus leaned back into the shivering corridor, grabbed the man by the ankles, and pulled him into the bay. He leaned his back against the wall and gulped air. "Charles!" he heaved. "They're after us again. We're only a few feet from the van, okay?" Gander rolled his head to the side and coughed out blood.

Sighing again, Sephus stood up and heaved the man onto his back. He marched to the van, unlocked it, and hurled Gander's slack body into the passenger's seat. He skirted the hood and jammed himself into his seat behind the steering wheel, slamming the door shut behind him.

Hillary threw herself against the hood, furiously beating on the van with her fists. "Let me in! Let me in!"

"It's unlocked!" Sephus shouted. She leapt into the back seat and pulled the sliding door to the van shut.

"They wouldn't let me inside the other spaceship," she panted. "Karl is dead. Maybe James and the others, too, I don't know. Frank is in their ship."

Sephus nodded. "Charles!" he said, shaking Gander by the shoulders. "Charles, I don't know how to pilot this thing."

Gander's head bobbed as one listless eye concentrated on him. Blood and spittle dribbled down his chin. "It's not even a stick shift," he murmured.

The van trembled as a blob of neon aubergine collided with the back window. Sephus craned his neck to look abaft. Four Greys stormed the shuttle bay, all firing ray guns. He flung the gear into reverse and gunned the gas pedal. The van peeled out, thumping against the Greys' bony frames and scattering them across the bay.

"The doors," rasped Gander. "Shoot out the bay doors."

Sephus fiddled with the controls, trying to remember how Gander had worked the windshield wiper to propel volleys of energy out from the headlights. Large metal contraptions blasted apart. "Aha!" exclaimed Sephus. He shifted the van into drive and angled it toward the bay doors. The van wobbled as more ray gun fire bathed its starboard side.

Sephus blasted the bay doors, denting them. He pulled back the windshield wiper stick repeatedly, releasing round after round of invisible cannonade into their flaps. Purple lightning bathed the trembling van. An alarm sounded over the radio. Smoke seeped out of the CD player. He continued launching salvos from the headlights, wiping perspiration from his eyes.

With a final pull, the bay doors crumpled and blasted apart. The van lurched forward in the ensuing vacuum. Random metal parts flew by, sucked into space. A Grey slammed its head against Sephus's side mirror before joining another flailing companion in the unwelcome nothingness beyond.

"Charles," said Sephus, watching blue

atmospheric force fields flicker on in tight electric sheets around the regrouping Greys. "Does the Windstar have some kind of tractor beam? Hillary says James and the others are incapacitated."

Gander nodded. He pointed a shaky finger at a switch next to the air-conditioning dial. A doodle of a tractor had been scribbled onto it with a permanent marker. Sephus flipped the switch. Bright blue beams shone out from the headlights, groping a nearby probe, which lifted into the air.

He flipped the switch off and rolled the van in reverse until its aft pointed toward the gaping bay doors. He further angled the vehicle until it faced James's skiff, and flipped the tractor beams on. The van rolled forward as the blue rays of light pulled the vehicles toward one another. The Windstar vibrated and lurched as another volley of purple dug into its side.

Sephus hit the gas. The Windstar lurched backwards, wheeling across the deck, plunging into the maw of space beyond. The skiff followed.

The Grey cruiser fell away from view as the Windstar and skiff shot backwards into dark nullity. The Earth loomed behind them, 50,000 miles from the rear bumper. Sephus shifted the Windstar into drive, then thrust the van and nearby skiff forward and away.

CHAPTER 57

It had been there for three hours. Corporal Snyder lit his final cigarette and stared up in disbelief. "Has it done anything?" he asked Private Albers.

"Not a damn thing, sir."

"This is one of those incidents they swear us to secrecy about," growled Snyder. "Though Army Intelligence is going to have one hell of a time covering it up." Half of the men at Ft. Sill were positioned across the air strip. Tanks, rocket launchers, anti-aircraft missiles, and machine guns stretched from one end to the other. "The damn thing's as a big as a football field," Snyder said, craning his neck back. "Surely folks in Lawton can see it." He turned to Private Albers. "Do you have any more cigarettes on you?"

"Sir!" Albers said, pointing up. Snyder looked skywards. The hovering monolith was awkwardly descending toward the ground. One end of the triangle dropped before the other two, making the behemoth wobble as it sank. Snyder's cigarette butt dropped from his mouth and bounced off his gleaming boot.

The craft stabilized twenty feet over the air strip. It hung there for another five minutes as the entirety of Ft. Sill held its breath. Finally, a hatch on its underside opened up and a stainless steel ladder poked out. It unfolded, refolded, withdrew into the craft entirely, then crashed out of ship, its legs bouncing on the ground below.

A jeep careened through the assembled units of tanks and missile launchers. Snyder recognized Colonel Horwitz in the passenger's seat, adjusting his tie and glancing at a clipboard. He jumped out of the vehicle and dashed toward the ladder, with three guards armed with AK-47s close behind.

A boot made its first unsteady step at the top of the ladder. Gradually, a bleeding, shirtless old man with a green ray gun slung over his shoulder limped down the rungs and onto the red soil of Comanche County. He turned and faced the gaping Colonel and heavily armed unit, then saluted. "Sergeant Leland F. McCorvick, 19th Infantry Regiment, 24th Infantry Division, retired."

Horwitz returned the salute, then dropped his hand and jaw. "Colonel John Horwitz, 428th Field Artillery Brigade."

"Colonel Horwitz," McCorvick said, surveying the assembled tanks and army, "I have commandeered a hostile vessel and hereby turn it over to the United States Army. Its crew is tied up and gagged inside."

"Um . . ." Horwitz said, looking up.

"I'd like to request a ride back to Hoople."

CHAPTER 58

Hillary hugged herself as the unforgiving December wind crept up her skirt like a pervert. She shivered and jogged to her Nissan, fumbling in her pockets for the new keys to her used car. Strapping herself in, she double-checked her purse for the paycheck. The fifth installment of her new promotions job at the Oklahoma City Philharmonic remained tucked safely inside her day calendar. She planned to get an apartment downtown within the week.

The radio kept her company as she waited for the engine to warm up. "And we're back," crooned Charles Gander over the airwaves. "Folks, I have a special treat for you tonight. Now, we're all going to miss Steven Hornswild, and I wish him well with his new show. No one could fill his shoes. But all the same, I think I've found a young man who will do well to replace him.

"Many of you will recall last September when I nearly died from a head-on collision following Labor Day. Well, I've stayed in touch with the fellow who pulled me from the wreckage. And he's *sharp*, folks. Bright young guy. Anyway, I've coaxed him to take on Steven's spot over the weekends. He's going to co-host with me tonight while he gets a feel for things. Welcome to the show, Sephus."

"Thank you, Charles, it's a pleasure to be here." Sephus sounded like he was getting married. His grin extended well beyond the frequency *Midnight Chat* broadcasted on, edging into a jazz show and an

NPR special on narwhals. "I only hope I can live up to the high standards you and Mr. Hornswild have set over the years."

Hillary pulled into reverse and exited the parking lot. She half-listened to the radio's amiable banter as she drove to Nichols Hills. A few minutes later, James opened the door to his house on Harvard Court, kissed her, and pulled her in.

"How was work?" he asked, taking her coat.

"Pretty good," she said, kicking her shoes off. "I stayed late to take care of some filing. I hope I didn't keep you up."

"No, not at all." James walked to the kitchen. He uncorked a bottle of wine, his finest, and let it breathe on the counter.

Hillary stared at it. "James, that's a mighty expensive jug of grape juice for a Monday night."

"Sort of a special occasion," he said. "Would you like to sit down?" he asked, gesturing to the kitchen table. He took a seat next to her.

Hillary looked at him warily. "What's up?"

"Hillary, I'm . . ." He sighed. "I practiced a speech in my head all day but I'm just going to cut to the chase." He stared at the table. "Hillary, we're leaving Earth."

Hillary stared at the same spot on the table. "When?" James glanced at his watch. "That soon?"

"I spoke to Montgomery and Vincent earlier today, and we're all feeling the same thing." He rubbed his forehead. "We share a subconscious, you know? When Karl died, his memories sort of, I don't know, *spilled* into the collective subliminal pool." He locked eyes with Hillary. "It's pretty awful, really. The nightmares are . . . horrific. I can see his victims .

. . I know what it feels like to die. Isn't that weird?" Hillary nodded. "We're going to rejoin, and head back to Zeta Reticuli."

"I thought you couldn't rejoin without Karl."

"No, we can rejoin," said James, "just not in full. We're missing our fourth lobe. Once we reconstitute we'll be functional, but temporary. We figure five or ten years, at best."

"Then?" Hillary asked, wide-eyed.

"We'll shuffle off this mortal coil." He smiled. "Amidst *tremendous* media coverage. Death is a rarity on Zeta Reticuli. We're going to be celebrities. Monty is thrilled."

Hillary held his hand. "What if you stay here?"

James frowned. "Same story, sadly. Without Karl to stabilize the three of us, our minds will start to get out of kilter. We'll go stark raving mad." He grinned maniacally. "I can already feel it *just* a bit."

"Wow," Hillary said, tears brimming. "This is all a lot to take in."

"I know," James said. His grin fell away as he stroked her hand.

"So I guess we're breaking up?" She laughed, wiping tears away.

"I mean, unless you want to try for a long-distance relationship with a terminal Zeta Reticulan."

She shook her head and smiled. "No, I don't think my phone plan is intergalactic." She snorted warm, tear-induced snot and suddenly felt very embarrassed. "I had sort of thought that, since you were stuck with mortality and everything, you might finish up here on Earth." She looked at him. "With me."

"Hillary," James returned, "I love you. You

know that. But we don't have a lot of sparks, you know? Even if I stuck around, even if I *could*, there wouldn't be much passion. And you deserve better than a husband by default."

Hillary snapped. She threw her arms around him and cried. "James! I'm so, so sorry you have to die!"

He brushed her hair. "Don't be, Hil. If I hadn't killed Karl, he would have killed you. Besides," he said, removing a strand of hair from her eyes, "I get to explore the final phase of humanity: death. It sucks, but it's human. It's what I came here for."

"James!" Mascara gushed down her cheeks. "I just—"

He put a hand over her mouth. "Listen, Hillary, we could discuss this all night. But it's my last on Earth, so we should make the most of it."

"What do you want to do?" she said, wiping her eyes again. She forced a tiny smile.

He stood up and sauntered toward the wine bottle. "Try this wine. Then gorge ourselves at the International House of Pancakes, leaving a hundred-dollar tip. Then," he said, pulling out his wallet, "I'm going to distribute $12,000 among hobos downtown. After that," he continued as he poured two glasses, "we'll come back, finish off this bottle, start another, and call my closest friends to let them know how much I love them and to apologize for waking them up. Then we leaf through *National Geographic* magazines on the couch."

"*National Geographic*?" Hillary asked.

"Last glimpse of a beautiful planet."

"Anything else?" she said, suggestively.

"Then I was thinking we could burn the house

down. I really want to see what that will look like."

"Okay."

"Finally, after we watch the sunrise, you drive me to Norman, we have crazy sex in the back of my car, and I retrieve my skiff from Griffin Memorial Hospital." Hillary giggled. "Oh, and you'll be topless while we're reading the *National Geographic's*, too. Sound good?"

Hillary grinned and tilted her head. "Well, let's get started. We haven't even burned the house down yet."

EPILOGUE

Hillary parked her Nissan behind an old Chevy in front of her mother's house. Her eyes were puffy from sleep deprivation and her makeup was smeared in multiple directions from the uncontrolled sobbing on the drive home from Griffin Memorial Hospital.

She took a deep breath and stepped out of her car. Outside, the frosty morning air nipped at her ears and nose. The door to the Chevy opened and a man warily stepped out. He adjusted his trench coat and shivered, releasing his breath into the atmosphere like smoke. He turned to face Hillary and gave a tiny, sheepish grin.

"Dad?" Hillary asked. "Dad?!" She ran across the frost to hug him. She stepped back and gaped at him.

"Oh, hey Hil," he said casually. He put his hands in his pockets and acted like he was about to whistle. His trousers did not quite reach his shoes; evidence of lingering suspicions that he was really a sixteen-year-old.

"Where the *hell* have you been?" she demanded. She slapped him across the face.

Arthur reeled back, repositioned himself, then jiggled his car keys. "It's really cold out . . ."

Hillary sighed. "Let's go inside." She linked elbows with her moronic father and maneuvered the icy steps to the porch. "Mom thought the Rectum Thief gutted you like a fish. You've got a lot of explaining to do." She unlocked the door and pushed him inside.

293

He surveyed the home and hung his Redhawks baseball cap on a hook. His graying, full head of hair remained, warming his mint condition brain. "Uh, nope. I just sort of, you know, had a moment. For a year or so. Listen, is your mom around?"

"Yes," Hillary said, pointing to his former bedroom. "Would you like me to go get her?"

He shook his head. "No, I think I'll surprise her. Is she, um, through with menopause?"

"I think so." Hillary tapped her foot. "Listen, why don't you go talk to Mom, and in a week or two, after she's through ripping you to shreds, I'll explain how amazingly pissed off *I* am."

"Okie-doke," he responded, walking toward his bedroom. He stopped and turned around to face her. "You're . . . okay and everything?"

"Yes. My boyfriend and I broke up last night, but I think it's for the best. Otherwise I'm doing pretty well. I'm working for the Philharmonic orchestra," she added.

"Oh," he said, rocking back on his heels. "That's super. Excuse me."

Hillary grabbed his elbow before he reached the end of the hall. "Dad, wait," she cautioned.

"Yes?"

"This is going to sound weird, but . . . just tell Mom you were abducted by aliens. It'll actually go over pretty well."

Arthur stared at her blankly. "Like Mexicans?"

"The kind from space," she corrected.

He pondered this for several moments and shrugged. "Whatever." He opened the door to his bedroom and poked a cautionary head in to see if his spouse was awake. "Helen?" he asked. She responded with a mangled sob of joy. He stepped into the room and shut the door behind him. "I was kidnapped by space Mexicans."

ACKNOWLEDGMENTS

A special thanks to Mr. J. M. Jennings for his creative input and support. To Ms. Sara Daly, for her advice to scrap what would have been a horrifically cornball ending. To Jim Swift and Melody Jones for their editorial prowess.

And to the talented hosts of Coast to Coast AM, who bring news of the weird and paranormal to curious humans across the world. Were it not for their ongoing efforts, this book would have very little to lampoon.

Made in the USA
Columbia, SC
06 April 2019